I0651856

Umar ibn Muhammad Nafzawi

The Perfumed gGarden of the Cheikh Nefzaoui

A Manual of Arabian erotology

Umar ibn Muhammad Nafzawi

The Perfumed gGarden of the Cheikh Nefzaoui
A Manual of Arabian erotology

ISBN/EAN: 9783744757546

Printed in Europe, USA, Canada, Australia, Japan

Cover: Foto ©Andreas Hilbeck / pixelio.de

More available books at **www.hansebooks.com**

THE PERFUMED GARDEN
OF THE
CHEIKH NEFZAOUI

NOTE

The "Perfumed Garden" was translated into French before the year 1850, by a Staff Officer of the French army in Algeria. An autograph edition, printed in the italic character, was printed in 1876, but, as only twenty-five copies are said to have been made, the book is both rare and costly, while, from the peculiarity of its type, it is difficult and fatiguing to read. An admirable reprint has, however, been recently issued in Paris, with the translator's notes and remarks, revised and corrected by the light of the fuller knowledge of Algeria which has been acquired since the translation was made. From that last edition the present translation (an exact and literal one) has been made, and it is the first time that the work,—one of the most remarkable of its kind,— has appeared in the English language.

THE
PERFUMED GARDEN

OF THE

CHEIKH NEFZAOUI

A MANUAL OF ARABIAN EROTOLOGY
(XVI. Century)

REVISED AND CORRECTED TRANSLATION

Cosmopoli: MDCCCLXXXVI: for the Kama Shastra Society of London and Benares, and for Private circulation only.

Alencon: Imprimerie Veuve Felix Guy et Cie.

CONTENTS

NOTES OF THE TRANSLATOR

RESPECTING THE

CHEIKH NEFZAOUI [1]

The name of the Cheikh has become known to posterity as the author of this work, which is the only one attributed to him.

In spite of the subject-matter of the book and the manifold errors found in it, and caused by the negligence and ignorance of the copyists, it is manifest that this treatise comes from the pen of a man of great erudition, who had a better knowledge in general of literature and medicine than is commonly found with Arabs.

According to the historical notice contained in the first leaves of the manuscript, and notwithstanding the apparent error respecting the name of the Bey who was reigning in Tunis, it may be presumed that this work was written in the beginning of the sixth century, about the year 925 of the Hegira.

As regards the birthplace of the author, it may be taken for granted, considering that the Arabs habitually joined the name of their birthplace to their own, that he was born at Nefzaoua,[1] a town situated in the district of

[1] Note in the autograph edition, 1876.—The reader will bear in mind in perusing this work that the remarks and notes by the eminent translator were written before 1850, when Algiers was but little known, and Kabylia in particular not at all. He will therefore not be surprised to find that some slight details are not on a level with the knowledge acquired since.

that name on the shore of the lake Sebkha Melrir, in the south of the kingdom of Tunis.

The Cheikh himself records that he lived in Tunis, and it is probable the book was written there. According to tradition, a particular motive induced him to undertake a work at variance with his simple tastes and retired habits.

His knowledge of law and literature, as well as of medicine, having been reported to the Bey of Tunis, this ruler wished to invest him with the office of cadi, although he was unwilling to occupy himself with public functions.

As he, however, desired not to give the Bey cause for offence, whereby he might have incurred danger, he merely requested a short delay, in order to be able to finish a work which he had in hand.

This having been granted, he set himself to compose the treatise which was then occupying his mind, and which, becoming known, drew so much attention upon the author, that it became henceforth impossible to confide to him functions of the nature of those of a cadi.[2]

---

[1] The district of Nefzaoua contains many isolated villages, all on level ground, and surrounded by palm trees; with large reservoirs in their midst. The pilgrims believe that the land is called Nefzaoua, because there are in it thousand "zaoua" (a chapel in which a marabout is buried), and it is alleged that the name was first El Afoun Zaouia, later corrupted into Nefzaoua. But this Arabian etymology does not appear to be correct, as according to the Arabian historians the names of the localities are older than the establishment of Islamism. The town of Nefzaoua is surrounded by a wall built of stones and bricks; having six gateways, one mosque, baths, and a market; in the environs are many wells and gardens.

[2] It is not impossible that the book, written in these circumstances, was only an abridgement of the present one, an abridgement which he refers to in the first chapter of this book under the name of "Torch of the Universe."

But this version, which is not supported by any au-
thenticated proof, and which represents the Cheikh
Nefzaoui as a man of light morals, does not seem to be
admissable. One need only glance at the book to be
convinced that its author was animated by the most
praiseworthy intentions, and that, far from being in
fault, he deserves gratitude for the services he has rendered to humanity. Contrary to the habits of the Arabs,
there exists no commentary on this book; the reason
may, perhaps, be found in the nature of the subject of
which it treats, and which may have frightened, unnec-
essarily, the serious and the studious. I say unnecessar-
ily, because this book, more than any other, ought to
have commentaries; grave questions are treated in it,
and open out a large field for work and meditation.

What can be more important, in fact, than the study
of the principles upon which rest the happiness of man
and woman, by reason of their mutual relations; relations
which are themselves dependent upon character, health,
temperament and the constitution, all of which it is the
duty of philosophers to study.[1] I have endeavoured to
rectify this omission by notes, which, incomplete as I
know them to be, will still serve for guidance.

In doubtful and difficult cases, and where the ideas of
the author did not seem to be clearly set out, I have not
hesitated to look for enlightment to the savants of
sundry confessions, and by their kind assistance many
difficulties, which I believed insurmountable, were con-

---

[1] "We need not fear to compare the pleasures of the senses
with the most intellectual pleasures; let us not fall into the
delusion of believing that there are natural pleasures of two
sorts, the one more ignoble than the other; the noblest pleasures are the greatest."—Essai de Philosophie Morale, par M. de
Maupertius, Berlin, 1749.)

Notes of the Translator

quered. I am glad to render them here my thanks.

Amongst the authors who have treated of similar subjects, there is not one that can be entirely compared with
the Cheikh; for his book reminds you, at the same time,
of Aretin, of the book "Conjugal Love," and of Rabelais; the resemblance to this last is sometimes so striking
that I could not resist the temptation to quote, in several places, analogous passages.

But what makes this treatise unique as a book of its
kind, is the seriousness with which the most lascivious
and obscene matters are presented. It is evident that the
author is convinced of the importance of his subject, and
that the desire to be of use to his fellow-men is the sole
motive of his efforts.

With the view to give more weight to his recommendations, he does not hesitate to multiply his religious
citations and in many cases invokes even the authority
of the Koran, the most sacred book of the Mussulmans.

It may be assumed that this book, without being exactly a compilation, is not entirely due to the genius of
the Cheikh Nefzaoui, and that several parts may have
been borrowed from Arabian and Indian writers. For
instance, all the record of Mocailama and of Chedja is
taken from the work of Mohammed ben Djerir el Ta-
beri; the description of the different positions for coition,
as well as the movements applicable to them, are borrowed from Indian works; finally, the book of "Birds
and Flowers," by Azeddine el Mocadecci, seems to have
been consulted with respect to the interpretation of
dreams. But an author certainly is to be commended for
having surrounded himself with the lights of former
savants, and it would be ingratitude not to acknowledge

the benefit which his books have conferred upon people who were still in their infancy to the art of love.

It is only to be regretted that this work, so complete in many respects, is defective in so far as it makes no mention of a custom too common with the Arabs not to deserve particular attention. I speak of the taste so universal with the old Greeks and Romans, namely, the preference they give to a boy before a woman, or even to treat the latter as a boy.

There might have been given on this subject sound advice as well with regard to the pleasures mutually enjoyed by the women called tribades. The same silence has been preserved by the author respecting bestiality. Nevertheless the two stories which he relates, and which speak, one of the mutual caresses of two women, and the other of a woman provoking the caresses of an ass, show that he knew of such matters. It is, therefore, inexcusable that he should not have spoken more particularly on those points. It would certainly have been interesting to know which animals, by reason of their nature and conformation, are fittest to give pleasure either to man or woman, and what would be the result of such copulation.

Lastly, the Cheikh does not mention the pleasures which the mouth or the hand of a pretty woman can, give, nor the cunnilinges.[1]

---

[1] Paediconibus os olere dicis;
  Hoc si, sicut ais, Fabulle, verum est,
  Quid credis olere cunnilingis?

The mouths of paederasts, you say, smell badly;
If such be true, as you aver, Fabulus,
What about those, think you, that lick the vulva?
            MARTIALIS, Book xii., Epig. 86.

parts of the two bellies,[1] the enjoyment soon comes to pass. The man is at work as with a pestle, while the woman seconds him by lascivious movements;[2] finally comes the ejaculation.

The kiss on the mouth, on the two cheeks, upon the neck, as well as the sucking up of fresh lips, are gifts of God, destined to provoke erection at the favourable moment. God also was it who has embellished the chest of the woman with breasts, has furnished her with a double chin,[3] and has given brilliant colours to her cheeks.

He has also gifted her with eyes that inspire love, and with eyelashes like polished blades.

He has furnished her with a rounded belly and a beautiful navel, and with a majestic crupper; and all these wonders are borne up by the thighs. It is between these latter that God has placed the arena of combat; when the same is provided with ample flesh, it resembles the head of a lion. It is called vulva. Oh! how many men's deaths lie at her door? Amongst them how many heroes!

---

[1] The Arabic word "ana" designates the lower parts of the belly, where the hairs grow, which are near to the generating organs.

[2] In order to express the movement which takes place in the act of coition, the author uses the word "dok" with reference to the man, and "hez" for the woman. The first of these words means to concuss, to stamp, to pound; it is the action of the pestle in the mortar; the second word signifies a swinging movement, at once exciting, exhilarating, and lascivious.

[3] The word "gheba" means a double chin. The Arabs have a decided preference for fat women, consequently everything pointing to that coition is with them a beauty. Thus, the ridges forming upon the stomach of a woman by the development of their stoutness are a very seductive sight in the eyes of Arabs.

God has furnished this object with a mouth, a tongue,[1] two lips: it is like the impression of the hoof of the gazelle in the sands of the desert.

The whole is supported by two marvellous columns, testifying to the might and the wisdom of God; they are not too long nor too short; and they are graced with knees, calves, ankles, and heels, upon which rest precious rings.

Then the Almighty has plunged woman into a sea of splendours, of voluptuousness, and of delights, and covered her with precious vestments, with brilliant girdles and provoking smiles.

So let us praise and exalt him who has created woman and her beauties, with her appetising flesh; who has given her hairs, a beautiful figure, a bosom with breasts which are swelling, and amorous ways, which awaken desires.

The master of the Universe has bestowed upon them the empire of seduction; all men, weak or strong, are subjected to the weakness for the love of woman. Through woman we have society or dispersion, sojourn or emigration.

The state of humility in which are the hearts of those who love and are separated from the object of their love, makes their hearts burn with love's fire; they are oppressed with a feeling of servitude, contempt and misery; they suffer under the vicissitudes of their passion: and all this as a consequence of their burning desire of contact.

I, the servant of God, am thankful to Him that no one can help falling in love with beautiful women, and that no one can escape the desire to possess them, neither by change, nor flight, nor separation.

[1] Meaning of the clitoris.

I testify that there is only one God, and that he has no associate. I shall adhere to his precious testimony to the days of the last judgment.

I likewise testify as to our lord and master, Moham-med, the servant and ambassador of God, the greatest of the prophets (the benediction and pity of God be with him and with his family and disciples!).[1] I keep pray-ers and benedictions for the day of retribution, that terrible moment.

THE ORIGIN OF THIS WORK.

I have written this magnificent work after a small book, called "The Torch of the World," which treats of the mysteries of generation.

This latter work came to the knowledge of the Vizir of our master Abd-el-Aziz, the ruler of Tunis.

This illustrious Vizir was his poet, his companion, his friend and private secretary. He was good in council, true, sagacious and wise, the best learned man of his time, and well acquainted with all things. He called himself Mohammed ben Ouana ez Zonaoui, and traced his origin from Zonaoua.[2] He had been brought up at Algiers, and in that town our master Abd-el-Aziz el

---

[1] Mohammed, in verse 56, chap. xxxiii., with the heading "The Confederates," asks the believers to pray for him to God, and salute his name. It is in pursuance of this precept that the Mussulmans neither pronounce nor write the name of their prophet, without adding the sacramental formula, which runs: "Upon whom be benedictions and blessings of God."

[2] The Zonaoua were an independent Kabyl tribe, occupying the high peaks of Djurjura. The land of Kon-kon, represented by the Spanish writers as a kingdom, is simply the district be-longing to the Zonaoua tribe, who had frequent conflicts with the Turks on their first arrival in Tunis.

Hafsi had made his acquaintance.[1]

On the day when Algiers was taken, that ruler took flight with him to Tunis (which land may God preserve in his power till the day of resurrection), and named him his Grand Vizir.

When the above mentioned book came into his hands, he sent for me and invited me pressingly to come and see him. I went forthwith to his house, and he received me most honorably.

Three days after he came to me, and showing me my book, said, "This is your work." Seeing me blush, he added, "You need not be ashamed; everything you have said in it is true: no one need be shocked at your words. Moreover, you are not the first who has treated of this matter; and I swear by God that it is necessary to know this book. It is only the shameless boor and the enemy of all science who will not read it, or make fun of it.

---

[1] The period spoken of here can only be that of the submission of Algiers to Spain, when that city in 1510 (916 of the Hegira) acknowledged the supremacy of Spain and promised to pay her tribute, or that of the establishment of the Turkish domination in 1515 (921 of the Hegira). These are the only two cases of submission related by the old historians; and at neither of these periods was an Abd-el-Aziz reigning in Tunis. It is, however, very probable that the Author speaks of the Turkish occupation, when Barbarossa, having been invited by the Emir of Algiers to help him with his Turks in the war with the Spaniards, arrived at the city, put the Emir to death, and caused himself to be proclaimed King of Algiers instead.

The ruler of Tunis was then Abou Omar Amane Mohammed. The Bey of the name Abd-el-ziz, who, according to the period of his reign, came nearest to the events named by the author, was Abou Omar Abd-el-Aziz, who died in 893, and was one of the best Khelifar of the dynasty of the Beni Hafs. This error or difference will not surprise those who know how inaccurate the Arabs are in their quotations.

But there are sundry things which you will have to treat about yet." I asked him what these things were, and he answered, "I wish that you would add to the work a supplement, treating of the remedies of which you have said nothing, and adding all the facts appertaining there-to, omitting nothing. You will describe in the same the motives of the act of generation, as well as the matters that prevent it. You will mention the means for undo-ing spelle (aiguillette), and the way to increase the size of the verile member, when too small, and to make it resplendent. You will further cite those means which remove the unpleasant smells from the armpits and the natural parts of women, and those which will contract those parts. You will further speak of pregnancy, so as to make your book perfect and wanting in nothing. And, finally, you will have done your work, if your book sat-isfy all wishes."

I replied to the Vizir: "O, my master, all you have said is not difficult to do, if it is the pleasure of God on high." [1]

I forthwith went to work with the composition of this book, imploring the assistance of God (may He pour His blessing on His prophet, and may happiness and pity be with Him).

[1] The Arabs never say they will do a thing, without adding "If it please God." The prescriptions of the Koran (verse 23, chap. xviii) run: "Never say, I shall do so and so to-morrow," without "If it please God."

The origin of this verse is ascribed to the momentary trouble in which Mohammed was, when answering questions put to him by Jews. He had promised to answer them the next day, forgetting to add, "If it please God." As punishment the reve-lations did not come till some days after. Their verse runs as follows:

"Never say, 'I shall do a thing to-morrow,' without adding 'If it be the will of God.' Remember God, if you should forget this, and say: 'Perhaps God will help me to the true knowledge of things.'"

I have called this work "The Perfumed Garden for the Soul's Recreation" (Er Roud el Aater p'nezaha el Khater).

And we pray to God, who directs everything for the best (and there is no other God than He, and there is nothing good that does not come from Him), to lend us His help, and lead us in good ways; for there is no power nor joy but in the high and mighty God.

I have divided this book into twenty-one chapters, in order to make it easier reading for the taleb (student) who wishes to learn, and to facilitate his search for what he wants. Each chapter relates to a particular subject, be it physical, or anecdotical, or treating of the wiles and deceits of women.

TABLE (LIST) OF CHAPTERS.

I have made the above table to facilitate the research for readers as they may desire.

CHAPTER I

CONCERNING PRAISEWORTHY MEN

Learn, O Vizir (God's blessing be upon you), that there are different sorts of men and women, that amongst these are those who are worthy of praise, and those who deserve reproach.

When a meritorious man finds himself near to women, his member grows, gets strong, vigorous and hard; he is not quick to discharge, and after the trembling caused by the emission of the sperm, he is soon stiff again.

Such a man is liked and appreciated by the women; this is, because the woman loves the man only for the sake of the coition. His member should, therefore, be of ample dimensions and length. Such a man ought to be broad in the chest, and heavy in the crupper; he should know how to regulate his emissions, and ready as to erection; his member should reach to the end of the canal of the female, and completely fill the same in all its parts. Such an one will be well loved by women, for as the poet says.—

"I have seen women trying to find in young men
The durable qualities which grace the man of full power,
The beauty, the enjoyment, the reserve, the strength,
The full-formed member providing a lengthened coition,
A heavy crupper, a slowly coming emission,
A lightsome chest, as it were floating upon them;
The spermal ejaculation slow to arrive, so as
To furnish forth a long drawn-out enjoyment.
His member soon to be prone again for erection,
To ply the plane[1] again and again and again on their vulvas,
Such is the man whose cult gives pleasure to women,
And who will ever stand high in their esteem."

[1] Note of the edition of 1876. The Arab word signifies, "He flies, he works all around, he planes roundly through space." This is a poetical image, difficult to render in translation.

QUALITIES WHICH WOMEN ARE LOOKING FOR IN MEN

The tale goes, that on a certain day, Abd-el-Melik ben Merouane,[1] went to see Leilla, his mistress,[2] and put various questions to her. Amongst other things, he asked her what were the qualities which women looked for in men.

Leilla answered him: "Oh my master, they must have cheeks like ours." "And what besides?" said Ben Merouane. She continued: "And hairs like ours; finally they should be like to you, O prince of believers, for surely, if a man is not strong and rich he will obtain nothing from women."

VARIOUS LENGTHS OF THE VIRILE MEMBER

The virile member, to please women, must have at most a length of the breadth of twelve fingers, or three hand-breadths, and at least six fingers, or a hand and a half breadth.

There are men with members of twelve, or three hand-breadths; others of ten fingers, or two and a half hands. And others measure eight fingers, or two hands. A man whose member is of less dimensions cannot please women.

[1] Abd-el-Melik ben Merouane was Kalif of Damascus; he reigned over Arabia, Syria, and part of the Orient. He lived about the year 76, for history reports that in that year he caused money to be coined with the legend, "God is unique, God is alone." His name is besides found on some coins older than from the year 75.

[2] Leilla is a poetess, who lived at the time of the Kalif, Abd-el-Melik, the son of Merouane. She was called Akhegalia, as belonging to an Arab family named "the children of Akhegal." She is celebrated for the love she inspired Medjenoun with, and which was the subject of many romances.

USE OF PERFUMES FOR THE COITION. THE HISTORY

OF MOCAILAMA

The use of perfumes by men as well as by women, excites to the act of copulation. The woman inhaling the perfumes employed by the man gets like into a swoon; and the use of scents has often proved a strong help to man, and assisted him in getting possession of a woman.

On this subject it is told of Mocailama,[1] the imposter, the son of Kaiss (whom God may curse!), that he pretended to have the gift of prophecy, and imitated the Prophet of God (blessings and salutations to him). For which reasons he and a great number of Arabs have incurred the ire of the Almighty.

Mocailama, the son of Kaiss, the imposter, misconstrued likewise the Koran by his lies and impostures; and on the subject of a chapter of the Koran, which the angel Gabriel (Hail be to him) and brought to the Prophet (the mercy of God and hail to him), people of bad faith had gone to see Mocailama, who had told them, "To me also has the angel Gabriel[2] brought a similar chapter.

---

[1] This Mocailama was one of the strongest competitors of Mohammed. He sprang from the tribe of Honcifa, in the province of Yamama. He was the head of a deputation sent by his tribe to the prophet Mohammed, and embraced Islamism in the year 9 of the Hegira.

[2] This angel plays a great part in the Koran, and consequently in the Oriental books. He conveyed to Mohammed the heavenly revelations. He forms part of that order of spirits which the Mussulmans call "Mokarrabine," which means approaching nearest to God.

He derided the chapter headed "the Elephant," [1] saying, "In this chapter of the Elephant I see the elephant.
What is the elephant? What does it mean? What is this
quadruped? It has a tail and a long trunk. Surely it is
a creation of our God, the magnificent."

The chapter of the Koran named the Kouter [2] is also
an object of his controversy. He said, "We have given
you precious stones for yourself, and in preference to
any other man, but take care not to be proud of them."

Mocailama had thus perverted sundry chapters in the
Koran by his lies and impostures.

He had been at this work when he heard the Prophet
(the salutation and mercy of God be with him) spoken
of. He heard that after he had placed his venerable
hands upon a bald head, the hair had forthwith sprung
up again; that when he spat into a pit, the water came
in abundantly, and that the dirty water turned at once
clean and good for drinking: that when he spat into an
eye that was blind or obscure, the sight was at once restored to it, and when he placed his hands upon the
head of a child, saying, "Live for a century," the child
lived to be a hundred years old.

When the disciples of Mocailama saw these things or

---

[1] There is in fact a chapter of the Koran with the heading
"The Elephant." This chapter, the 105th, originated with a
victory of the Prophet over an Ethiopian prince; the white
Elephant, on which the prince was mounted, having knelt down
as a sign of adoration at the sight of Mecca. Hence the name
of the chapter, which perpetuates the name of this victory. It
was this name that Mocailama tries to turn into ridicule, by
pretending to see only the name of an animal, and not to understand its real sense.

[2] The title of Chapter 108 of the Koran, "el Kouter," signifies "generosity," "liberality." Mocailama pretended in his
controversy that all the articles which the first verse of the
chapter declares to have been given to Mohammed had been
previously placed at his disposition, so that he might reserve
for himself the best.

heard speak of them, they came to him and said, "Have you no knowledge of Mohammed and his doings?" He replied, "I shall do better than that."

Now, Mocailama was an enemy of God, and when he put his luckless hand on the head of someone who had not much hair, the man was at once quite bald; when he spat into a well with a scanty supply of water, sweet as it was, it was turned dirty by the will of God; if he spat into a suffering eye, that eye lost its sight at once, and when he laid his hand upon the head of an infant, saying, "Live a hundred years," the infant died within an hour.

Observe, my brethren, what happens to those whose eyes remain closed to the light, and who are deprived of the assistance of the Almighty!

And thus acted that woman of the Beni-Temin, called Chedja et Temimia, who pretended to be a prophetess. She had heard of Mocailama, and he likewise of her.

This woman was powerful, for the Beni-Temim form a numerous tribe. She said, "Prophecy cannot belong to two persons. Either he is a prophet, and then I and my disciples will follow his laws, or I am a prophetess, and then he and his disciples will follow my laws."

This happened after the death of the Prophet (the salutation and mercy of God be with him).

Chedja then wrote to Mocailama a letter, in which she told him, "It is not proper that two persons should at one and the same time profess prophecy; it is for one only to be a prophet. We and our disciples will meet and examine each other. We shall discuss about that which has come to us from God (the Koran), and we will follow the laws of him who shall be acknowledged as the true prophet."

She then closed her letter and gave it to a messenger, saying to him: "Betake yourself, with this missive, to Yamama, and give it to Mocailama ben Kaiss. As for myself, I follow you, with the army."

Next day the prophetess mounted horse with her goum [1] and followed the spoor of her envoy. When the latter arrived at Mocailama's place, he greeted him and gave him the letter.

Mocailama opened and read it, and understood its contents. He was dismayed, and began to advise with the people of his goum, one after another, but he did not see anything in their advice or in their views that could rid him of his embarrassment.

While he was in this perplexity, one of the superior men of his goum came forward and said to him. "Oh, Mocailama, calm your soul and cool your eye.[2] I will give you the advice of a father to his son."

Mocailama said to him: "Speak, and may thy words be true."

And the other one said: "To-morrow morning erect outside the city a tent of coloured brocades, provided with silk furniture of all sorts.[3] Fill the tent afterwards

---

[1] Goum.—Meeting of cavaliers, who form an escort, sometimes representing the war-forces of great Arab chiefs. Perhaps in the sense used by the author the word may be rendered as disciples.

[2] One hears frequently, "May God refresh his eyes," which means: "May God by contentment refresh his eyes, which is hot with tears."

[3] It will, perhaps, not be useless to observe here that among the nomadical Arabs the custom obtains that the man who wants to cohabit with his wife erects a tent over her. Hence a man who is going to be married is called "bani," building; and of a man who has just been married it is said, "Bena ala Ahlihi," which means: "He has built over his wife."

with a variety of different perfumes, amber, musk, and all sorts of scents, as rose, orange flowers, jonquils, jessamine, hyacinth, carnation and other plants. This done, have then placed there several gold censers filled with green aloes, ambergris, neddle [1] and so on. Then fix the hangings so that nothing of these perfumes can escape out of the tent. Then, when you find the vapor strong enough to impregnate water,[2] sit down on your throne, and send for the prophetess to come and see you in the tent, where she will be alone with you. When you are thus together there, and she inhales the perfumes, she will delight in the same, all her bones will be relaxed in a soft repose, and finally she will be swooning. When you see her thus far gone, ask her to grant you her favours; she will not hesitate to accord them. Having once possessed her, you will be freed of the embarrassment caused to you by her and her goum."

Mocailama exclaimed: "You have spoken well. As God lives, your advice is good and well thought out." And he had everything arranged accordingly.

When he saw that the perfumed vapour was dense enough to impregnate the water in the tent he sat down upon his throne and sent for the prophetess. On her

---

[1] The "nedde" is a mixture of various perfumes, amongst which benzoin and amber predominate. This mixture, which is black, is formed into a small cylinder. It is burnt upon coals, or like the pastils of the serail by lighting one end. According to some authors, "neddle" is only a preparation of amber.

[2] That is to say that the vapours of the perfumes have been long enough in the place and thick enough to communicate their odour to water placed in the tent. The text says only "when the water shall be mixed with the fumes."

arrival he gave orders to admit her into the tent; she entered and remained alone with him. He engaged her in conversation.

While Mocailama spoke to her she lost all her presence of mind, and became embarrassed and confused.

When he saw her in that state he knew that she desired cohabitation, and he said: "Come, rise and let me have possession of you; this place has been prepared for that purpose. If you like you may lie on your back, or you can place yourself on all fours, or kneel as in prayer, with your brow touching the ground, and your crupper in the air, forming a tripod.[1] Whichever position you prefer, speak, and you shall be satisfied."

The prophetess answered, "I want it done in all ways. Let the revelation of God descend upon me, O Prophet of the Almighty."

He at once precipitated himself upon her, and enjoyed her as he liked. She then said to him, "When I am gone from here, ask my goum to give me to you in marriage."

When she left the tent and met her disciples, they said to her "What is the result of the conference, O

---

[1] To understand this passage properly it must be known that the Arabs, when praying, kneel on the ground with the face bent low down and the hands on the knees.

The tripod is then formed by the two knees and the head touching the ground. It is easy to see that this position causes the posterior part of the body to project very much backwards. The way how to practice cohabitation thus is stated in the 69th manner, chapter vi. "Hoc mihi tradidit Deus: foemines Deus condidit rimosas, virosque iis dedit maritos, qui mentulas in ipsas immittunt; eas que deinde simul ac volunt retrahunt: quo facto illae catulos nobis pariunt."

prophetess of God?" and she replied, "Mocailama has shown me what has been revealed to him, and I found it to be the truth, so obey him."

Then Mocailama asked her in marriage from the goum, which was accorded to him. When the goum asked about the marriage-dowry of his future wife, he told them, "I dispense you from saying that prayer 'aceur'" (which is said at three or four o'clock). Ever from that time the Beni-Temin do not pray at that hour; and when they are asked the reason, they answer, "It is on account of our prophetess; she only knows the way to the truth." And, in fact, they recognize no other prophet.

On this subject a poet has said—

> For us a female prophet has arisen;
> Her laws we follow; for the rest of mankind
> The prophets that appeared were always men.[1]

The death of Mocailama was foretold by the prophecy of Abou Beker [2] (to whom God be good). He was, in fact, killed by Zeid ben Khettab. Other people say it

---

[1] This history of the encounter between Mocailama and Chedja, whose proper name was Fedja bent el Harents ben Souard, is reproduced in the work of Abou Djaferi Mohammed ben Djerir el Teberi, where it is told with the minutest particulars, and bears the signs of a veritable religious truth.

[2] Abou Beker is the father of Aicha, the wife of Mohammed. He followed the latter in the year 11 of the Hegira. By his and Omar's authority, a great many Mussulmans were turned from their design to apostasize. He was the first Kalif, and remained in power, in spite of the pretensions of the partisans of Ali Mohammed's son-in-law, who maintained that the Prophet had long before his death assigned Ali as his successor.

was done by Ouhcha, one of his disciples. God only knows whether it was Ouhcha. He himself says on this point, "I have killed in my ignorance the best of men, Haman ben Abd el Mosaleb,[1] and then I killed the worst of men, Mocailama. I hope that God will pardon one of these actions in consideration of the other."

The meaning of these words, "I have killed the best of men" is, that Ouhcha, before having yet known the prophet, had killed Hamza (to whom God be good), and having afterwards embraced Islamism, he killed Mocailama.

As regards Chedja et Temimia, she repented by God's grace, and took to the Islamitic faith; she married one of the Prophet's followers (God be good to her hus-band).

Thus finishes the story.

The man who deserves favours is in the eyes of women, the one who is anxious to please them. He must be of good presence, excel in beauty those around him, be of good shape and well-formed proportions; true and sin-cere in his speech with women; he must likewise be gen-erous and brave, not vainglorious, and pleasant in con-versation. A slave to his promise, he must always keep his word, ever speak the truth, and do what he has said.

---

[1] These facts concur with the historical ones. Hamza, the uncle of the Prophet, was certainly killed in the battle of Ohod, in the year 4 of the Hegira, by a negro, Ouhcha, who after-wards killed Mocailama.

The man who boasts of his relations to women, of their acquaintance and good will to him, is a dastard. He will be spoken of in the next chapter.

There is a story that once there lived a king named Mamoum,[1] who had a court fool of the name of Bahloul,[2] who amused the princes and Vizirs.

One day this buffoon appeared before the King, who was amusing himself. The King bade him sit down, and then asked him, turning away, "Why hast thou come, O son of a bad woman?"

Bahloul answered, "I have come to see what has come to our Lord, whom may God make victorious."

"And what has come to thee?" replied the King, "and how art thou getting on with thy new and with thy old wife?" For Bahloul, not content with one wife, had married a second one.

"I am not happy," he answered, "neither with the old one, nor with the new one; and moreover poverty overpowers me."

The King said, "Can you recite any verses on this subject?"

---

[1] Abdallah ben Namoum, one of the sons of Haroun er Kachid. Having for a long time made war upon his brother el Amine for the empire, and the latter having been vanquished and killed in a battle near Bagdad, el Mamoum was unanimously proclaimed Kalif in the year 178 of the Hegira. He was one of the most distinguished Abyssidian rulers with respect to science, wisdom, and goodness.

[2] The word Bahloul, of Persian origin, signifies a man that laughs, derides; a knave, a sort of fool in the Orient.

The buffoon having answered in the affirmative, Mamoum commanded him to recite those he knew, and Bahloul began as follows:—

> "Poverty holds me in chains; misery torments me.
> I am being scourged with all misfortunes;
> Ill luck has cast me in trouble and peril,
> And has drawn upon me the contempt of man.
> God does not favour a poverty like mine;
> That is approbrious in every one's eyes.
> Misfortune and misery for a long time
> Have held me tightly; and no doubt of it
> My dwelling house will soon not know me more."

Mamoum said to him, "Where are you going to?"

He replied, "To God and his Prophet, O prince of the believers."

"That is well!" said the King; "those who take refuge in God and his Prophet, and then in us, will be made welcome. But can you now tell me some more verses about your two wives, and about what comes to pass with them?"

"Certainly," said Bahloul.

"Then let us hear what you have to say!"
Bahloul then began thus with poetical words:
"By reason of my ignorance, I have married two wives—
And why do you complain, O husband of two wives?
I said to myself, I shall be like a lamb between them;
I shall take my pleasure upon the bosoms of my two sheep,
And I have become like a ram between two female jackals.
Days follow upon days, and nights upon nights,
And their yoke bears me down both during days and nights.
If I am kind to one, the other gets vexed.

And so I cannot escape from these two furies.
If you want to live well and with a free heart,
And with your hands unclenched, then do not marry.
If you must wed, then marry one wife only.
One alone is enough to satisfy two armies."

When Mamoum heard these words he began to laugh, till he nearly tumbled over. Then as a proof of his kindness, he gave to Bahloul his golden robe, a most beautiful vestment.

Bahloul went in high spirits towards the dwelling of the Grand Vizir. Just then Hamdonna [1] looked from the height of her palace in that direction, and saw him. She said to her negress, "By the God of the temple of Mecca! There is Bahloul dressed in a fine gold-worked robe! How can I manage to get possession of the same?"

The negress said, "Oh, my mistress, you would not know how to get hold of that robe."

Hamdonna answered, "I have thought of a trick to do it, and I shall get the robe from him."

"Bahloul is a sly man," replied the negress. "People think generally that they can make fun of him; but, for God, it is he who makes fun of them. Give the idea up, mistress mine, and take care that you do not fall into the snare which you intend setting for him."

But Hamdonna said again, "It must be done!" She then sent her negress to Bahloul, to tell him that he should come to her. He said, "By the blessing of God,

---

[1] Hamdona from the Arabic root hamd, which means to praise; hence Ahmed, the most praiseworthy. From the same root comes the name of Mohammed, corrupted into Mahomet.

to him who calls you, you shall make answer," and went to Hamdonna.[1]

Hamdonna welcomed him and said: "Oh, Bahloul, I believe you come to hear me sing." He replied. "Most certainly, oh, my mistress! She has a marvelous gift for singing," he continued. "I also think that after having listened to my songs, you will be pleased to take some refreshments." "Yes," said he.

Then she began to sing admirably, so as to make people who listened die with love.

After Bahloul had heard her sing, refreshments were served; he ate and he drank. Then she said to him. "I do not know why but I fancy you would gladly take off your robe, to make me a present of it." And Bahloul answered: "Oh, my mistress! I have sworn to give it to her to whom I have done as a man does to a woman."

"What! you know what that is, Bahloul?" said she.

"Whether I know it?" replied he. "I, who am instructing God's creatures in that science? It is I who make them copulate in love, who initiate them in the delights a female can give, show them how you must caress a woman, and what will excite and satisfy her. Oh, my mistress, who should know the art of coition if it is not I?"

Hamdonna was the daughter of Mamoum, and the wife of the Grand Vizir. She was endowed with the most perfect beauty; of superb figure and harmonious form. No one in her time surpassed her in grace and

---

[1] "To him who calls you make answer." This sentence is taken from the Hadits, or Traditions of Mohammed. Sometimes it is used in conversation in the same sense as above, but its true meaning is obscure. The words "By the blessing of God" in the same sentence is a form of acceptance or consent.

perfection. Heroes on seeing her became humble and submissive and looked down to the ground for fear of temptation, so many charms and perfections had God lavished on her. Those who looked steadily at her were troubled in their mind, and oh! how many heroes imper-illed themselves for her sake. For this very reason Bahloul had always avoided meeting her for fear of succumbing to the temptation, and, apprehensive of his peace of mind, he had never, until then, been in her presence.

Bahloul began to converse with her. Now he looked at her and anon bent his eyes to the ground, fearful of not being able to command his passion. Hamdonna burnt with desire to have the robe, and he would not give it up without being paid for it.

"What price do you demand," she asked. To which he replied, "Coition, O apple of my eye."

"You know what that is, O Bahloul?" said she.

"By God," he cried; "no man knows women better than I; they are the occupation of my life. No one has studied all their concerns more than I. I know what they are fond of; for learn, oh, lady mine, that men choose different occupations according to their genius and their bent. The one takes, the other gives; this one sells, the other buys. My only thought is of love and of the possession of beautiful women. I heal those that are lovesick, and carry a solace to their thirsting vaginas."

Hamdonna was surprised at his words and the sweet-ness of his language. "Could you recite me some verses on this subject?" she asked.

"Certainly," he answered.

"Very well, O Bahloul, let me hear what you have to say."

Bahloul recited as follows:—

"Men are divided according to their affairs and doings;
Some are always in spirits and joyful, others in tears.
There are those whose life is restless and full of misery,
While, on the contrary, others are steeped in good fortune,
Always in luck's happy way, and favoured in all things.
I alone am indifferent to all such matters.
What care I for Turkomans, Persians, and Arabs?
My whole ambition is in love and coition with women,
No doubt nor mistake about that!
If my member is without vulva, my state becomes frightful,
My heart then burns with a fire which cannot be quenched.
Look at my member erect! There it is—admire its beauty!
It calms the heat of love and quenches the hottest fires
By its movement in and out between your thighs.
Oh, my hope and my apple, oh, noble and generous lady,
If one time will not suffice to appease thy fire,
I shall do it again, so as to give satisfaction;
No one may reproach thee, for all the world does the same.
But if you choose to deny me, then send me away!
Chase me away from thy presence without fear or remorse!
Yet bethink thee, and speak and augment not my trouble,
But, in the name of God, forgive me and do not reproach me.
While I am here let thy words be kind and forgiving.
Let them not fall upon me like sword-blades, keen and cutting!
Let me come to you and do not repel me.
Let me come to you like one that brings drink to the thirsty;
Hasten and let my hungry eyes look at thy bosom.
Do not withhold from me love's joys, and do not be bashful,
Give yourself up to me—I shall never cause you a trouble,
Even were you to fill me with sickness from head to foot.
I shall always remain as I am, and you as you are,
Knowing, that we are the servants, and you are the mistress.
Then shall our love be veiled? It shall be hidden for all time,
For I keep it a secret and I shall be mute and muzzled.
It's by the will of God, that everything is to happen,
He has filled me with love, and to-day I am in ill-luck."

While Hamdonna was listening she nearly swooned, and set herself to examine the member of Bahloul, which stood erect like a column between his thighs. Now she said to herself: "I shall give myself up to him," and now "No I will not." During this uncertainty she felt a yearning for pleasure between her thighs, and Eblis made flow from her natural parts a moisture, the fore-runner of pleasure.[1] She then no longer combated her desire to cohabit with him, and reassured herself by the thought: "If this Bahloul, after having had his pleasure with me, should divulge it no one will believe his words."

She requested him to divest himself of his robe and to come into her room, but Bahloul replied. "I shall not undress till I have stated my desire, O apple of my eye."

Then Hamdonna rose, trembling with excitement for what was to follow; she undid her girdle and left the room, Bahloul following her and thinking: "Am I really awake or is this a dream?" He walked after her till she had entered her boudoir. Then she threw herself on a couch of silk, which was rounded on the top like a vault, lifted her clothes up over her thighs, trembling all over, and all the beauty which God had given her was in Bahloul's arms.

Bahloul examined the belly of Hamdonna, round like an elegant cupola, his eyes dwelt upon a navel which was like a pearl in a golden cup; and descending lower

---

[1] The words "Eblis made flow a moisture" (djera Eblis menha madjera el dem) is an Arabian idiom, expressing that a woman is getting lusty; the sexual parts get moist. Eblis is a rebellious angel who refused to bow down before Adam when God ordered him to do so. Sometimes Eblis is also used as a general name for the devil, Satan, demon.

down there was a beautiful piece of nature's workman-
ship, and the whiteness and shape of her thighs surprised him.

Then he pressed Hamdonna in a passionate embrace,
and soon saw the animation leave her face; she seemed
to be almost unconscious. She had lost her head; and
holding Bahloul's member in her hands excited and fired
him more and more.

Bahloul said to her: "Why do I see you so troubled
and beside yourself?" And she answered: "Leave me, O
son of the debauched woman! By God, I am like a mare
in heat, and you continue to excite me still more with
your words, and what words! They would set any
woman on fire, if she was the purest creature in the
world. You will insist in making me succumb by your
talk and your verses."

Bahloul answered: "Am I then not like your husband?" "Yes," she said, "but a woman gets in heat on
account of the man, as a mare on account of the horse,
whether the man be the husband or not; with this difference, however, that the mare gets lusty only at certain periods of the year, and only then receives the stallion, while a woman can always be made rampant by
words of love.[1] Both these dispositions have met within
me, and, as my husband is absent, make haste, for he
will soon be back."

Bahloul replied: "Oh, my mistress, my loins hurt me

---

[1] Rabelais says on the subject of women who, against the
laws of nature, go on receiving the embraces of men after
having conceived: "And if anybody should blame them for
allowing men to explore them when full, considering that beasts
in the like case never endure the male to enter, they will say
that those are beasts; but they are women, making use of their
right of superfetation."

and prevent me mounting upon you. You take the man's position, and then take my robe and let me depart.

Then he laid himself down in the position the woman takes in receiving a man; and his verge was standing up like a column.

Hamdonna threw herself upon Bahloul, took his member between her hands and began to look at it. She was astonished at its size, strength and firmness, and cried: "Here we have the ruin of all women and the cause of many troubles. O Bahloul! I never saw a more beautiful dart than yours!" Still she continued keeping hold of it, and rubbed its head against the lips of her vulva till the latter part seemed to say: "O member, come into me."

Then Bahloul inserted his member into the vagina of the Sultan's daughter, and she, settling down upon his engine, allowed it to penetrate entirely into her furnace till nothing more could be seen of it, not the slightest trace, and she said. "How lascivious has God made woman, and how indefatigable after her pleasures." She then gave herself up to an up-and-down dance, moving her bottom like a riddle; to the right and left, and forward and backward; never was there such a dance as this.

The Sultan's daughter continued her ride upon Bahloul's member till the moment of enjoyment arrived, and the attraction [1] of the vulva seemed to pump the member as though by suction: just as an infant sucks the teat of the mother. The acme of the enjoyment came to both

---

[1] The word djadeba (attraction) comes from an Arab root, djedeb, which means "attract, drain, pump." It appears several times in this work, and I believe it corresponds with a peculiarity found in some favoured woman called "nut-cracker."

simultaneously, and each took the pleasure with avidity.

Then Hamdonna seized the member in order to withdraw it, and slowly, slowly she made it come out, saying: "This is the deed of a vigorous man." Then she dried it and her own private parts with a silken kerchief and arose.

Bahloul also got up and prepared to depart, but she said, "And the robe?"

He answered, "Why, O mistress! You have been riding me, and still want a present?"

"But," said she, "did you not tell me that you could not mount me on account of the pains in your loins?"

"It matters but little," said Bahloul. "The first time it was your turn, the second will be mine, and the price for it will be the robe, and then I will go."

Hamdonna thought to herself, "As he began he may now go on; afterwards he will go away."

So she laid herself down, but Bahloul, "I shall not lie with you unless you undress entirely."

Then she undressed until she was quite naked, and Bahloul fell into an ecstasy in seeing the beauty and perfection of her form. He looked at her magnificent thighs and rebounding navel, at her belly vaulted like an arch, her plump breasts standing out like hyacinths. Her neck was like a gazelle's, the opening of her mouth like a ring, her lips fresh and red like a gory sabre. Her teeth might have been taken for pearls and her cheeks for roses. Her eyes were black and well slit, and her eyebrows of ebony resembled the rounded flourish of the noun [1] traced by

---

[1] Noun is a letter of the Arabian alphabet corresponding to our N. Its half-circular form explains the comparison made by the author with reference to arched eyebrows.

the hand of a skilful writer. Her forehead was like the full moon in the night.

Bahloul began to embrace her, to suck her lips and to kiss her bosom: he drew her fresh saliva and bit her thighs. So he went on till she was ready to swoon, and could scarcely stammer, and her eyes got veiled. Then he kissed her vulva, and she moved neither hand nor foot. He looked lovingly upon the secret parts of Ham-donna, beautiful enough to attract all eyes with their purple centre.[1]

Bahloul cried, "Oh, the temptation of man!" and still he bit her and kissed her till the desire was roused to its full pitch. Her sighs came quicker, and grasping his member with her hand she made it disappear in her vagina.

Then it was he who moved hard, and she responded hotly; the overwhelming pleasure simultaneously calmed their fervour.

Then Bahloul got off her, dried his pestle and her mortar, and prepared to retire. But Hamdonna said, "Where is the robe? You mock me, O Bahloul." He answered, "O my mistress, I shall only part with it for a consideration. You have had your dues and I mine. The first time was for you, the second time for me, now the third time shall be for the robe."

This said, he took it off, folded it, and put it in Ham-donna's hands, who, having risen, laid down again on the couch and said, "Do what you like!"

---

[1] The word, which really means "biting," is used for all sorts of caresses in which the lips, the teeth, and even the tongue take part. It is, therefore, wrong to conclude from this passage that Bahloul indulged in the exercise of cunnilinge.

Forthwith Bahloul threw himself upon her, and with one push completely buried his member in her vagina; then he began to work as with a pestle, and she to move her bottom, until both again did flow over at the same time. Then he rose from her side, left his robe, and went.

The negress said to Hamdonna, "O my mistress, is it not as I have told you? Bahloul is a bad man, and you could not get the better of him. They consider him as a subject for mockery, but, before God, he is making fun of them. Why would you not believe me?"

Hamdonna turned to her and said, "Do not tire me with your remarks. It came to pass what had to come to pass, and on the opening of each vulva is inscribed the name of the man who is to enter [1] it, right or wrong, for love or for hatred. If Bahloul's name had not been inscribed on my vulva he would never have got into it, had he offered me the universe with all it contains."

As they were thus talking there came a knock at the door. The negress asked who was there, and in answer the voice of Bahloul said, "It is I." Hamdonna, in doubt as to what the buffoon wanted to do, got frightened. The negress asked Bahloul what he wanted, and received the reply, "Bring me a little water." She went out of the house with a cup full of water. Bahloul drank, and then let the cup slip out of his hands, and it was broken. The negress shut the door upon Bahloul, who sat himself down on the threshold.

---

[1] These words, "each vulva, etc." (Koul ferdj mektoub ali esm nakahon) allude to the phrase taken from the traditions left by Mohammed and often repeated by Mussulmans, "Each man has his destiny written on his forehead, and no one can take it off."

The buffoon being thus close to the door, the Vizir, Hamdonna's husband, arrived, who said to him, "Why do I see you here, O Bahloul?" And he answered, "O my lord, I was passing through this street. when I was overcome by a great thirst. A negress came and brought me a cup of water. The cup slipped from my hands and got broken. Then our Lady Hamdonna took my robe, which the Sultan our Master had given me as indemnification."

Then said the Vizir, "Let him have his robe." Hamdonna at this moment came out, and her husband asked her whether it was true that she had taken the robe in payment for the cup. Hamdonna then cried, beating her hands together, "What have you done, O Bahloul?" He answered, "I have talked to your husband the language of my folly; talk to him, you, the language of thy wisdom." And she, enraptured with the cunning he had displayed, gave him his robe back, and he departed.

CHAPTER II

CONCERNING WOMEN WHO DESERVE TO BE PRAISED

Know, oh Vizir (and the mercy of God be with you!) that there are women of all sorts; that there are such as are worthy of praise, and such as deserve nothing but contempt.

In order that a woman may be relished by men, she must have a perfect waist, and must be plump and lusty. Her hair will be black, her forehead wide, she will have eyebrows of Ethiopian blackness, large black eyes, with the whites in them very limpid. With cheeks of a perfect oval, she will have an elegant nose and a graceful mouth; lips and tongue vermillion; her breath will be of pleasant odour, her throat long, her neck strong, her bust and her belly large; her breasts must be full and firm; her belly in good proportion, and her navel well-developed and marked; the lower part of the belly is to be large, the vulva projecting and fleshy from the point where the hairs grow to the buttocks; the conduit must be narrow and not moist, soft to the touch, and emitting a strong heat and no bad smell; she must have the thighs and buttocks hard, the hips large and full, a waist of fine shape, hands and feet of striking elegance, plump arms and well-developed shoulders.

If one looks at a woman with those qualities in front, one is fascinated; if from behind, one dies with pleasure. Looked at sitting, she is a rounded dome; lying, a soft bed; standing, the staff of a standard. When she is walking, her natural parts appear as set off under her clothing. She speaks and laughs rarely, and never without a reason. She never leaves the house even to see neighbours of her acquaintance. She has no woman friends, gives her confidence to nobody, and her husband is her sole reliance. She takes nothing from anyone, excepting from her husband and her parents. If she sees relatives she does not meddle with their affairs. She is not treacherous, and has no faults to hide, nor bad reasons to proffer. She does not try to entice people. If her husband shows the intention to fulfil the conjugal rite, she is agreeable to his desire and occasionally even provokes them. She assists him always in his affairs, and is sparing in complaints and tears; she does not laugh or rejoice when she sees her husband moody or sorrowful, but shares his troubles, and wheedles him into good humour, till he is quite content again. She does not surrender herself to anybody but her husband, even if abstinence would kill her. She hides her secret parts, and does not allow them to be seen; she is always elegantly attired, of the utmost personal propriety, and takes care not to let her husband see what might be repugnant to him. She perfumes herself with scents, uses antimony for her toilet, and cleans her teeth with souak.[1]

Such a woman is cherished by all men.

---

[1] Souak is the bark of the walnut tree, which has the quality to clean the teeth and redden the lips and gums. Souak means also toothpicks.

THE STORY OF THE NEGRO DORERAME [1]

The story goes, and God knows its truth, that there was once a powerful king who had a large kingdom, armies and allies. His name was Ali ben Direme.

One night, not being able to sleep at all, he called his vizir, the chief of police, and the commander of his guards. They presented themselves before him without delay, and he ordered them to arm themselves with their swords. They did so at once, and asked him, "What news is there?"

He told them. "The sleep will not come to me; I wish to walk through the town to-night, and I must have you ready to my hand during my round."

"To hear is to obey," they said.

The King then went, saying: "In the name of God! and may the blessing of the prophet be with us, and benediction and mercy be with him."

His suite followed, and accompanied him everywhere from street to street.

So they went on, when they heard a noise in one of the streets, and saw a man in the most violent passion stretched on the ground, face downwards, beating his breast with a stone and crying, "Ah there is no longer any justice here below! Is there nobody who will tell the King what is going on in his states?" And he repeated incessantly: "There is no longer any justice! she has disappeared and the whole world is in mourning."

The King said to his attendants, "Bring this man to

[1] This name is derived from an Arab word, which means to be ferocious, hard, etc., etc.

me quietly, and be careful not to frighten him." They went to him, took him by the hand, and said to him, "Rise and have no fear—no harm will come to you."

To which the man made answer, "You tell me that I shall not come to harm, and have nothing to be afraid of, and still you do not bid me welcome! And you know that the welcome of a believer is a warrant of security and forgiveness.[1] Then, if the believer does not welcome the believer there is certainly ground for fear." He then got up, and went with them towards the King.

The King stood still, hiding his face with his kaïk, as also did his attendants. The latter had their swords in their hands, and leant upon them.

When the man had come close to the King, he said, "Hail be with you, O man!" The King answered, "I return your hail, O man!" Then the man, "Why say you 'O man?'" The King, "And why did you say 'O man?'" "It is because I do not know your name." "And likewise I do not know yours!"

The King then asked him, "What mean those words I have heard: 'Ah! there is no more justice here below! Nobody tells the King what is going on in his states!' Tell me what has happened to you." "I shall tell it only to that man that can avenge me and free me from oppression and shame, if it so please the Almighty God!"

The King said to him, "May God place me at your disposal for your revenge and deliverance from oppression and shame?"

---

[1] The author plays with the word selam, which has two meanings—Security, the state of a man who is right and safe; and greeting, welcome. Es selam alik is the formula employed as welcome.

"What I shall now tell you," said the man, "is mar-vellous and surprising. I loved a woman, who loved me also, and we were united in love. These relations lasted a long while, until an old woman enticed my mistress and took her away to a house of misfortune, shame and debauchery. Then sleep fled from my couch; I have lost all my happiness, and I have fallen into the abyss of misfortune."

The King then said to him, "Which is that house of ill omen, and with whom is the woman?"

The man replied, "She is with a negro of the name of Dorerame, who has at his house women beautiful as the moon, the likes of whom the King has not in his place. He has a mistress who has a profound love for him, is entirely devoted to him, and who sends him all he wants in the way of silver, beverages and clothing."

Then the man stopped speaking. The King was much surprised at what he had heard, but the Vizir, who had not missed a word of this conversation, had certainly made out, from what the man had said that the negro was no other than his own.

The King requested the man to show him the house. "If I show it you, what will you do?" asked the man.

"You will see what I shall do," said the King. "You will not be able to do anything," replied the man, "for it is a place which must be respected and feared. If you want to enter it by force you will risk death, for its master is redoubtable by means of his strength and courage."

"Show me the place," said the King, "and have no fear." The man said, "So be it as God will!"

He then rose, and walked before them. They followed him to a wide street, where he stopped in front of a house with lofty doors, the walls being on all sides high and inaccessible.

They examined the walls, looking for a place where they might be scaled, but with no result. To their surprise they found the house to be as close as a breastplate.

The King turned to the man and asked him, "What is your name?"

"Omar ben Isad," he replied.

The King said to him, "Omar, are you demented?"

"Yes, my brother," answered he, "if it so pleases God on high!" And turning to the King he added, "May God assist you to-night!"

Then the King, addressing his attendants, said, "Are you determined? Is there one amongst you who could scale these walls?"

"Impossible!" they all replied.

Then said the King, "I myself will scale this wall, so please God on high! but by means of an expedient for which I require your assistance, and if you lend me the same I shall scale the wall, if it pleases God on high."

They said, "What is there to be done?"

"Tell me," said the King, "who is the strongest amongst you." They replied, "The chief of the police, who is your chaouch."

The King said, "And who next?"

"The commander of the guards."

"And after him, who?" asked the King.

"The Grand Vizir."

Omar listened with astonishment. He knew now that it was the King, and his joy was great.

The King said, "Who is there yet?"

Omar replied, "I, O my master."

The King said to him, "Omar, you have found out who we are; but do not betray our disguise, and you will be absolved from blame."

"To hear is to obey," said Omar.

The King then said to the chaouch, "Rest your hands against the wall so that your back projects."

The chaouch did so.

Then said the King to the commander of the guards, "Mount upon the back of the chaouch." He did so, and stood with his feet on the other men's shoulders. Then the King ordered the Vizir to mount, and he got on the shoulders of the commander of the guards, and put his hands against the wall.

Then said the King, "O Omar, mount upon the high-est place!" And Omar, surprised by this expedient, cried, "May God lend you his help, O our master, and assist you in your just enterprise!" He then got on to the shoulders of the chaouch, and from there upon the back of the commander of the guards, and then upon that of the Vizir, and, standing upon the shoulders of the latter, he took the same position as the others. There was now only the King left.

Then the King said, "In the name of God! and his blessing be with the prophet, upon whom the mercy and salutation of God!" and, placing his hand upon the back of the chaouch, he said, "Have a moment's pa-tience; if I succeed you will be compensated!" He then did the same with the others, until he got upon Omar's back, to whom he also said, "O Omar, have a moment's patience with me, and I shall name you my private sec-retary. And, of all things do not move!" Then, placing his feet upon Omar's shoulders, the King could with his hands grasp the terrace, and crying, "In the name of God! may he pour his blessings upon the prophet, to whom come the mercy and salutation of God!" And with that he made a spring, and stood upon the terrace.

Then he said to his attendants, "Descend now from each other's shoulders!"

And they got down one after another, and they could not help admiring the ingenious idea of the King, as well as the strength of the chaouch who carried four men at once.

The King then began to look for a place for descend-ing, but found no passage. He unrolled his turban, fixed one end with a single knot at the place where he was, and let himself down into the courtyard, which he ex-plored until he found the portal in the middle of the house fastened with an enormous lock. The solidity of this lock, and the obstacle it created, gave him a dis-agreeable surprise. He said to himself, "I am now in a difficulty, but all comes from God; it was he who gave me the strength and the idea that brought me here; he will also provide the means for me to return to my companions."

He then set himself to examine the place where he found himself, and counted the chambers one after an-other. He found seventeen chambers or rooms, fur-nished in different styles, with tapestries and velvet hangings of various colours, from the first to the last.

Examining all round, he saw a place raised by seven stair-steps, from which issued a great noise from voices. He went up to it, saying, "O God! favour my project, and let me come safe and sound out of here.

He mounted on the first step, saying, "In the name of God the mild and merciful!" Then he began to look at the steps, which were of variously coloured marble—black, red, white, green and other shades.

Mounting the second step, he said, "He whom God helps is invincible!"

On the third step he said, "With the aid of God the victory is near."

And on the fourth, "I have asked for victory of God, who is the most auxiliary."

Finally he mounted the fifth, sixth, and seventh step invoking the prophet (with whom be the mercy and salvation of God).

He arrived then at the curtain hanging at the entrance; it was of red brocade. From there he examined the room, which was bathed in light, filled with many chandeliers, and candles burning in golden sconces. In the middle of this saloon played a jet of musk-water. A table-cloth extended from end to end,[1] covered with sundry meats and fruits.

The saloon was provided with gilt furniture, the splendour of which dazzled the eye. In fact, everywhere there were ornaments of all kinds.

On looking closer the King ascertained that round that table-cloth there were twelve maidens and seven women, all like moons; he was astonished at their beauty and grace. There were likewise with them seven negroes, and this view filled him with surprise. His attention was above all attracted by a woman like the full moon, of perfect beauty, with black eyes, oval cheeks, and a lithe

---

[1] The Arabs eat lying on carpets and cushions; they do not make use of tables, but have a table-cloth made of leather or stuff which is stretched on the ground for putting the dishes on. This table-cloth is called sefra.

and graceful waist; she humbled the hearts of those who got enamoured with her.

Stupified by her beauty, the King was like stunned. He then said to himself, "How is there any getting out of this place? O my spirit, do not give way to love!"

And continuing his inspection of the room, he perceived in the hands of those who were present glasses filled with wine. They were drinking and eating, and it was easy to see they were overcome with drink.

While the King was thinking how to get out of his embarrassment he heard one of the women saying to one of her companions, calling her by name, "Oh, so and so, rise and light a torch, so that we can go to bed, for the sleep is overpowering us. Come, light the torch and let us retire to the other chamber."

They rose and lifted up the curtain to leave the room. The King hid himself to let them pass out; then, perceiving that they had left their chamber to do a thing necessary and obligatory to human kind, he took advantage of their absence, entered their apartment, and hid himself in a cupboard.

Whilst the King was thus in hiding the women returned and shut the doors. Their reason was obscure by the fumes of wine; they pulled off all their clothes and began to caress each other mutually.[1]

The King said to himself, "Omar has told me true about this house of misfortune as an abyss of debauchery."

When the women had fallen asleep the King rose, ex-

---

[1] The text says literally, "They set to work on each other mutually."

tinguished the light, undressed, and laid down between the two. He had taken care during their conversation to impress their names on his memory. So he was able to say to one of them, "You—so and so—where have you put the door-keys?" speaking very low.

The woman answered, "Go to sleep, you whore, the keys are at their usual place."

The King said to himself, "There is no might and strength but in God the Almighty and Benevolent!" and was much troubled.

And again he asked the woman about the keys, saying, "Daylight is coming. I must open the doors. There is the sun. I am going to open the house."

And she answered, "The keys are in the usual place. Why do you thus bother me? Sleep, I say, till it is day."

And again the King said to himself, "There is no might and strength but in God the Almighty and Benevolent, and surely if it were not for the fear of God I should run my sword through her." Then he began again, "Oh, you so and so!"

She said, "What do you want?"

"I am uneasy," said the King, "about the keys; tell me where they are?"

And she answered, "You hussy! Does your vulva itch for coition? Cannot you do without for a single night? Look! the Vizir's wife has withstood all the entreaties of the negro, and repelled him since six months! Go, the keys are in the negro's pocket. Do not say to him, 'Give me the keys'; but say, 'Give me your member.' You know his name is Dorerame."

The King was now silent, for he knew what to do. He waited a short time till the woman was asleep; then he dressed himself in her clothes, and concealed his sword under them; his face he hid under a veil of red silk. Thus dressed he looked like other women. He then opened the door, stole softly out, and placed himself behind the curtains of the saloon entrance. He saw only some people sitting there; the remainder were asleep.

The King made the following silent prayer, "O my soul, let me follow the right way, and let all those people among whom I find myself be stunned with drunkenness, so that they cannot know the King from his subjects, and God give me strength."

He then entered the saloon saying: "In the name of God!" and he tottered towards the bed of the negro as if drunk. The negroes and the women took him to be the woman whose attire he had taken.

Dorerame had a great desire to have his pleasure with that woman, and when he saw her sit down by the bed he thought that she had broken her sleep to come to him, perhaps for love games. So he said, "Oh, you, so-and-so, undress and get into my bed, I shall soon be back."

The King said to himself, "There is no might and strength but in the High God, the Benevolent!" Then he searched for the keys in the clothes and pockets of the negro, but found nothing. He said, "God's will be done!" Then raising his eyes, he saw a high window; he reached up with his arm, and found gold embroidered garments there; he slipped his hands into the pockets, and, oh, surprised! he found the keys there. He examined them and counted seven, corresponding to the number of the doors of the house, and in his joy, he exclaimed, "God be praised and glorified!" Then he said, "I can only get out of here by a ruse." Then feigning sickness, and appearing as if he wanted to vomit violently, he held his hand before his mouth, and hurried to the centre of the courtyard. The negro said to him, "God bless you! oh, so-and-so! any other women would have been sick into the bed!"

The King then went to the inner door of the house, and opened it; he closed it behind him, and so from one door to the other, till he came to the seventh, which opened upon the street. Here he found his companions again, who had been in great anxiety, and who asked him what he had seen?

Then said the King: "This is not the time to answer. Let us go into this house with the blessing of God and with his help."

They resolved to be upon their guard, there being in the house seven negroes, twelve maidens and seven women, beautiful as moons.

The Vizir asked the King, "What garments are these?" And the King answered, "Be silent; without them I should never have got the keys."

He then went to the chamber where the two women were, with whom he had been lying, took off the clothes in which he was dressed, and resumed his own, taking good care of his sword. He then went to the saloon, where the negroes and the women were, and he and his companions ranged themselves behind the door-curtain.

After having had a look into the saloon, they said, "Amongst all these women there is none more beautiful than the one seated on the elevated cushion!" The King said, "I reserve her for myself, if she does not belong to someone else."

While they were examining the interior of the saloon, Dorerame descended from the bed, and after him one of the beautiful women. Then another negro got on the bed with another woman, and so on till to the seventh. They rode them in this way one after the other, excepting the beautiful woman mentioned above, and the maidens. Each of these women appeared to mount upon the bed with marked reluctance, and descended, after the coition was finished, with the head bent down.

However, the negroes were lusting after, and pressing one after the other, the beautiful woman. But she spurned them all, saying, "I shall never consent to it, and as to these virgins, I take them also under my protection."

Dorerame then rose and went up to her, holding in his hands his member in full erection, stiff as a pillar.[1] He hit her with it on the face and head, saying, "Six times this night I was pressing you to cede to my desires, and you always refuse; but now I must have you, even this night."

When the woman saw the stubbornness of the negro and the state of drunkenness he was in, she tried to soften him by promises. "Sit down here by me," she said, "and tonight thy desires shall be contented."

The negro sat down near her with his member still erect as a column. The King could scarcely master his surprise.

---

[1] The Arabian text has it literally, Ou airouhou kaime bine iadihi ki el eumoud. Eumoud signifies "pillar, column."

The woman began to sing the following verses, inton-
ing them from the bottom of her heart:

"I prefer the young man for coition, and him only;
He is of courage full—he is my sole ambition,
His member is strong to deflower the virgin,
And richly proportioned in all its dimensions;
It has a head alike to a brazier,
Enormous, and none like it in creation;
Strong it is and hard, and with the head rounded off,
It is always ready for action and does not die down;
It never sleeps, owing to the violence of its love.
It sighs to enter my vulva, and sheds tears on my belly;
It asks not for help, not being in want of any;
It needs no ally, and stands alone the greatest fatigues,
And nobody can be sure of what will result from its efforts.
Full of vigour and life, it bores into my vagina,
And it works about there in action constant and splendid.
First from the front to the back, and then from right to left;
Now it is crammed hard in by vigorous pressure,
Now it rubs its head on the orifice of my vagina.
And he strokes my back, my stomach, my sides,
Kisses my cheeks, and anon begins to suck at my lips.
He embraces me close, and makes me roll on the bed,
And between his arms I am like a corpse without life.
Every part of my body receives in turn his love-bites,
And he covers me with kisses of fire;
When he sees me in heat he quickly comes to me,
Then he opens my thighs and kisses my belly,
And he puts his tool in my hand to make it knock at my door.
Soon he is in the cave, and I feel the pleasure approaching.
He shakes me and thrills me, and hotly we both are working,
And he says, 'Receive my seed!' and I answer, 'Oh give it,
    beloved one!
It shall be welcome to me, you light of my eyes!
Oh, you man of all men, who fillest me with pleasure.
Oh, you soul of my soul, go on with fresh vigour,
For you must not yet withdraw it from me; leave it there,
And this day will then be finished free of all sorrow.'
He has sworn to God to have me for seventy nights,
And what he wished for he did in the way of kisses and em-
    braces during all those nights."

When she had finished the King, in great surprise, said, "How lascivious has God made this woman." And turning to his companions, "There is no doubt that this woman has no husband, and has not been debauched, for, certainly that negro is in love with her, and she has nevertheless repulsed him."

Omar ben Isad took the word, "This is true, O King! Her husband has been now away for nearly a year, and many men have endeavoured to debauch her, but she has resisted.

The King asked, "Who is her husband?" And after his companions answered, "She is the wife of the son of your father's Vizir."

The King replied, "You speak true; I have indeed heard it said that the son of my father's Vizir had a wife without fault, endowed with beauty and perfection and of exquisite shape; not adulterous and innocent of debauchery."

"This is the same woman," they said.

The King said, "No matter how, but I must have her," and turning to Omar, he added, "Where, amongst these women, is your mistress?" Omar answered, "I do not see her, O King!" Upon which the King said, "Have patience, I will show her to you." Omar was quite surprised to find that the King knew so much. "And this then is the negro Dorerame?" asked the King. "Yes, and he is a slave of mine," answered the Vizir. "Be silent, this is not the time to speak," said the King.

While this discourse was going on, the negro Dorerame, still desirous of obtaining the favours of that lady, said to her, "I am tired of your lies, O Beder el Bedour" (full moon of the full moons), for so she called herself.

The King said, "He who called her so called her by
her true name, for she is the full moon of the full moons,
afore God!"

However, the negro wanted to draw the woman away
with him, and hit her in the face.

The King, mad with jealousy, and with his heart full
of ire, said to the Vizir, "Look what your negro is doing! By God! he shall die the death of a villain, and I
shall make an example of him, and a warning to those
who would imitate him!"

At that moment the King heard the lady say to the
negro, "You are betraying your master the Vizir with his
wife, and now you betray her, in spite of your intimacy
with her and the favours she grants to you.[1] And surely
she loves you passionately, and you are pursuing another
woman!"

The King said to the Vizir, "Listen, and do not speak
a word."

The lady then rose and returned to the place where
she had been before, and began to recite:

"Oh, men! listen to what I say on the subject of women,[2]
For her thirst for coition is written between her eyes.
Do not put trust in her vows, and were she the Sultan's
     daughter.
Woman's malice is boundless; not even the King of kings
Would suffice to subdue it, what'er be his might.
Men, take heed and shun the love of woman!
Do not say, 'Such a one is my well beloved';

[1] You are betraying your master," etc., etc. By this phrase
is rendered a passage in the text which runs, "You betray the
salt, and you betray the wife of the Vizir." "To betray the
salt" is a figurative phrase in allusion to the Oriental usage of
hospitality in offering salt, and signifies "betraying the host, the
master, the hand that nourishes."

[2] "Women's nature is represented to us by the moon."—
(Rabelais, book iii., chap. xxxii.)

Do not say, 'She is my life's companion.'
If I deceive you, then say my words are untruths.
As long as she is with you in bed, you have her love,
But a woman's love is not enduring, believe me.
Lying upon her breast, you are her love-treasure;
Whilst the coition goes on, you have her love, poor fool!
But, anon, she looks upon you as a fiend;
And this is a fact undoubted and certain.
The wife receives the slave in the bed of the master,
And the serving-men allay upon her their lust.
Certain it is, such conduct is not to be praised and honored.
But the virtue of women is frail and changeful,
And the man thus deceived is looked upon with contempt.
Therefore a man with a heart should not put trust in a woman."

At these words the Vizir began to cry, but the King
bade him to be quiet. Then the negro recited the following verses in response to those of the lady:

"We negroes have had our fill of women,
We fear not their tricks, however subtle they be.
Men confide in us with regard to what they cherish.[1]
This is no lie remember, but is the truth, as you know.
Oh, you women all! for sure you have no patience when the
    virile member you are wanting,
For in the same resides your life and death;
It is the end and all of your wishes, secret or open.
If your choler and ire are aroused against your husbands,
They appease you simply by introducing their members.
Your religion resides in your vulva, and the manly member is
    your soul.
Such you will always find in the nature of woman."

[1] This verse alludes to the fact that negroes, as domestics,
are considered as an inferior class, who are allowed to come
near women, as incapable of making an impression.

With that, the negro threw himself upon the woman, who pushed him back.

At this moment the King felt his heart oppressed: he drew his sword, as did his companions, and they entered the room. The negroes and women saw nothing but brandished swords.

One of the negroes rose, and rushed upon the King and his companions, but the Chaouch severed with one blow his head from his body. The King cried, "God's blessing upon you! Your arm is not withered and your mother has not borne a weakling. You have struck down your enemies, and the paradise shall be your dwelling and place of rest!"

Another negro got up and aimed a blow at the Chaouch, which broke the sword of the Chaouch in twain. It had been a beautiful weapon, and the Chaouch, on seeing it ruined, broke out into the most violent passion; he seized the negro by the arm, lifted him up, and threw him against the wall, breaking his bones. Then the King cried, "God is great. He has not dried up your hand. Oh, what a Chaouch! God grant you his blessings."

The negroes, when they saw this, were cowed and silent, and the King, master now of their lives, said, "The man that lifts his hand only, shall lose his head!" And he commanded that the remaining five negroes should have their hands tied behind their backs.

This having been done, he turned to Beder el Bedour and asked her, "Whose wife are you, and who is this negro?"

She then told him on that subject what he had heard already from Omar. And the King thanked her saying,

"May God give you his blessing." He then asked her, "Ho long can a woman patiently do without coition?" She seemed amazed, but the King said, "Speak, and do not be abashed."

She then answered, "A well-born lady of high origin can remain for six months without; but a lowly woman of no race nor high blood, who does not respect herself when she can lay her hand upon a man, will have him upon her; his stomach and his member will know her vagina."

Then said the King, pointing to one of the women, "Who is this one?" She answered, "This is the wife of the Kadi." "And this one?" "The wife of the second Vizir." "And this?" "The wife of the chief of the Muftis." "And that one?" "The Treasurer's." "And those two women that are in the other room?" She answered, "They have received the hospitality of the house, and one of them was brought here yesterday by an old woman; the negro has so far not got possession of her."

Then said Omar. "This is the one I spoke to you about, O my master."

"And the other woman? To whom does she belong?" said the King.

"She is the wife of the Amine [1] of the carpenters," answered she.

Then said the King, "And these girls, who are they?" She answered, "This one is the daughter of the clerk of the treasury; this other one the daughter of the

---

[1] The title Amine corresponds to our councillor; syndic.

Mohtesib,[1] the third is the daughter of the Bouab;[2] the next one the daughter of the Amine of the Moueddin;[3] that one the daughter of the colour-keeper."[4]   At the invitation of the King, she passed them thus all in review.

The King then asked for the reason of so many women being brought together there.

Beder el Bedour replied, "O master of ours, the negro knows no other passions than for coition and good wine. He keeps making love night and day, and his member rests only when he is asleep himself."

The King asked further, "What does he live upon?"

She said, "Upon yolks of eggs fried in fat and swimming in honey, and upon white bread; he drinks nothing but old muscatel wine."

The King said, "Who has brought these women here, who, all of them, belong to officials of the State?"

She replied, "O master of ours, he has in his service an old woman who has had the run of the houses in the town; she chooses and brings to him any woman of superior beauty and perfection; but she serves him only against good consideration in silver, dresses, etc., precious stones, rubies, and other objects of value."

---

[1] The Mohtesib is a commissioner of the police, charged with surveying weights and measures.

[2] Bouab signifies an usher.

[3] The Moueddin are the criers, who call from the top of the Mosques the true believers to prayers.

[4] The Oriental sovereigns having a great number of flags, standards, etc., which are carried before them on the occasions of state ceremonials, and which they take with them to their wars, the keeper of those colours is a man of importance.

"And whence does the negro get the silver?" asked the King. The lady remaining silent, he added, "Give me some information, please."

She signified with a sign from the corner of her eye that he had got it all from the wife of the Grand Vizir.

The King understood her, and continued, "O Beder el Bedour! I have faith and confidence in you, and your testimony will have in my eyes the value of that of the two Adels.[1] Speak to me without reserve as to what concerns yourself."

She answered him, "I have not been touched, and however long this might have lasted the negro would not have got his desire satisfied."

"Is this so?" asked the King.

She replied, "It is so!" She had understood what the King wanted to say, and the King has seized the meaning of her words.

"Has the negro respected my honour? Inform me about that," said the King.

She answered, "He has respected your honour as far as your wives are concerned. He has not pushed his criminal deeds that far; but if God has spared his days there is no certainty that he would not have tried to soil what he should have respected."

The King having asked her then who those negroes were, she answered, "They are his companions. After he has quite surfeited himself with the women which he had got brought to him, he handed them over to them, as you have seen. If it were not for the protection of a woman where would that man be?"

---

[1] The two Adels (Adeline) are the two sworn witnesses who assist the Cadi when he sits in judgment.

Then spoke the King, "O Beder el Bedour, why did not your husband ask my help against this oppression? Why did you not complain?"

She replied, "O King of the time, O beloved Sultan, O master of numerous armies and allies! As regards my husband I was so far unable to inform him of my lot; as to myself I have nothing to say but what you know by the verses I sung just now. I have given advice to men about women from the first verse to the last."

The King said, "O Beder el Bedour! I like you, I have put the question to you in the name of the chosen Prophet (the benediction and mercy of God be with him!). Inform me of everything; you have nothing to fear; I give you the aman [1] complete. Has this negro not enjoyed you? For I presume that none of you were out of reach of his attempts and had your honours safe."

She replied, "O King of our time, in the name of your high rank and your power! Look! He, about whom you ask me, I would not have accepted him as a legimate husband; how could I have consented to grant him the favour of an illicit love?"

The King said, "You appear to be sincere, but the verses I heard you sing have roused doubts in my soul."

She replied, "I had three motives to hold that language. Firstly, I was at that moment in heat, like a young mare; secondly, Eblis had excited my natural parts, and lastly, I wanted to quiet the negro and make him have patience, so that he should grant me some delay and leave me in peace until God would deliver me of him."

---

[1] The aman, that is the pardon, absolution, protection; this is a compact or treaty of indemnity.

The King said, "Do you speak seriously?" She was silent. Then the King cried, "O Beder el Bedour, you alone shall be pardoned!" She understood that it was she only that the King would spare from the punishment of death. He then cautioned her that she must keep the secret, and said he wanted to leave now.

Then all the women and virgins approached Beder el Bedour and implored her, saying, "Intercede for us, for you have power over the King"; and they shed tears over her hands, and in despair threw themselves down.

Beder el Bedour then called the King back, who was going, and said to him, "O our master! you have not granted me any favour yet." "How," said he, "I have sent for a beautiful mule for you; you will mount her and come with us. As for these women, they must all of them die."

She then said, "O our master! I ask you and conjure you to authorize me to make a stipulation which you will accept." The King made oath that he would fulfil it. Then she said, "I ask as a gift the pardon of all these women and of all these maidens. Their deaths would moreover throw the most terrible consternation over the whole town."

The King said, "There is no might nor power but in God, the merciful!" He then ordered the negroes to be taken out and beheaded. The only exception he made was with the negro Dorerame, who was enormously stout and had a neck like a bull. They cut off his ears, nose, and lips; likewise his virile member, which they put into his mouth, and then hung him on a gallows.

Then the King ordered the seven doors of the house to be closed, and returned to his palace.

At sunrise he sent a mule to Beder el Bedour, in order to let her be brought to him. He made her dwell with him, and found her to be excelling all those who excel.

Then the King caused the wife of Omar ben Isad to be restored to him, and he made him his private secretary. Then he ordered the Vizir to repudiate his wife. He did not forget the Chaouch and the commander of the guards, to whom he made large presents, as he had promised, using for that purpose the negro's hoards. He sent the son of his father's Vizir to prison. He also caused the old go-between to be brought before him, and then asked her, "Give me all the particulars about the conduct of the negro, and tell me whether it was well done to bring in that way women to men." She answered, "This is the trade of nearly all old women." He then had her executed, as well as all old women who followed that trade, and thus cut off in his State the tree of panderism as the root, and burnt the trunk.

He besides sent back to their families the women and girls, and bade them repent in the name of God.

This story presents but a small part of the tricks and stratagems used by women against their husbands.

The moral of the tale is, that a man who falls in love with a woman imperils himself, and exposes himself to the greatest troubles.

CHAPTER III

ABOUT MEN WHO ARE TO BE HELD IN CONTEMPT

Know, O my brother (to whom God be merciful), that a man who is misshapen, of coarse appearance, and whose member is short, thin and flabby, is contemptible in the eyes of women.

When such a man has a bout with a woman, he does not do her business with the vigour and in a manner to give her enjoyment. He lays himself down upon her without previous toying, he does not kiss her, nor twine himself round her, he does not bite her, nor suck her lips, nor tickle her.

He gets upon her before she has begun longing for pleasure, and then he introduces with infinite trouble a member soft and nerveless. Scarcely has he commenced when he is already done for; he makes one or two move- ments, and then sinks upon the woman's breast to spend his sperm, and that is the most he can do. This done he withdraws his affair, and makes all haste to get down again from her.

Such a man—as was said by a writer—is quick in ejaculation and slow as to erection; after the trembling, which follows the ejaculation of the seed, his chest is heavy and his sides ache.

Qualities like those are no recommendations with women. Despicable also is the man who is false to his words; who does not fulfil the promise he has made; who never speaks without telling lies, and who conceals from his wife all his doings, except the adulterous exploits which he commits.

Women cannot esteem such men, as they cannot procure them any enjoyment.

It is said that a man of the name of Abbès, whose member was extremely small and slight, had a very corpulent wife, whom he could not contrive to satisfy in coition, so that she soon began to complain to her female friends about it.

This woman possessed a considerable fortune, whilst Abbès was very poor; and when he wanted anything, she was sure not to let him have what he wanted.

One day he went to see a wise man, and submitted his case to him.

The sage told him: "If you had a fine member you might dispose of her fortune. Do you not know that women's religion is in their vulva's? But I will prescribe you a remedy which will do away with your troubles."

Abbès lost no time to make up the remedy according to the recipe of the wise man, and after he had used it his member grew to be long and thick. When his wife saw it in that state she was surprised, but it came still better when he made her feel in the matter of enjoyment quite another thing than she had been accustomed to experience; he began in fact to work her with his tool in a quite remarkable manner to such point that she rattled and sighed and sobbed and cried out during the operation.

As soon as the wife found in her husband such eminently good qualities she gave him her fortune, and placed her person and all she had at his disposal.

CHAPTER IV

ABOUT WOMEN WHO ARE TO BE HELD IN CONTEMPT

Know, O Vizir (to whom God be merciful), that women differ in their natural dispositions: there are women who are worthy of all praise; and there are, on the other hand, women who only merit contempt.

The woman who merits the contempt of the men is ugly and garrulous; her hair is wooly, her forehead projecting, her eyes are small and blear, the nose is enormous, the lips lead-coloured, the mouth large, the cheeks wrinkled and she shows gaps in her teeth; her cheekbones shine purple, and she sports bristles on her chin; her head sits on a meagre neck, with very much developed tendons; her shoulders are contracted and her chest is narrow, with flabby pendulous breasts, and her belly is like an empty leather-bottle, with the navel standing out like a heap of stones; her flanks are shaped like arcades; the bones of her spinal column may be counted; there is no flesh upon her croup; her vulva is large and cold, and exhales an odour of carrion; it is hairless, pale and wet, with a long hard, greasy clitoris projecting out of it.

Finally, such a woman has large knees and feet,[1] big hands and emaciated legs.

A woman with such blemishes can give no pleasure to men in general, and least of all to him who is her husband or who enjoys her favours.

---

[1] "Feet like a guitar."—(Rabelais, book iv., chap. xxxi.)

The man who approaches a woman like that with his member in erection will find it presently soft and relaxed, as though he was only close to a beast of burden. May God keep us from a woman of that description!

Contemptible is likewise the woman who is constantly laughing out; for, as it was said by an author, "If you see a woman who is always laughing, found of gaming and jesting, always running to her neighbours, meddling with matters that are no concern of hers, plaguing her husband with constant complaints, leaguing herself with other women against him, playing the grand lady, accepting gifts from everybody, know that that woman is a whore without shame."

And again to be despised is the woman of a sombre, frowning nature, and one who is prolific in talk; the woman who is lightheaded in her relations with men, or contentious, or fond of tittle-tattle and unable to keep her husband's secrets, or who is malicious. The woman of a malicious nature talks only to tell lies; if she makes a promise she does so only to break it, and if anybody confides in her, she betrays him; she is debauched, thievish, a scold, coarse and violent; she cannot give good advice; she is always occupied with the affairs of other people, and with such as bring harm, and is always on the watch for frivolous news; she is fond of repose, but not of work; she uses unbecoming words in addressing a Mussulman, even to her husband; invectives are always at her tongue's end; she exhales a bad odour which infects you, and sticks to you even after you have left her.

And no less contemptible is she who talks to no purpose, who is a hypocrite and does no good act; she, who, when her husband asks her to fulfil the conjugal office, refuses to listen to his demand; the woman who does not assist her husband in his affairs; and finally, she who plagues him with unceasing complaints and tears.

A woman of that sort, seeing her husband irritated or in trouble does not share his affliction; on the contrary, she laughs and jests all the more, and does not try to drive away his ill-humour by endearments. She is more prodigal with her person to other men than to her husband; it is not for his sake that she adorns herself, and it is not to please him that she tries to look well. Far from that; with him she is very untidy, and does not care to let him see things and habits about her person which must be repugnant to him. Lastly, she never uses either Atsmed nor Souak.[1]

No happiness can be hoped for a man with such a wife. God keep us from such a one!

---

[1] Atsmed is antimony, of which an eye-salve is made. The women blacken the inside of the eyelids with it, to make the eyes appear to look larger and more brilliant.

CHAPTER V

RELATING TO THE ACT OF GENERATION

Know, O Vizir (and God protect you!), that if you wish for coition, that in joining the woman you should have your stomach not loaded with food and drink, only in that condition will your cohabitation be wholesome and good. If your stomach is full, only harm can come of it to both of you; you will have symptoms of apoplexy and gout, and the least evil that will be the consequence of it will be the inability of passing your urine or weak-ness of sight.

Let your stomach then be free from excessive food and drink, and you need not apprehend any illness.

Before setting to work with your wife excite her with toying, so that the copulation will finish to your mutual satisfaction.

Thus it will be well to play with her before you intro-duce your verge and accomplish the cohabitation. You will excite her by kissing her cheeks, sucking her lips and nibbling at her breasts. Lavish kisses on her navel and thighs, and titillate the lower parts. Bite her arms, and neglect no part of her body; cling close to her chest, and show your love and submission. Interlace your legs with hers, and press her in your arms, for, as the poet has said:

"Under her neck my right hand has served her for a cushion,
And to draw her to me
I have sent out my left hand,
Which bore her up as a bed."

When you are close to a woman, and you see her eyes getting dim, and hear her, yearning for coition, heave deep sighs, then let your and her yearning be joined into one, and let your lubricity rise to the highest point; for this will be the moment most favourable to the game of love. The pleasure which the woman then feels will be extreme; as for yourself, you will cherish her all the more, and she will continue her affection for you, for it has been said:

"If you see a woman heaving deep sighs, with her lips getting red and her eyes languishing, when her mouth half opens and her movements get heedless; when she appears to be disposed to go to sleep, vascillating in her steps and prone to yawn, know that this is the moment for coition, and if you there and then make your way into her you will procure for her an unquestionable treat. You yourself will find the mouth of her womb clasping your article, which is undoubtedly the crown-ing pleasure for both, for this before everything begets affection and love."

The following precepts, coming from a profound con-noisseur in love affairs, are well known:

"Woman is like a fruit, which will not yield its sweet-ness until you rub it between your hands. Look at the basil plant; if you do not rub it warm with your fingers it will not emit any scent. Do you not know that the amber, unless it be handled and warmed, keeps hidden within its pores the aroma contained in it? It is the same with woman. If you do not animate her with your toying, intermixed with kissing, nibbling and touching, you will not obtain from her what you are wishing; you will feel no enjoyment when you share her couch, and you will waken in her heart neither inclination nor affec-tion, nor love for you; all her qualities will remain hid-den.

It is reported that a man, having asked a woman what means were the most likely to create affection in the female heart, with respect to the pleasures of coition, received confidentially the following answer:—

"O you who question me, what develops the taste for coition are the toyings and touches which precede it, and then the close embrace at the moment of the ejaculation!

"Believe me, the kisses, nibblings, suction of the lips, the close embrace, the visits of the mouth to the nipples of the bosom, and the sipping of the fresh saliva, these are the things to render affection lasting.

"In acting thus, the two ejaculations take place simultaneously, and the enjoyment comes to the man and woman at the same moment. Then the man feels the womb grasping his member, which gives to each of them the most exquisite pleasure.

"This it is which gives birth to love, and if matters have not been managed this way the woman has not had her full share of pleasure, and the delights of the womb are wanting. Know that the woman will not feel her desires satisfied, and will not love her rider unless he is able to act up to her womb; but when the womb is made to enter into action she will feel the most violent love for her cavalier, even if he be unsightly in appearance.

"Then do all you can to cause a simultaneous discharge of the two spermal fluids; herein lies the secret of love."

One of the savants who has occupied himself with this subject thus relates the confidences a woman made to him:

"O you men, one and all, who are soliciting the love of woman and her affection, and who wish that sentiment in her heart to be of an enduring nature, toy with her previous to coition; prepare her for the enjoyment, and neglect nothing to attain that end. Explore her with the greater assiduity, and, entirely occupied with her, let nothing else engage your thoughts. Do not let the propitious moment for enjoyment pass away; that moment will be when you see her eyes humid, half open. Then go to work, but, remember, not till your kisses and toyings have taken effect.

"After you have got the woman into a proper state of excitement, O men! put your member into her, and, if you then observe the proper movements, she will experience a pleasure which will satisfy all her desires.

"Lie on her breast, rain kisses on her cheeks, and let not your member quit her vagina. Push for the mouth of her womb. This will crown your labour.

"If, by God's favour, you have found it, take good care not to withdraw your member, but let it remain there, and imbibe an endless pleasure! Listen to the sighs and heavy breathing of the woman. They witness the violence of the bliss you have given her.

"And after the enjoyment is over, and your amorous struggle has come to an end, be careful not to get up at once, but withdraw your member cautiously. Remain close to the woman, and lie down on the right side of the bed that witnessed your enjoyment. You will find this pleasant, and you will not be like a fellow who mounts the woman after the fashion of a mule, without any regard to refinement, and who, after the emission, hastens to get his member out, and to rise. Avoid such manners, for they rob the woman of all her pleasure."

In short, the true lover of coition will not fail to observe all what I have recommended; for, from the observance of my recommendations will result the pleasure of the woman, and these rules comprise everything essential in that respect.

God has made everything for the best!

CHAPTER VI

CONCERNING EVERYTHING THAT IS FAVOURABLE
TO THE ACT OF COITION

Know, O Vizir (God be good to you!), if you would
have a pleasant coition, which ought to give an equal
share of happiness to the two combatants and be satisfactory to both, you must first of all toy with the woman, excite her with kisses, by nibbling and sucking her
lips, by caressing her neck and cheeks. Turn her over
in bed, now on her back, now on her stomach, till you
see by her eyes that the time for pleasure is near, as I
have mentioned in the preceding chapter, and certainly
I have not been sparing with my observations thereupon.

Then when you observe the lips of a woman to tremble and get red, and her eyes to become languishing, and
her sighs to become quicker, know that she is hot for
coition, then get between her thighs, so that your member can enter into her vagina. If you have followed my
advice, you will have both a pleasant coition, which will
give you the greatest satisfaction, and leave to you a
delicious remembrance.

Someone has said:

"If you desire the coition, place the woman on the
ground, cling closely to her bosom, with her lips close
to yours; then clasp her to you, such her breath, bite
her; kiss her breasts, her stomach, her flanks, press her
close in your arms, so as to make her faint with pleasure;
when you see her so far gone, then push your member
into her. If you have done as I said, the enjoyment will

come to both of you simultaneously. This it is which makes the pleasure. of the woman so sweet. But if you neglect my advice the woman will not be satisfied and you will not have procured her any pleasure."

The coition being finished, do not get up at once, but come down softly on her right side, and if she has con-ceived, she will bear a male child, if it please God on high!

Sages and Savants (may God grant to all his forgive-ness!) have said:

"If anyone placing his hand upon the vulva of a wo-mon that is with child pronounces the following words. 'In the name of God! may he grant salutation and mercy to his Prophet (salutation and mercy be with him). Oh! my God! I pray thee in the name of the Prophet to let a boy issue from this conception,' it will come to pass by the will of God, and in consideration for our lord Mo-hammed (the salutation and grace of God be with him), the woman will be delivered of a boy."

Do not drink rain-water directly after copulation, be-cause this beverage weakens the kidneys.

If you want to repeat the coition, perfume yourself with sweet scents, then close with the woman, and you will arrive at a happy result.

Do not let the woman perform the act of coition mounted upon you, for fear that in that position some drops of her seminal fluid might enter the canal of your verge and cause a sharp uretritis.[1]

Do not work hard directly after coition; this might affect your health badly, but go to rest for some time.

---

[1] Although the dictionary gives no clue with respect to this illness, I thought it well, in conformity with the information I took, to call it sharp uretritis, a disease which is vulgarly called gonorrhoea with stricture.

Do not wash your verge directly after having with-drawn it from the vagina of the woman; until the irritat-tion has gone down somewhat; then wash it and its opening carefully. Otherwise, do not wash your mem-ber frequently. Do not leave the vulva directly after the emission, as this may cause canker.[1]

SUNDRY POISONS FOR THE COITUS

The ways of doing it to women are numerous and variable. And now is the time to make known to you the different positions which are usual.

God, the magnificent, has said:

"The women are your field. Go upon your field as you like." [2]   According to your wish you can choose the position you like best, of course provided that the coition takes place in the spot destined for it, that is, in the vulva.

Manner the first.—Make the woman lie upon her back, with her thighs raised, then getting between her legs, introduce your member into her. Then pressing your toes to the ground, you can rummage her in a con-venient, measured way.[3]   This is a good position for a man with a long verge.

---

[1] Although I have translated the word with canker it may, according to the dictum of some practitioners, signify also an affection that is known under the names of seña, otherwise

putrefaction, which is simply gonorrhea.

[2] This passage is an extract from the 223rd verse, chap. ii. of the Koran. The same runs: "The women are your field. Go out upon your field as you list, but do previously some deed for your soul's sake. Fear God and be mindful of the day when you shall be in his presence."

[3] This position for the coition, which may be called the nat-ural one, is called by the Arabs hannechi, which means "the manner of serpents."

Manner the second.—If your member is a short one, let the woman lie on her back, lift her legs into the air, so that her right leg be near her right ear, and the left one near her left ear, and in this posture, with her but-tock lifted up, her vulva will project forward. Then put in your member.

Manner the third.—Let the woman stretch herself upon the ground, and place yourself between her thighs; then putting one of her legs upon your shoulder, and the other under your arm, near the armpit, get into her.

Manner the fourth.—Let her lie down, and put her legs on your shoulders; in this position your member will just face her vulva, which must not touch the ground. And then introduce your member.

Manner the fifth.—Let her lie down on her side, then lie yourself down by her on the side, and getting be-tween her thighs, put your member into her vagina. But the sidelong coition predisposes for rheumatic pains and sciatica.[1]

Manner the sixth.—Make her get down on her knees and elbows, as if kneeling in prayer. In this position the vulva is projected backwards; you then attack her from that side, and put your member into her.[2]

Manner the seventh.—Place the woman on her side, and squat between her thighs, with one of her legs on your shoulder and the other between your thighs, while she remains lying on her side. Then you enter her va-gina, and make her move by drawing her towards your chest by means of your hands, with which you hold her embraced.

[1] The name of the side-coition is in Arabic djenabi, from djeneb, which means "side, sidewards."

[2] In vulgar Arabic, this manner of enjoying woman is called begouri, that is to say, after the fashion of a bull.

Manner the eighth.—Let her stretch herself upon the ground, on her back, with her legs crossed; then mount her like a cavalier on horseback, being on your knees, while her legs are placed under her thighs, and put your member into her vagina.

Manner the ninth.—Place the woman so that she leans with her front, or, if you prefer it, her back upon a moderate elevation, with her feet set upon the ground. She thus offers her vulva to the introduction of your member.[1]

Manner the tenth.—Place the woman near to a low divan, the back of which she can take hold of with her hands; then, getting under her, lift her legs to the height of your navel, and let her clasp you with her legs on each side of your body; in this position plant your verge into her, seizing with your hands the back of the divan. When you begin the action your movements must respond to those of the woman.

Manner the eleventh.—Let her lie upon her back on the ground with a cushion under her posterior; then getting between her legs, and letting her place the sole of her right foot against the sole of her left, introduce your member.

There are other positions besides the above named in use among the peoples of India. It is well for you to know that the inhabitants of those parts have multiplied the different ways to enjoy women, and they have advanced further than we in knowledge and investigation of the coitus.

[1] Note in the autographic edition: It is necessary to observe that in all these descriptions the couch where the encounter takes place is only an Arabian bed, generally formed by several carpets laid one over the other, or covering a mattress, which lies upon the ground. Such a bed is very low, for which reason the author suggests an elevation (platform), when the tryste requires a support of the height of our beds.

Amongst those manners are the following, called:

1. El asemeud, the stopperage.
2. El modefeda, frog-fashion.
3. El mokefa, with the toes cramped.
4. El mokeurmeutt, with the legs in the air.
5. Es setouri, he-goat-fashion.
6. El loulabi, the screw of Archimedes.
7. Ez zedjadja, piercing with the lance.
8. El hedouli, hanging.
9. El kelouci, the somerset.
10. Hachou en nekanok, the tail of the ostrich.
11. Lebeuss el djoureb, in head over heel.
12. Kechef el astine, reciprocal sight of the posteriors.
13. Neza el kouss, the bent of the rainbow.
14. Nesedj el kheuzz, alternative boring.
15. Dok el arz, pounding on the spot.
16. Nik el kohoul, the coition at the back.
17. El keurchi, belly to belly.
18. El kepachi, ram-fashion.
19. El kouri, the camel's hump.
20. Dok el outed, driving the peg home.
21. Sebek el heub, love's fusion.
22. El morteseb, rape.
23. Tred ech chate, sheep-fashion.
24. Kaleb el miche, interchange in coition.
25. Rekeud el air, the tilting of the member.
26. El modakheli, the fitter in.
27. El khouariki, the one who stops in the house.
28. Nik el haddadi, the smith's coition.
29. El moheundi, the seducer.

The first manner.—El asemeud (the stopperage). Place the woman on her back with a cushion under her buttocks, then get between her legs, resting the points of your feet against the ground; bend her thighs against her chest as far as you can; place your hands under her arms so as to enfold her or cramp her shoulders. Then introduce your member, and at the moment of ejaculation draw her towards you. This position is painful for woman, for her thighs being bent upwards and her buttocks raised by the cushion, the walls of her vagina tighten, and the uterus tending forward there is no much room for movement, and scarcely space enough for the intruder; consequently the latter enters with difficulty and strikes against the uterus. This position should therefore not be adopted, unless the man's member is short or soft.

Second manner.—El modefeda (frog fashion). Place the woman on her back, and arrange her thighs so that they touch the heels, which latter are thus coming close to the buttocks; then you sit down in this kind of merry thought,[1] facing the vulva, in which you insert your member; you then place her knees under your arm-pits; and taking firm hold of the upper part of her arms, you draw her towards you at the crisis.

Third manner.—El mokefa (with the toes cramped). Place the woman on her back, and squat on your knees, between her thighs, gripping the ground with the toes; raise her knees as high as your sides, in order that she may cross her legs over your back, and then pass her arms round your neck.

----

[1] The Arab text says mokorfeuss, which signifies the manner to squat on the ground with the arms slung round the legs. The root is a word of four letters, signifying: to tie somebody up by fastening his hands under his feet.

Fourth manner.—El mokeurmeutt (the legs in the air). The woman lying on her back, you put her thighs together and raise her legs up until the soles of her feet look at the ceiling; then enfolding her within your thighs you insert your member, holding her legs up with your hands.

Fifth manner.—Es setouri (he-goat fashion [1]). The woman being crouched on her side, you let her stretch out the leg on which she is resting, and squat down between her thighs with your calves bent under you; [2] then you lift her uppermost leg so that it rests on your back, and introduce your member. During the action you take hold of her shoulders, or, if you prefer it, by the arms.

Sixth manner.—El loulabi (the screw of Archimedes [3]). The man being stretched on his back the woman sits on his member, facing him; she then places her hands upon the bed so that she can keep her stomach from touching the man's, she then moves up and downwards, and if the man is supple he assists her from below. If in this position she wants to kiss him, she need only stretch her arms along the bed.

Seventh manner.—Er zedjadja (piercing with the lance). [4] You suspend the woman from the ceiling by

---

[1] The root of the word setouri is seteur, which means a he-goat.

[2] Note of the autograph edition.   Here occurs the word mokorfeuss, mentioned in note 1, p. 72, and which has been translated with "bending the calves."   This expression recurs frequently, preceded generally by the word djeleuss, "to sit down."

[3] The root of el loulabi is louleb, which means the pipe of a fountain, through which the water is forced, issuing out of a narrow opening, after a system which, like the screw of Archimedes, serves to raise water.

[4] The word ezzedjadja is derived from zedj, to beat, pierce with the zoudj, that is, with the point of the lance.

means of four cords attached to her hands and feet; the middle of her body is supported by a fifth cord, arranged so as not to hurt her back. Her position should be so that if you stand upright before her, her vagina should just face your member, which you introduce into her. You then communicate to the apparatus a swinging motion, first pushing it slightly from you and then drawing it towards you again; in this way your weapon will alternately enter and retire from its sheath, you taking care to hit the entrance on her approach. This action you continue till the ejaculation arrives.

Eighth manner.—El hedouli (suspension). The man brings the woman's hands and feet together in the direction of her neck, so that her vulva is standing out like a dome, and then raises her up by means of a pulley which is fixed in the ceiling. Then he stretches himself out below her, holding in his hand the other end of the cord, by means of which he can lower her down upon himself, and so is able to penetrate into her. He thus causes her alternately to rise and descend upon his tool until the ejaculation takes place.

Ninth Manner.—El kelouci (the summerset). The woman must have a pair of pantaloons on, which she lets drop down upon her heels; she then stoops down, placing her head between her feet, so that her neck is in the pantaloons. At that moment the man, seizing her legs, turns her upon her back, making her perform a summerset; then he brings his member right against her vulva, and, slipping it between her legs, inserts it.

It is alleged that there are women who, lying on their back, can place their feet under the head without the help of pantaloons or of their hands.

Tenth manner.—Hacou en nekanok (the tail of the ostrich). The woman lying on her back along the bed, the man kneels in front of her, and lifts up her legs until her head and shoulders only are resting on the bed; his member sets into motion the buttocks of the woman who, on her part, twines her legs round his neck.[1]

Eleventh manner.—Lebeuss el djoureb (fitting on of the sock).[2] The woman lies on her back, you sit down between her legs and place your member between the lips of her vulva, which you fit over it with your thumb and first finger; then you move so as to procure for your member as far as it is in contact with the woman a lively rubbing, which action you continue until her vulva gets moistened with the liquid emitted from your verge. When she is thus amply prepared for the enjoyment by the alternate coming and going of your weapon in her scabbard, put it into her full length.

Twelfth manner.—Kechef el astine (reciprocal sight of the posteriors).[3] The man lying stretched out on his back, the woman sits down upon his member with her back to the man's face, who presses her sides between his

---

[1] In taking notice of the position, it is easy to understand that the two legs of the woman raised up with the man's head between them may, to a certain extent, appear somewhat like an Ostrich's tail.

[2] The author compares the virile member, which the man with the help of his hand envelopes, so to say, with the lips of the vulva before pushing in, to the foot round which the Arab winds a piece of linen, called djoureb, previous to putting on his shoe.

[3] This posture has received the above name, because during the action each party can see the other's posterior. The name usually employed, has ou kaa, literally signifying head and bottom, can be rendered in French "tete-beche."

thighs and legs, whilst she places her hands upon the bed as a support for her movements, and stooping her head, her eyes are turned towards the buttocks of the man.[1]

Thirteenth manner.—Neza el kouss (the bend of the arch). The woman is lying on her side; the man also on his side, with his face towards her back, pushes in between her legs and introduces his member, with his hands lying on the upper part of her back. As to the woman, she then gets hold of the man's feet, which she lifts up as far as she can, drawing him close to her; thus she forms with the body of the man an arch, of which she is the rise.

Fourteenth manner.—Nesedj el kheuzz (the alternate movement of piercing).[2] The man in sitting attitude places the soles of his feet together, and lowering his thighs, draws his feet nearer to his member; the woman sits down upon his feet, which he takes care to keep firm together. In this position the two thighs of the woman are pressed against the man's flanks, and she puts her arms round his neck. Then the man clasps the woman's ankles, and drawing his feet nearer to his body, brings also the woman sitting on them, within range of his member, which then enters her vagina. By moving his feet he sends her back and brings her forward again, without ever withdrawing his member entirely.

The woman makes herself as light as possible, and assists as well as she can in this come-and-go exercise; her

[1] Ast, translated with foundation, means the posterior; hence the word setani, meaning paederast.

[2] The word nesedj expresses the coming and going movement of the shuttle in weaving, the same being sent to and fro from one side to the other. The word Kheuzz means to perforate, to pierce through and through.

cooperation is indispensable for it. If the man apprehends that his member may come out entirely, he takes her round the waist, and she receives otherwise no other impulse than that which is imparted to her by the feet of the man upon which she is sitting.

Fifteenth manner.—Dok el arz (the pounding on the spot).[1] The man sits down with his legs stretched out; the woman then places herself astride on his thighs, crossing her legs behind the back of the man, and places her vulva opposite his member, which latter she guides into her vagina; she then places her arms round his neck, and he embraces her sides and waist, and helps her to rise and descend upon his verge. She must assist in his work.

Sixteenth manner.—Nik el kohoul (coitus from the back). The woman lies down on her stomach and raises her buttocks by help of a cushion; the man approaches from behind, stretches himself on her back and inserts his tool, while the woman twines her arms round the man's elbows. This is the easiest of all methods.

Seventeenth manner.—El keurchi (belly to belly). The man and the woman are standing upright, face to face; she opens her thighs; the man then brings his feet forward between those of the woman, who also advances hers a little. In this position the man must have one of his feet somewhat in advance of the other. Each of the two has the arms round the other's hips, the man introduces his verge, and the two move thus intertwined after a manner called neza' el dela, which I shall explain later on, please God the Almighty. (See first manner.)

---

[1] The vulgar expression of this position is nekahet el gada, signifying the coitus whilst sitting.

Eighteenth manner.—El kebachi (after the fashion of the ram). The woman is on her knees, with her fore-arms on the ground; the man approaches from behind, kneels down, and lets his member penetrate into her vagina, which she presses out as much as possible; he will do well in placing his hands on the woman's shoulders.

Nineteenth manner.—El houri (the hump of the camel). The woman, standing on her feet, places her hands on the ground, and elevates her hinder parts; the man, standing behind her, explores her, taking hold of her thighs in front of her buttocks.

If in this position the man, after having introduced his member, withdraws it, and the woman remains steady in her attitude, there will escape from her vagina a sound resembling the lowing of a calf. But this kind of coitus is not easy to obtain, as women who know that circumstance refuse to lend themselves for it.

Twentieth manner.—Dok el (driving the pin in). The woman enlaces with her legs the waist of the man, steadying herself by leaning against the wall. Whilst she who is standing, with her arms passed round his neck, and is thus suspended the man inserts his pin into her vulva.

Twenty-first manner.—Sebek el heub (love's fusion). While the woman is lying on her right side you extend yourself on your left side; your left leg remains extended, and you raise your right one till it is up to her flank, when you lay her upper leg upon your side. Thus her uppermost leg serves the woman as a support for her back. After having introduced your member you move as you please, and she responds to your action as she pleases.

Twenty-second manner.—El morteseb (the coition by

violence). The man approaches the woman from behind, so as to take her unawares; he passes his hands under her armpits; and seizing hers, draws them up towards her throat, so as to paralyze all resistance on her part. He can intertwine his fingers with hers, and thus bring her hands behind her neck by making her bend her head down.

If she has no drawers on, he tries to raise her robe with his knees towards the middle of the body, fixing one of her legs with his, so that she cannot turn away her receptacle from his weapon, nor make any resistance to its introduction. If she has drawers on and is strong, the man will be obliged to hold her two hands with one of his while he undoes her drawers with the other.

This manner will prove convenient for a man who wants to enjoy a woman, and can only get her by force and against her will.

Twenty-third manner.—Tred ech chate (coitus of the sheep).[1] The woman is on her hands and knees; the man behind her lifts her thighs till her vulva is on a level with his member, which he then inserts. In this position she ought to place her head between her arms.

Twenty-fourth manner.—Kaleb el miche (the inversion in coition). The man is lying on his back, and the woman gliding in between his legs, places herself upon him with her toe-nails against the ground; she lifts up the man's thighs, turning them against his own body, so that his virile member faces her vulva, into which she glides it; she then places her hands upon the bed by the sides of the man. It is, however, indispensable that the

[1] The name tred ech chate—sheep's courtship—has received this name, because the sheep in receiving the caresses of the ram puts its head between its legs, as is done by the woman in the position as described.

woman's feet rest upon a cushion to enable her to keep her vulva in accordance with his member.

In this position the parts are exchanged, the woman fulfilling that of the man, and vice versa.

There is a variation to this manner. The man stretches himself out upon his back, while the woman kneels with her legs under her between his legs. The remainder conforms exactly to what has been said above.

Twenty-fifth manner.—Rekeud el air (the race of the member). The man on his back supports himself with a cushion under his shoulders, but his posterior must keep touch of the bed. Thus placed, he draws up his thighs until his knees are on a level with his face; then the woman sits down, impaling herself on his member; she must not lie down, but keep seated as if on horseback, the saddle being represented by the knees and the stomach of the man. In that position she can by the play of her knees work up and down and down and up. She can beside place her knees on the bed, in which case the man accentuates the movement by plying his thighs, whilst she holds with her left hand on to his right shoulder.

Twenty-sixth manner.—El modakheli (the fitter-in). The woman is seated on her coccyx, with only the points of her buttocks touching the ground; the man takes the same position, her vulva facing his member, then the woman puts her right thigh over the left thigh of the man, whilst he on his part puts his right thigh over her left one.

The woman, seizing with her hands the man's arms, gets his member into her vulva; and each of them leaning alternately a little back, and holding each other by the upper part of the arms, they get into a swaying movement, acting by way of little concussions,[1] and keeping their movements in exact rhythm by the assist-ance of their heels, which are resting on the ground.

Twenty-seventh manner.—El khouariki (the one that stops at home). The woman being couched on her back, the man lies down on her, with cushions held in his hands.

After the member has got in, the woman raises her buttocks as high as she can off the bed, the man follow-ing her up with his member well inside; then the woman lowers herself again upon the bed, giving some short shocks, and although they do not embrace, the man must stick like glue to her. This movement they continue, but the man must make himself light and must not be pon-derous, and the bed must be soft; in default of which the exercise cannot be kept up without break.

Twenty-eighth manner.—Nik el haddadi (the coition of the blacksmith). The woman lies on her back with a cushion under her buttocks, with her knees raised as far as possible towards her chest, so that her vulva stands out as a target; she then guides his member in.

The man then executes for some time the usual action of the coition, then draws his tool out of the vulva, and glides it for a moment between the thighs of the woman, as the smith withdraws the glowing iron from the fur-nace in order to plunge it into cold water. This man-ner is called sferdgeli, position of the quince.

Twenty-ninth manner.—El moheundi (the seductive). The woman lying on her back, the man sits between her legs, with his croupe on his feet; then he raises and sepa-rates the woman's thighs, placing her legs under his

[1] The author makes use of the word nitha, derived from netah, and which is spoken of in note 1, p. 1.

arms or over his shoulders; he then takes her round the
waist, or seizes her shoulders.

The preceding descriptions furnish a large number of
procedures that cannot well be all put to the proof; but
with such a variety to choose from, the man who finds
one of them difficult to practise can easily find plenty of
others more to his convenience.

I have not made mention of positions which appeared
to me to be impossible to realize, and if there be anybody who thinks that those which I have described are
not exhaustive he has only to look for new ones.

It cannot be gainsaid that the Indians have surmounted the greatest difficulties in respect to coition. As a
grand exploit, originating with them, the following may
be cited:

"The woman being stretched out on her back, the man
sits down on her chest with his back turned to her face,
his knees turned forward and his nails gripping the
ground; he then raises her hips, arching her back until
he has brought her vulva to face with his member,
which he then inserts, and thus gains his purpose."

This position, as you perceive, is very fatiguing and
very difficult to attain. I even believe that the only realization of it consists in words and designs. With regard
to the other methods, as described above, they can only
be practised if both man and woman are free from physical defects, and of analogous construction; for instance,
one or the other of them must not be humpbacked or
very little, or very tall, or too fat. And I repeat, that
both must be in perfect health.

I shall now treat of the coition between two persons
of different conformation. I shall particularize the positions that will suit them in treating each of them sev-
erally.

I shall first discourse of the coition of a lean man and a corpulent woman, and the different postures they can take for the operation, assuming the woman to be lying down, and being turned successively over on her four sides.

If the man wants to work her sideways he takes the thigh of the woman which is uppermost, and raises it as high as possible on his flank, so that it rests over his waist; he employs her undermost arm as a pillow for the support of his head, and he takes care to place a stout cushion under his undermost hip, so as to elevate his member to the necessary height, which is indispensable on account of the thickness of the woman's thighs.

But if the man has an enormous stomach, projecting by reason of its obesity, over her thighs and flanks it will be best to lay her on her back, and to lift up her thighs toward her belly; the man kneels between them, with his hands having hold of her waist, and drawing her towards him, and if he cannot manage her in consequence of the obesity of her belly and thighs, he must with his two arms encircle her buttocks. But it is impossible for him to work her conveniently, owing to the want of mobility as to her thighs, which are impeded by her belly. He may, however, support them with his hands, but let him take care not to place them over his own thighs, as, owing to their weight, he would not have the power nor the facility to move. As the poet has said:

"If you have to explore her, lift up her buttocks,
In order to work like the rope thrown to a drowning man.
You will then seem between her thighs
Like a rower seated at the end of the boat."

The man can likewise couch the woman on her side, with the undermost leg in front; then he sits down on the thigh of that leg, his member being opposite her vulva, and lets her raise the upper leg, which she must bend at the knee. Then, with his hands seizing her legs and thighs, he introduces his member, with his body lying between her legs, his knees bent, and the points of his feet between the ground, so that he can elevate his posterior, and prevent her thighs from impeding the entrance. In this attitude they can enter into action.

If the woman's belly is enlarged by reason of her being with child, the man lets her lie down on one of her sides; then placing one of her thighs over the other, he raises them both towards the stomach, without their touching the latter; he then lies down behind her on the same side, and thus can fit his member in. He can in this way get his tool in entirely, particularly by raising his foot, which is under the woman's leg, to the height of her thigh. The same may be done with a barren woman; but it is particularly to be recommended for the woman who is enceinte, as the above position offers the advantage of procuring her the pleasure she wants without exposing her to danger.

In case of the man being obese, with a very pronounced rotundity of stomach, and the woman being thin, the best course to take is to let the woman take the active part. To this end, the man lies down on his back with his thighs close together, and the woman lets herself down upon his member, astride of him; she rests her hands upon the bed, and he seizes her arms with his hands. If she knows how to move, she can thus, in turn, rise and sink upon his member; if she is not adroit enough for that movement, the man imparts a movement to her buttocks by the play of one of his thighs behind them. Only, if the man takes that position, it may become sometimes prejudicial to him, inasmuch as some of the female sperm may penetrate into his urethra, and grave malady may ensue that the man's sperm cannot pass out, and returns into therefrom. It may also happen that the man's sperm cannot pass out, and returns into the urethra.

If the man prefers that the woman should lie on her back, he places himself, with his legs folded under him, between her legs, which she parts only moderately. Thus, his buttocks are between the women's legs, with his heels touching them. In doing that way he will, however, feel fatigue, owing to the position of his stomach resting upon the woman's and the inconvenience resulting therefrom; and, besides, he will not be able to get his whole member in the vulva.

It will be about the same when both lie on their sides as mentioned above in the case of pregnant women, where the manner is described.

When both man and woman are fat, and are wanting to unite themselves in coition, they cannot contrive to do it without trouble, particularly when both have prominent stomachs. In these circumstances the best way to go about it is for the woman to be on her knees with her hands on the ground, so that her posterior is elevated; then the man separates her legs, leaving the points of the feet close together and the heels parted asunder; he then attacks her from behind, kneeling and holding up his stomach with his hand, and so introduces his member. Resting his stomach upon her buttocks he holds during the act the thighs or the waist of the woman with his hands. If the posterior of the woman is too low for his stomach to rest upon, he must place a cushion under her knees to remedy this.

I know of no other position so favourable as this for coition of a fat man and a fat woman.

In fact, if the man gets between the legs of the woman on her back under the above named circumstances, his stomach, encountering the woman's thighs, will not allow him to make free use of his tool. He cannot even see her vulva, or only in part; it may be almost said that it will be impossible for him to accomplish the act.

On the other hand, if the man makes the woman lie upon her side and he places himself, with his legs bent behind her, pressing his stomach upon the upper part of her posterior, she must draw her legs and thighs up to her stomach, in order to lay bare her vagina and allow the introduction of his member; but if she cannot sufficiently bend her knees, the man can neither see her vulva, nor explore it.

If, however, the stomach of each person is not extremely large, they can manage very well all positions. Only they must not be too long in coming to the crisis, as they will soon feel fatigue and lose their breath.

In the case of a very big man and a very little woman, the difficulty to be solved is how to contrive that their organs of generation and their mouths can meet at the same time. To gain this end the woman had best lie on her back; the man places himself on his side near her, passes one of his hands under her neck, and with the other raises her thighs till he can put his member against her vulva from behind, the woman remaining still on her back. In this position he holds her up with his hands by the neck and the thighs. He can then enter her body, while the woman on her part puts her arms round his neck, and approaches her lips to his.

If the man wishes the woman to lie on her side he gets between her legs, and placing her thighs so that they are in contact with his sides, one above and one under, he glides in between them till his member is facing her vulva from behind; he then presses his thighs against her buttocks, which he seizes with one hand in order to import movement to them; the other hand he has round her neck. If the man then likes, he can get his thighs over those of the woman, and press her towards him; this will make it easier for him to move.

As regards the copulation of a very small man and a tall woman, the two actors cannot kiss each other while in action unless they take one of the three following positions, and even then they will get fatigued.

First position.—The woman lies on her back, with a thick cushion under her buttocks, and a similar one under her head; she then draws up her thighs as far as possible towards her chest. The man lies down upon her, introduces his member, and takes hold of her shoulders, drawing himself up towards them. The woman winds her arms and legs round over his back, whilst he holds on to her shoulders, or, if he can, to her neck.

Second position.—Man and woman both lie on their sides, face to face; the woman slips her undermost thigh under the man's flank, drawing it at the same time higher up; she does the like with her other thigh over his; then she arches her stomach out, while his member is penetrating into her. Both should have hold of the other's neck, and the woman, crossing her legs over his back, should draw the man towards her.

Third position.—The man lies on his back, with his legs stretched out; the woman sits on his member, and, stretching herself down over him, draws up her knees to the height of her stomach; then, laying her hands over his shoulders, she draws herself up, and presses her lips to his.

All these postures are more or less fatiguing for both; they can, however, choose any other position they like, only they must be able to kiss each other during the act.

I will now speak to you of people who are little, in consequence of being humpbacked. Of these there are several kinds.

First, there is the man who is crookbacked, but whose spine and neck are straight. For him it is most convenient to unite himself with a little woman, but not otherwise than from behind. Placing himself behind her posterior, he thus introduces his member into her vulva. But if the woman is in a stooping attitude, on her hands and feet, he will do still better. If the woman be afflicted with a hump and the man is straight, the same position is right.

If both of them are crookbacked they can take what position they like for the coition. They cannot, however, embrace; and if they lie on their side, face to face, there will be left an empty space between them. And if one or the other lies down on the back, a cushion must be placed under the head and the shoulder, to hold them up, and fill the place which is left vacant.

In the case of a man whose malformation is only affecting his neck, so as to press the chin towards his chest, but who is otherwise straight, he can take any position he likes for doing the business, and give himself up to any embraces and caresses, always excepting the kisses on the mouth. If the woman is lying on her back, he will appear in the action as if he was butting at her

like a ram. If the woman has her neck deformed in similar manner, their coition will resemble the mutual attack
of two horned beasts with their heads. The most convenient position for them will be that the woman should
stoop down, and he attack her from behind. The man
whose hump appears on his back in the shape of only
the half of a jar is not so much disfigured as the one of
whom the poet has said—

> "Lying on his back he is a dish;
> Turn him over, and you have a dish-cover."

In his case the coition can take place as with any other
man who is small in stature and straight; he can, however, not well lie on his back.

If a little woman is lying on her back, with such a
humpbacked man upon her belly, he will look like the
cover over a vase. If, on the contrary, the woman is
large-sized, he will have the appearance of a carpenter's
plane in action. I have made the following verses on
this subject:

> "The humpback is vaulted like an arch;
> In seeing him you cry, 'Glory be to God!'
> You ask him how he manages the coitus?
> 'It is the retribution for my sins,' he says,
> The woman under him is like a board of deal;
> The humpback, who explores her, does the planing."

I have also said in verse:—

> "The humpback's dorsal cord is tied in knots,
> The angels tire with writing all his sins:[1]
> In trying for a wife of proper shape;
> And for her favours, she repulses him,
> And says, 'Who bears the wrongs we shall commit?'
> And he, 'I bear them well upon my hump!'
> And then she mocks him saying, 'Oh, you plane!
> Destined for making shavings, take a deal board;' "

[1] Note in the autograph edition. The angels, according to
the creed of the Mussulmans, are incessantly busy in writing
down, whilst standing behind or before a man, his good and
bad actions. (See the "Koran," chap. vi., verse 61, and chap.
xiii., verse 12.

If the woman has a hump as well as the man, they may take any of the various positions for the coition, always observing that if one of them lies on the back, the hump must be environed with cushion, as with a turban, thus having a nest to lie in, which guards its top, which is very tender. In this way they can embrace closely.

If the man is humped both on back and chest he must renounce the embrace and clinging, and can otherwise take any position he likes for coition. But, generally speaking, the action must always be troublesome for himself and the woman. I have written on this subject:

> "The humpback engaged in the act of coition
> Is like a vase provided with two handles.
> If he is burning for a woman, she will tell him,
> 'Your hump is in the way; you cannot do it;
> Your verge would find a place to rummage in,
> But on your chest the hump, where would it be?' "

If both the woman and the man have double humps, the best position they can take for the coitus is the following. "Whilst the woman is lying on her side, the man introduces his member after the fashion described previously in respect to pregnant women. Thus the two humps do not encounter. Both are lying on their sides, and the man attacks from behind. Should the woman be on her back, her hump must be supported by a cushion, whilst the man kneels between her legs, she holding up her posterior. Thus placed, their two humps are not near each other, and all inconvenience is avoided.

The same is the case if the woman stoops down with her head, with her croup in the air, after the manner of El kouri, which position will suit both of them, if they have the chest malformed, but not the back. One of them then performs the action of come-and-go.

But the most curious and amusing description in this respect which I have ever met is contained in these verses.

> "Their two extremities are close together,
> And nature made a laughing stock of them;
> Foreshortened he appears as if cut off;
> He looks like someone bending to escape a blow,
> Or like a man who has received a blow
> And shrivels down so as to miss a second."

If a man's spine is curved about the hips and his back is straight, so that he looks as though he was in prayer, half prostrated, coition is for him very difficult; owing to the reciprocal positions of his thighs and his stomach, he cannot possibly insert his member entirely, as it lies so far back between his thighs. The best for him to do is to stand up. The woman stoops down before him with her hands to the ground, and her posterior in the air; he can thus introduce his member as a pivot for the woman to move upon, for, be it observed, he cannot well move himself. It is the manner El kouri, with the difference, that it is the woman who moves.

A man may be attacked by the illness called ikaad, or zamana (paralysis), which compels him to be constantly seated. If this malady only affects his knees and legs, his thighs and spinal column remaining sound, he can use all the sundry positions for coition, except those where he would have to stand up. In case his buttocks are affected, even if he is otherwise perfectly well, it is the woman who will have to make all the movements.

Know, that the most enjoyable coitus does not always exist in the manners described here; I only gave them so as to render the work as complete as possible. Sometimes most enjoyable coition takes place between lovers, who, not quite perfect in their proportions, find their own means for their mutual gratification.

It is said that there are women of great experience who, lying with a man, elevate one of their feet vertically in the air, and upon that foot a lamp is set full of oil, and with the wick burning. While the man is ramming them, they keep the lamp burning, and the oil is not spilled.

Their coition is in no way impeded by this exhibition, but it must require great practice on the part of both.

Assuredly the Indian writers have in their works described a great many ways of making love, but the majority of them do not yield enjoyment, and give more pain than pleasure. That which is to be looked for in coition, the crowning point of it, is the enjoyment, the embrace, the kisses. This is the distinction between the coitus of men and that of animals. No one is indifferent to the enjoyment which proceeds from the difference between the sexes, and man finds his highest felicity in it.

If the desire of love in man is roused to its highest pitch, all the pleasures of coition become easy for him, and he satisfies his yearning in any way.

It is well for the lover of coition to put all these manners to the proof, so as to ascertain which is the position that gives the greatest pleasure to both combatants. Then he will know which to choose for the tryst, and in satisfying his desires retain the woman's affection.

Many people have essayed all the positions I have described, but none has been as much approved of as the Dok el arz.

A story is told on this subject of a man who had a mistress of incomparable beauty, graceful and accomplished. He used to explore her in the ordinary manner, never having recourse to any other. The woman experienced none of the pleasure which ought to accompany the act, and was consequently generally very moody after the coition was over.

The man complained about this to an old dame, who told him, "Try different ways in uniting yourself to her, until you find the one which best satisfies her. Then work her in this fashion only, and her affection for you will know no limit."

The man then tried upon his wife various manners of coition, and when he came to the one called Dok el arz he saw her in violent transports of love, and at the crisis of the pleasure he felt her womb grasp his verge energetically, and she said to him, biting his lips, "This is the veritable manner of making love!"

These demonstrations proved to the lover, in fact, that his mistress felt in that position the most lively pleasure and he always after worked with her in that way. Thus he attained his end, and made the woman love him to folly.

Therefore try different manners; for every woman likes one in preference to all others for her pleasure. The majority of them have, however, a predilection for the Dok el arz, as, in the application of the same, belly is pressed to belly, mouth glued to mouth, and the action of the womb is rarely absent.

I have now only to mention the various movements practised for the coitus, and shall describe some of them.

First movement, called Neza el dela (the bucket in the well). The man and woman join in close embrace after the introduction. Then he gives a push, and withdraws a little; the woman then follows him with a push, and also retires. They continue their alternate movement, keeping proper time. Placing foot against foot, and hand against hand, they keep up the motion of a bucket in a well.

Second movement.—En netahi (the mutual shock). After the introduction, they each draw back, but with-out dislodging the member completely. Then they both push tightly together, and thus go on keeping time.

Third movement.—El motadani (the approach). The man moves as usual, and then stops. Then the woman, with the member in her receptacle, begins to move like the man, and then stops. And they continue this way until the ejaculation comes.

Fourth movement.—Khiate el heub (Love's tailor). The man, with his member being only partially inserted in the vulva, keeps first up a sort of quick friction with the part that is in, and then suddenly plunges his whole member in up to its root. This is the movement of the needle in the hands of the tailor, of which the man and woman must take cognisance.

This movement only suits such men and women who can at will retard the crisis. With those who are other-wise constituted it would act too quickly.

Fifth movement.—Souak et feurdj (the toothpick in the vulva). The man introduces his member between the walls of the vulva, and then drives it up and down, and right and left. Only a man with a very vigorous member can execute this movement.

Sixth movement.—Tachik el heub (the boxing up of love). The man introduces his member entirely into the vagina, so closely that his hairs are completely mixed up with the woman's. In that position he must now move forcibly, without withdrawing his tool in the least.

This is the best of all the movements, and is particularly well adapted to the position Dok el arz. The women prefer it to any other kind, as it procures them the extreme pleasure of seizing the member with their womb; and appeases their lust most completely.

The woman called tribades always use this movement in their mutual caresses. And it provokes prompt ejaculation both with man and woman.

Without kissing, no kind of position or movement procures the full pleasure; and the positions in which the kiss is not practicable are not entirely satisfactory, considering that the kiss is one of the most powerful stimulants to the work of love.

I have said in verse:—

> "The languishing eye
>   Puts in connection soul with soul,
>   And the tender kiss
>   Takes the message from member to vulva."

The kiss is assumed to be an integral part of the coition. The best kiss is the one impressed on humid lips combined with the suction of the lips and tongue, which latter particularly provokes the flow of sweet and fresh saliva. It is for the man to bring this about by slightly and softly nibbling her tongue, when her saliva will flow sweet and exquisite, more pleasant than refined honey, and which will not mix with the saliva of her mouth. This manouevre will give the man a trembling emotion, which will run all through his body, and is more intoxicating than wine drunk to excess.

A poet has said:—

"In kissing her, I have drunk from my mouth
Like a camel that drinks from the redir;[1]
Her embrace and the freshness of her mouth
Give me a languor that goes to my marrow."

The kiss should be sonorous; it originates with the tongue touching the palate, lubricated by saliva. It is produced by the movement of the tongue in the mouth and by the displacement of the saliva, provoked by the suction.

The kiss given to the superficial outer part of the lips, and making a noise comparable to the one by which you call your cat, gives no pleasure. It is well enough thus applied to children and hands.

The kiss I have described above is the one for the coitus and is full of voluptuousness.

A vulgar proverb says:—

"A humid kiss
Is better than a hurried coitus."

I have composed on this subject the following lines:

"You kiss my hand—my mouth should be the place!
O woman, thou who art my idol!
It was a fond kiss you gave me, but it is lost,
The hand cannot appreciate the nature of a kiss."

The three words, Kobla, letsem, and bouss are used indifferently to indicate the kiss on the hand or mouth. The word ferame means specially the kiss on the mouth.

An Arab poet has said:—

"The heart of love can find no remedy
In witching sorcery nor amulets,
Nor in the fond embrace without a kiss,
Nor in kiss without the coitus."

---

[1] Note of the autograph edition. The redir is a natural reservoir in the hot plains, in which the rainwater collects. It is a precious hoard for nomadic populations.

And the author of the work, "The Jewels of the Bride and the Rejoicing of Souls," has added to the above as complement and commentary the two following verses:

"Nor in converce, however unrestrained,
  But by the placing legs on legs (the coition)."

Remember that all caresses and all sorts of kisses, as described, are of no account without the introduction of the member. Therefore abstain from them, if you do not want action; they only fan a fire at no purpose. The passion which is getting excited resembles in fact a fire which is being lighted; and just as water only can extinguish the latter, so the emission of the sperm only can calm the lust and appease the heat.

The woman is not more advantaged than the man by caresses without coition.

It is said that Dahama bent Mesedjel appeared before the Governor of the province of Yamama, with her father and her husband, El Adjadje, alleging that the latter was impotent, and did not cohabit with her nor come near her.

Her father, who assisted her in her case, was reproached for mixing himself up with her plaint by the people of Yamama, who said to him, "Are you not ashamed to help your daughter bring a claim for coition?"

To which he answered, "It is my wish that she should have children; if she loses them it will be by God's will; if she brings them up they will be useful to her."

Dahama formulated her claim thus in coming before the Governor: "There stands my husband, and until now he has never touched me." The Governor interposed, saying, "No doubt this will be because you have been unwilling?" "On the contrary," she replied, "it is for him that I open my thighs and lie down on my back." Then cried the husband, "O Emir, she tells untruth; in order to possess her I have to fight with her." The Emir pronounced the following judgment: "I give you, he said, a year's time to prove her allegation to be false." He decides thus out of regard for the man. El Adjadje then went away reciting these verses:

> "Dahama and her father Mesedjel thought,
> The Emir would decide upon my impotence.
> Is not the stallion sometimes lazy-minded?
> And yet he is so large and vigorous."

Returned to his house he began to kiss and caress his wife; but his efforts went no farther, he remained incapable of giving proofs of his virility. Dahama said to him, "Keep your caresses and embraces; they do not satisfy love. What I desire is a solid and stiff member, the sperm of which will flow into my matrix." And she recited to him the following verses:

> "Before God! it is in vain to try with kisses
> To entertain me, and with your embracings!
> To still my torments I must feel a member,
> Ejaculating sperm into my uterus."

El Adjadje, in despair, conducted her forthwith back to her family, and, to hide his shame, repudiated her that very night.

A poet said on that occasion:

> "What are caresses to an ardent woman,
> Or costly vestments and fine jewelry,[1]
> If the man's organs do not meet her own,
> And she is yearning for the virile verge!"

[1] Note of the autograph edition.—The author cites here two names of costly garments: "l'ouchahane" and the "djelbab." For the translation it appeared better not to cling to the latter, but to give the true sense, which is: "luxurious garments and jewelry."

Know then that the majority of women do not find full satisfaction in kisses and embraces without coition. For them it resides only in the member, and they only like the man who rummages them, even if he is ugly.

A story also goes on this subject that Moussa ben Mesab betook himself one day to a woman in the town who had a female slave, an excellent singer, whom he wanted to buy from her. The woman was resplendently beautiful, and independent of her charming appearance, she had a large fortune. He saw at the same time in the house a young man of bad shape and ungainly appearance, who went to and fro giving orders.

Moussa having asked who that man was, she told him, "This is my husband, and for him I would give my life!" "This is a hard slavery," he said, "to which you are reduced, and I am sorry for you. We belong to God, and shall return to him![1] but what a misfortune it is that such incomparable beauty and such delightful forms as I see in you should be for such a man!"

She made answer, "O son of my mother,[2] if he could do to you from behind what he does for me in front, you would sell your lately acquired fortune as well as your patrimony. He would appear to you beautiful, and his plain looks would be changed into beauty."

"May God preserve him to you!"[3] said Moussa.

It is also said that the poet Farazdak met one day a woman on whom he cast a glance burning with love, and

[1] Note of the autograph edition.—The Mussulman formula expressing resignation. (See Koran, chap. ii., verse 151.)

[2] Id. A familiar expression, not exactly implying that he who is thus addressed is the brother of the person who uses it.

[3] Id. Literally, "God bless you in this respect."

who for that reason thus addressed him: "What makes you look at me in this fashion? Had I a thousand vulvas there would be nothing to hope for you!" "And why?" said the poet. "Because your appearance is not prepossessing," she said, "and what you keep hidden will be no better." He replied, "If you would put me to the proof, you would find that my interior qualities are of a nature to make you forget my outer appearance." He then uncovered himself, and let her see a member the size of the arm of a young girl. At that sight she felt herself getting burning hot with amorous desire. He saw it, and asked her to let him caress her. Then she uncovered herself and showed him her mount of Venus, vaulted like a cupola.[1] He then did the business for her, and then recited these verses:—

> "I have plied in her my member, big as a virgin's arm;
> A member with a round head, and prompt to attack;
> Measuring in length a span and a half,
> And, oh! I felt as though I had put it in a brazier."

He who seeks the pleasure a woman can give must satisfy her amorous desires after hot caresses as described. He will see her swooning with lust, her vulva will get moist, her womb will stretch forward, and the two sperms will come together.

---

[1] Note of the autograph edition.—Here appears the taste of the Arabs for prominent pubis. The subject of this structural quality of women will appear frequently.

CHAPTER VII

OF MATTERS WHICH ARE INJURIOUS IN THE ACT OF GENERATION

Know, O Vizir (to whom God be good!), that the ills caused by coition are numerous. I will mention to you some of them, which are essential to know, to avoid them.

Let me tell you in the first place that the coition, if performed standing, affects the knee-joints and brings about nervous shiverings; and if performed sideways will predispose your system for gout and sciatica, which resides chiefly in the hip-joint.

Do not mount upon a woman fasting or immediately before making a meal, else you will have pains in your back, you will lose your vigor, and your eyesight will get weaker.

If you do it with the woman bestriding you, your dorsal cord will suffer and your heart will be affected; and if in that position the smallest drop of the secretions of the vagina enters your urethral canal, a stricture may result.

Do not leave your member in the vulva after ejaculation, as this might cause gravel, or softening of the vertebral column, or the rupture of the bloodvessels, or lastly inflammation of the lungs.

Too much exercise after coition is also detrimental.

Avoid washing your member after the copulation, as this may cause canker.

As to coition with old women, it acts like a fatal poison, and it has been said, "Do not rummage old women, were they as rich as Karoun." [1]   And it has further been said, "Beware of mounting old women; and if they cover you with favours."   And again, "The coitus of old women is a venomous meal."

Know that the man who works a woman younger than he is himself acquires new vigor; if she is of the same age as he is he will derive no advantage from it, and, finally, if it is a woman older than himself she will take all his strength out of him for herself.   The following verses treat on this subject:—

"Be on your guard and shun coition with old women;
In her bosom she bears the poison of the arakime." [2]

A proverb says also, "Do not serve an old woman, even, if she offers to feed you with semolina and almond bread."

The excessive practice of the coition injures the health on account of the expenditure of too much sperm.   For as butter made of cream represents the quitessence of the milk, and if you take the cream off, the milk loses its qualities, even so does the sperm form the quintessence of nutrition, and its loss is debilitating.   On the other hand, the condition of the body, and consequently the quality of the sperm depends directly upon the food you take.   If, therefore, a man will passionately give himself up to the enjoyment of coition, without undergoing too great fatigue, he must live upon strengthening food, ex-

---

[1] This Karoun, the Cora of the Bible, is reported by the expositors to have constructed a palace all covered with gold, the doors being of solid gold. He generally made a white mule covered with golden trappings.

[2] Note of the autograph edition.—Arakime is the plural of Arkeum, the name of a hedious serpent whose sting is fatal.

citing comfits,[1] aromatic plants, meat, honey, eggs, and other similar viands. He who follows such a regime is protected against the following accidents, to which excessive coition may lead.

Firstly, the loss of generation power.

Secondly, the deterioration of his sight; for although he may not become blind, he will at least have to suffer from eye diseases if he does not follow my advice.

Thirdly, the loss of his physical strength; he may become like the man who wants to fly but cannot, who, pursuing somebody cannot catch him, or who carrying a burden, or working, soon gets tired and prostrated.

He who does not want to feel the necessity for the coition uses camphor. Half a mitskal of this substance, macerated in water, makes the man who drinks it insensible to the pleasures of copulation. Many women use this remedy when in fits of jealousy against rivals,[3] or when they want repose after great exercise. Then they try to procure camphor that has been left after a burial, and shrink from no expense of money to get such from the old women who have the charge of the corpses.[4] They make also use of the flower of henna, which is called faria;[1] they macerate the same in water, until it

---

[1] These comfits are called madjoun, and are prepared from fruit, particularly from cherries and pears cooked with honey. According as they may be wanted more or less spiced there are added, in varying quantities, cinnamon, musk, etc.

[2] The mitskal is a weight of three-sevenths of a dirhem, corresponding to a drachm and a half of our old system of weights and is equal to one gramme and ninety centigrammes.

[3] The word derair—the singular number of which is derra, and which is rendered in the translation with rivals—comes from a root which signifies to be injurious.

[4] With the Mussulmans it is customary to wash the dead with the greatest assiduity with perfumed waters before they are buried.

turns yellow, and thus supply themselves with a beverage which has almost the same effect as camphor.

I have treated of these remedies in the present chapter, although this is not their proper place; but I thought
that this information, as here given, may be of use to
many.

There are certain things which will become injurious
if constantly indulged in and which in the end affect the
health. Such are: too much sleep, long voyages in unfavourable season, which latter, particularly in cold countries, may weaken the body and cause disease of the
spine. The same effects may arise from the habitual
handling of bodies which engender cold and humidity,
like plaster, etc.

For people who have difficulty in passing their water
the coitus is hurtful.

The habit of consuming acid food is debilitating.

To keep the member in the vulva of a woman after
the ejaculation has taken place, be it for a long or a short
time, enfeebles that organ and makes it less fit for coition.

If you are lying with a woman, do her business several times if you feel inclined, but take care not to over-
do it, for it is a true word that "He who plays the game
of love for his own sake, and to satisfy his desires, feels
the most intense and durable pleasure; but he who does
it to satisfy the lust of another person will languish, lose
all his desire, and finishes by becoming impotent for
coition."

The sense of these words is, that a man when he feels

¹ Henna is a plant which is in great demand with Arabs.
The dried leaves of it are reduced to a powder or stepped in
water, and are then used to rouge the nails, feet, hands, hair
and beard.

disposed for it can give himself up to the exercise of the coitus with more or less ardour according to his desires, and at the time which best suits him, without any fear of future impotence, if his enjoyment is provoked and regulated only by his feeling the want of lying with a woman.

But he who makes love for the sake of somebody else, that is to say, only to satisfy the passion of his mistress, and tries all he can to attain that impossibility, that man will act against his own interest and imperil his health to please another person.

As injurious may be considered coition in the bath or immediately after leaving the bath; after having been bled or purged or such like. The coitus after a heavy bout of drinking is likewise to be avoided. To exercise the coitus with a woman during her courses is detrimental to the man as to the woman herself, as at that time her blood is vitiated and her womb cold, and if the least drop of blood should get in the man's urinary canal numerous maladies may supervene. As to the woman, she feels no pleasure during her courses, and holds the coitus in aversion.

As regards the copulation in the bath, some say that there is no pleasure to be derived from it, if, as is believed, the degree of enjoyment is dependent upon the warmth of the vulva, and in the bath the vulva cannot be otherwise than cold, and consequently unfit for giving pleasure. And it is not to be forgotten that the water penetrating into the sexual parts of man or woman may lead to grave results.

It is pretended that to look into the cavity of the vagina is injurious to the eyes. This is a question for a physician and not for a mere advisor.

It is told with regard to this subject that Hacen ben

Isehac, Sultan of Damascus, was in the habit of examining the interior of women's parts, and being warned not
to do it he said, "Is there a pleasure preferable to this?"
And thus before long he was blind.

The coitus after a full meal may occasion rupture of
the intestines. It is also to be avoided after undergoing
much fatigue, or at a time of very hot or very cold
weather.

Amongst the accidents which may attend the act of
coition in hot countries may be mentioned sudden blindness without any previous symptoms.

The repetition of the coitus without washing the parts
ought to be shunned, as it may enfeeble the virile power.

The man must also abstain from copulation with his
wife if he is in a state of legal impurity,[1] for if she become pregnant by such coition the child could not be
sound.

After ejaculation do not remain close to the woman, as
the disposition for recommencing will suffer by doing so.

Care is to be taken not to carry heavy loads on one's
back or to over-exert the mind, if one does not want the
coitus to be impeded.   It is also not well to constantly
wear vestments made of silk [2] as they impair all the en-

---

[1] Note in the autograph edition.—Legal impurity is due to
different causes, enumerated by Sidi Khelil, in chap. i. of his
"Religious Jurisprudence."   The same disappears by ablution or
by lotion.   To give an example, I shall cite the following extract from that chapter.   "The lotion is obligatory for any male
person arrived at the age of puberty who has introduced only
the gland of his verge, be it in carnal connection with a woman,
or with an animal, or with a corpse, or (in case of malformation, or on account of flaccidity) who has thus introduced part
of his verge to the length of the gland."   (Translation of
Perron.)

[2] It is probably owing to the great warmth developed by silk
that the author thinks the wearing of silken stuffs to be injurious with respect to coition.   It may, in fact, be admitted that
they have that effect.

ergy for copulation. Silken cloths worn by women also affect injuriously the capacity for erection of the virile member.

Fasting, if prolonged, calms the sexual desires; but in the beginning it excites them.

Abstain from greasy liquids, as in the course of time they diminish the strength necessary for coition.

The effect of snuff, whether plain or scented, is similar.

It is bad to wash the sexual parts with cold water directly after copulation; in general, washing with cold water calms down the desire, while warm water strengthens it.

Conversation with a young woman excites in the man the rection and passion commensurate with the youthfulness of a woman.

An Arab addressed the following recommendations to his daughter at the time when he conducted her to her husband: "Perfume yourself with water!" meaning that she should frequently wash her body with water in preference to perfumes; which are not suitable to everyone.

It is also reported that a woman having said to her husband, "You are then a nobody, as you never perfume yourself!" he made answer, "Oh, you sloven! it is for the women to emit a sweet odour."

The abuse of coition is followed by the loss of the taste for its pleasures; and to remedy this loss the sufferer must anoint his member with a mixture of the blood of a he-goat with honey. This will procure for him a marvellous effect in making love.

It is said that reading the Koran also predisposes for copulation.

Remember that a prudent man will beware of abusing

the enjoyment of the coition. The sperm is the water of
life; if you use it economically you will be always ready
for love's pleasures; it is the light of your eye; do not be
lavish with it at all times and whenever you have a fancy
for enjoyment, for if you are not sparing with it you will
expose yourself to many ills. Wise medical men say, "A
robust constitution is indispensable for copulation, and
he who is endowed with it may give himself up to pleasure without danger; but it is otherwise with the weakly
man; he runs into danger by indulging freely with
women."

The sage, Es Sakli, has thus determined the limits to
be observed by man as to the indulgence of the pleasures
of coition: Man, be he phlegmatic or sanguine, should
not make love more than twice or thrice a month; bilious
or hypochondriac men only once or twice a month. It
is nevertheless a well established fact that nowadays men
of any of these four temperaments are insatiable as to
coition, and give themselves up to it day and night, taking no heed how they expose themselves to numerous
ills.

Women are more favoured than men in indulging
their passion for coition. It is in fact their specialty; and
for them it is all pleasure; while men run many risks in
abandoning themselves without reserve to the pleasures
of love.

Having thus treated of the dangers which may occur
from the coitus, I have considered it useful to bring to
your knowledge the following verses which contain hygi-
enic advice in this respect. These verses have been composed by the order of Haroun er Rachid [1] by the most
noted physicians of his time, whom he had asked to

---

[1] The Haroun er Rachid in question was Kalif in the year
170, and was acknowledged to have been one of the most
meritorious, eloquent, cultured and generous rulers.

inform him of the remedies for combating ills caused by coition.

> "Eat slowly, if your food shall do you good,
> And take good care, that it be well digested.
> Beware of things which want hard mastication;
> They are bad nourishment, so keep from them.
> Drink not directly after finishing your meal,
> Or else you go half way to meet an illness.
> Keep not within you what is of excess,
> And if you were in the most susceptible circles,
> Attend to this well before seeking your bed,
> For rest this is the first necessity.
> From medicines and drugs keep well away,
> And do not use them unless very ill.
> Use all precautions proper, for they keep
> Your body sound, and are the best support.
> Don't be too eager for round-breasted women;
> Excess of pleasure soon will make you feeble,
> And in coition you may find a sickness;
> And then you find too late that in coition
> Our spring of life runs into women's vulva.
> And before all beware of aged women,
> For their embraces will to you be poison.
> Each second day a bath should wash you clean;
> Remember these precepts and follow them."

Those were the rules given by the sages to the master of benevolence and goodness, to the generous of generous.

All sages and physicians agree in saying that the ills which afflict man originate with the abuse of coition. The man therefore who wishes to preserve his health, and particularly his sight, and who wants to lead a pleasant life will indulge with moderation in love's pleasures, aware that the greatest evils may spring therefrom.

CHAPTER VIII

THE SUNDRY NAMES TO THE SEXUAL PARTS
OF MAN

Know, O Vizir (to whom God be good!), that man's member bears different names, as: [1]

Ed de keur, the virile member.
El kamera, the penis.
El air, the member for generation.
El hamama, the pigeon.
Et teunnana, the tinkler.
El heurmak, the indomitable.
El ahlil, the liberator.
Ez zeub, the verge.
El hammache, the exciter.
El fadelak, the deceiver.
En naasse, the sleeper.
Ez zodamne, the crowbar.
El khiade, the tailor.
Mochefi el relil, the extinguisher of passion.
Ei khorrate, the turnabout.
El deukkak, the striker.
El aouame, the swimmer.
Ed dekhal, the housebreaker.
El khorradj, the sorter.
El aouar, the one-eyed.
El fortass, the bald.

[1] Rabelais also gives in his history of Pantagruel divers more or less curious names to the organ of generation of man.

Abou aine, the one with an eye.[1]

El atsar, the pusher.

Ed dommar, the strong-headed.

Abou rokba, the one with a neck.[1]

Abou quetaia, the hairy one.[1]

El besiss, the impudent one.

El mostahi, the shame-faced one.

El bekkai, the weeping one.

El hezzaz, the rummager.

El lezzaz, the unionist.

Abou laaba, the expectorant.

Ech chebbac, the chopper.

El hattack, the digger.

El fattache, the searcher.

El hakkak, the rubber.

El mourekhi, the flabby one.

El motela, the ransacker.

El mokcheuf, the discoverer.

As regards the names of kamera [2] and dekeur, their
meaning is plain. Dekeur is a word which signifies the
male of all creatures, and is also used in the sense of
"mention" and "memory." When a man has met with
an accident to his member, when it has been amputated,

---

[1] The word "abou" signifies father, and "abou aine," literally
translated, means father of the eye. But in reality the word
used in this way indicates the possession, and means who has.
See the "Chrestomathie Arabe" of Bresnier, page 67, second
edition, note 2 of No. xv.

There are a great many similar combinations of words forming surnames or nicknames. Frequent recurrences in this sense
will appear in this work.

[2] Kamera also signifies the "gland of the penis." The root of
it, kemeur, means, "to have a larger penis or gland than any
other man," and in a third form, "rivalling any body with respect to the size of the penis.

or has become weak, and he can, in consequence, no longer fulfil his conjugal duties, they say of him: "the member of such a one is dead"; which means: the remembrance of him will be lost, and his generation is cut off by the root. When he died they will say, "His member has been cut off," meaning, "His memory is departed from the world." [1]

The dekeur plays also an important part in dreams. The man who dreams that his member has been cut off is certain to live long after that dream, for, as said above, it presages his loss of memory and the extinction of his race.

I shall treat this subject more particularly in the explication of dreams. [2]

The teeth (senane) represent years (senine); if therefore a man sees in a dream a fine set of teeth, this is for him a sign of a long life.

If he sees his nail (defeur) reversed or upside down, this is an indication that the victory (defeur) which he has gained over his enemies will change sides; and from a victor; he will become the vanquished; inversely, if he sees the neal of his enemy turned the wrong way, he can conclude that the victory which had been with his enemy will soon return to him.

The sight of a lily (sonsana) is the prognostication of a misfortune lasting a year (son, misfortune; sena, year).

The appearance of ostriches (namate) in dreams is of bad augury, because their name being formed of naa and mate, signifies "news of death," namely, peril.

---

[1] Note of the autograph edition.—There is here a play of words respecting the different meanings of dekeur, and which it is impossible to give in English.

[2] The explication of these dreams turns generally upon words with several meanings, or upon references to the radical letters of which they are composed.

To dream of a shield (henafa) means the coming on of all sorts of misfortune, for this word, by a change of letters, gives koul afa, "all bad luck."

The sight of a fresh rose (ourarde) announces the arrival (oroud) of a pleasure to make the heart tremble with joy; a faded rose indicates deceitful news. It is the same with baldness of the temples, and similar things.[1]

The pessamine (yasmine) is formed of yas, signifying deception, or the happening of a thing contrary to your wish, and mine, which means untruth. The man, then, who sees a pessamine in his dream is to conclude that the deception, yas, in the name yasmine, is an untruth, and will thus be assured of the success of his enterprise.[2] However, the prognostications furnished by the jessamine have not the same character of certainty as those given by the rose. It differs greatly from this latter-flower, inasmuch as the slightest breath of wind will upset it.

The sight of a saucepan (beurma) announces the conclusion (anuberame) of affairs in which one is engaged. Abou Djahel[3] (God's curse be upon him!) has added that such conclusion would take place during the night.

A jar (khabia) is the sign of turpitude (khebets) in every kind of affair, unless it is one that has fallen into a

---

[1] Some Mussulmans have the hairs plucked from the temples in order to look younger. This operation, which does not realize, in the eyes of strangers, the appearance of a reality, is considered by the author as being like the announcements of lying news.

[2] This play of words upon jessamine is taken from the work of Azzedine el Mocadesi, called, "The Birds and the Flowers."

[3] Abou Djahel, one of the foremost men of the Koreichites, was a sworn enemy of Mohammed and of his doctrine. His real name is Amcur ben Heichame, of the family of Moukhzoum. He received also the surname of Abou el Heukoum, the man gifted with wisdom.

pit or river and got broken, so as to let escape all the calamities contained in it.

Sawing wood (nechara) means good news (bechara).

The inkstand (douaia) indicates the remedy (doua), namely, the cure of a malady, unless it be burnt, broken or lost, when it means the contrary.

The turban (amama) if seen to fall over the face and covering the eyes is a presage of blindness (aina), from which God preserve us!

The finding again in good condition a gem that has been lost or forgotten is a sign of success.

If one dreams that he gets out of a window (taga) he will know that he will come with advantage out of all transactions he may have, whether important or not. But if the window seen in the dream is narrow so that he had trouble to get out, it will be a sign to him that in order to be successful he will have to make efforts in proportion to the difficulty experienced by him in get-ting out.

The bitter orange signifies that from the place where it was seen calumnies will be issuing.[1]

Trees (achedjar) mean discussions (mechadjera).

The carrot (asefnaria) prognosticates misfortune (asef) and sorrow.

The turnip (cufte) means for the man that has seen it a matter that is past and gone (ameur fate), so that there is no going back to it. The matter is weighty if it ap-peared large, of no importance if seen small; in short, important in proportion to the size of the turnip seen.[2]

---

[1] The connection no doubt originates with the fact that cal-umny bears bitter fruits, like the one in question.

[2] It must be confessed, looking at the forced relationship be-tween "cufte" and "ameur fate," that the author gets easily over any difficulties in his explanations of dreams.

A musket seen without its being fired means a complot contrived in secret, and of no importance. But if it
is seen going off it is a sign that the moment has arrived for the realization of the complot.

The sight of fire is of bad augury.

If the pitcher (brik)[1] of a man who has turned to God
breaks, this is a sign that his repentance is in vain, but if
the glass out of which he drinks wine breaks, this means
that he returns to God.

If you have dreamed of feasts and sumptuous ban-
quets, be sure that quite contrary things will come to
pass.

If you have seen somebody bidding adieu to people
on their going away you may be certain that it will be
the later who will shortly wish him a good journey,
for the poet says:

"If you have seen your friend saying good-bye, rejoice;
Let your soul be content as to him who is far away,
For you may look forward to his speedy return,
And the heart of him who said adieu will come back to you."[2]

The coriander (keusbeur) signifies that the vulva
(keuss) is in proper condition.

On this subject there is a story that the Sultan Haroun
er Rachid having with him several persons of mark with
whom he was familiar, rose and left them to go to one of
his wives, with whom he wanted to enjoy himself. He

---

[1] The "brik" is a small earthenware pitcher provided with a
handle, which the Arab generally carries about with him filled
with water for quenching his thirst. It has a peculiar shaped
neck, which allows the water to be drunk easily.

[2] This is again a play of words by transposing letters, which
the author employs for explaining dreams, like the one given
in Note 2 on p. 117. The case here rests upon the words
"aoud" and "oudaa," adieu.

found her suffering from the courses, and returned to his companions, resigned to his disappointment.

Now it happened that a moment afterwards the woman found herself free from her discharge. When she had assured herself of this, she made forthwith her ablutions, and sent to the Sultan by a negress, a plate of coriander.[1]

Haroun er Rachid was seated amongst his friends when the negress brought the plate to him. He took it and examined it, but did not understand the meaning of its being sent to him by his wife. At last he handed it to one of his poets, who, having looked at it attentively, recited to him the following verses.

"She has sent you coriander (keusbeur),
White as sugar;
I have placed it in my palm,
And concentrated all my thoughts upon it,
In order to find out its meaning;
And I have seized it. O my master, what she wants to say,
It is, 'My vulva is restored to health' (keussi beuri)."

Er Rachid was surprised at the wit shown by the woman, and at the poet's penetration. Thus that which was to remain a mystery remained hidden, and that which was to be known was divulged.

A drawn sword is a sign of war, and the victory will remain with him who holds its hilt.

A bridle means servitude and oppression.

A long beard points to good fortune and prosperity; but it is a sign of death if it reaches down to the ground.

Others pretend that the intelligence of each man is in

---

[1] The coriander, "keusbeur," preserves viands, as salt does. The viands dried and seasoned with spices, are called "khelia." They will keep good for a year and longer. Coriander is, moreover, a stimulant.

an inverse proportion to the length of his beard: that is to say, a big beard denotes a small mind. A story goes in this respect, that a man who had a long beard saw one day a book with the following sentence inscribed on its back. "He whose chin is garnished with a large beard is as foolish as his beard is long." Afraid of being taken for a fool by his acquaintances, he thought of getting rid of what there was too much of his beard, and to this end, it being night time, he grasped a handful of his beard close to the chin, and set the remainder on fire by the light of the lamp. The flame ran rapidly up the beard and reached his hand, which he had to withdraw precipitately on account of the heat. Thus his beard was burnt off entirely. Then he wrote on the back of the book under the abovementioned sentence, "These words are entirely true. I, who am now writing this, have proved their truth." Being himself convinced that the weakness of the intellect is proportioned to the length of the beard.[1]

On the same subject it is related that Haroun er Rachid, being in a kiosk, saw a man with a long beard. He ordered the man to be brought before him, and when he was there he asked him, "What is your name?" "Abou Arouba," replied the man. "What is your profession?" "I am master in controversy.

Haroum then gave him the following case to solve. A

---

[1] This little tale brings out, not without humour, the double stupidity of the man who is its hero, and who, not content with burning off his whole beard, and probably also burning his skin, is writing down a certificate of his imbecility in the inscription which he adds with his own hand on the back of the book. One may, up to a certain point, discern here a connection between this demonstration and the famous argument: Epimenides says, "That the Cretans are liars." Now Epimenides is a Cretan.

man buys a he-goat, who, in voiding his excrements, hits the buyer's eye with part of it and injures the same. Who has to pay for the damages? "The seller," promptly says Abou Arouba. "And why?" asked the Kalif. "Because he had sold the animal without warning the buyer that it had a catupult in its anus," answered the man. At these words the Kalif began to laugh immoderately, and recited the following verses:

> "When the beard of the young man
> Has grown down to his navel,
> The shortness of his intellect is in my eyes
> Proportioned to the length his beard has grown."

It is averred by many authors that amongst proper names there are such as bring luck and others that bring ill luck, according to the meaning they bear.

The names Ahmed, Mohammed, Hamdouna, Hamdoun indicate in encounters and dreams the lucky issue arrived at in a transaction.[1] Ali, Alia indicate the height and elevation of rank.[2] Naserouna, Naseur, Mansour, Naseur Allah, signify triumph over enemies.[3] Salem, Salema Selim, Selimane indicate success in all affairs; also security for him who is in danger.[4] Fetah Allah, Fetah indicate victory, like all the other names which in their meaning speak of lucky things.[5] The names Rad,

---

[1] The root of these names is "hamd," which means to praise, glorify, to bear oneself worthy of praise.

[2] The root is "ala," signifying high, elevated both in reality and figuratively.

[3] From "neseur," meaning to help, and by extension to carry off the victory. The word God is understood; helped by God is being victorious.

[4] From the root "selem," which means to be right and well, to escape from a danger, to be safe.

[5] Ahmed, Mohammed, etc.

Raad signify thunder, tumult, and comprise everything in connection with this meaning.[1] Abou el Feurdj and Ferendj indicate joy; Ranem and Renime success, Khalf Allah and Khaleuf compensation for a loss, and benediction. The sense of Abder Rassi, Hafid and Mahfond is favourable. The names in which the words latif (benevolent), mourits (helpful), hanine (compassionate), aziz (beloved), carry with them, in conformity with the sense of these words, the ideas of benevolence, lateuf (charity), iratsa (compassion), hanana, and aiz (favour). As an example of words of an unfavourable omen I will cite el ouar, el ouara, which imply the idea of difficulties.

As supporting the truth of the preceding observations I will refer to this saying of the Prophet (the salutation and benevolence of God to him!). Compare the names appearing in your dreams with their significance, so that you may draw therefrom your conclusions." [2]

I must confess that this was not the place for treating of this subject, but one word leads on to more. I now return to the subject of this chapter, viz: the different names of the sexual parts of man.

The name of el air is derived from el kir (the smith's bellows). In fact if you turn in the latter word the K, kef, so that it faces the opposite way, you will find the word to read ei air.[3] The member is called so on ac-

---

[1] The root "rad" signifies to thunder, menace as a verb; and tumult, trembling, misfortune, calamity as a substantive.

[2] See the hadits, or traditions left by Mohammed.

[3] This origin of the word air, although ingenious, is unlikely. It rests upon turning the Arab letter kef, preceded by the letter lam making it lam alif. It is thus that kir, turning the kef the other way, will read air.

count of its alternate swelling and subsiding again. If swollen up it stands erect, and if not sinks down flaccid.

It is called el hamama (the pigeon), because after having been swelled out it resembles at the moment when it returns to repose a pigeon sitting on her eggs.[1]

El teunnana (the tinkler).—So called because when it enters or leaves the vulva in coition it makes a noise.

El heurmak (the indomitable).[2]—It has received this name because when in a state of erection it begins to move its head, searching for the entrance to the vulva till it has found it, and then walks in quite insolently, without asking leave.

El ahlil (the liberator).—Thus called because in penetrating into the vulva of a woman thrice repudiated it gives her the liberty to return to her first husband.[3]

Ez zeub (the verge).—From the word deub, which means creeping. This name was given to the member because when it gets between a woman's thighs and feels a plump vulva it begins to creep upon the thighs and the Mount of Venus, then approaches the entrance of the vulva, and keeps creeping in until it is in possession and is comfortably lodged, and having it all its own way penetrates into the middle of the vulva, there to ejaculate.[4]

---

[1] In Arabic the word which signifies eggs is also used for testicles, hence the comparison made by the author.

[2] Heurmak is not a common Arabian word. It signifies a fiery, violent, indomitable stallion.

[3] Note of the autograph edition.—According to the Mussulman law a wife that has been divorced by the thrice repeated formula cannot marry again her first husband until she has married another man, and been divorced from him.

[4] In several passages of this work the man is advised when in coition to place his member well in the centre of the vagina at the crisis. The Arabian sages are not agreed upon the sense of this advice.

El hammache (the exciter).—It has received this name because it irritates the vulva by frequent entries and exits.

El fadelak (the deceiver).—It takes this name from its ruses and deceits. This expression signifies liar. Calling somebody a fadelak means that he is a deceiver. When he desires coition he says, "If God gives me the chance to encounter a vulva I shall never part with it." And when he has got at one he is soon sated; his presumption is apparent, and he looks at it despairingly, because he has been boasting that, once in, he would not come out again.

In coming near a woman it is getting again into erection, and seems to say to the vulva, "To-day I shall quench my desires with you, O my soul!" The vulva, seeing it erect, and stiff, is surprised at its dimensions, and seems to say, "Who could take in such a member?" For any other answer, it gets its head into the lips of the vulva, makes it open its mouth, and penetrate to its bottom. When it begins to move about, the vulva makes fun of it, saying, "How deceitful your movements is!" for before it has been in long it retires again; and the two testicles seem to say to each other, "Our member is dead; it has succumbed after the arrival of the pleasure, the quenching of its passion, and the emission of the sperm!" The member itself, coming precipitately out of the vulva, tries to hold up its head, but it sinks down soft and sluggish. The testicles repeat, "Our brother is dead! our brother is dead!" It protests, saying, "Nothing of the sort"; but the vulva cries, "Why did you retire? Oh you liar! You had said if you were once in you would never come out again."

En naasse (the sleeper). From its deceitful appearance. When it gets into erection, it lengthens out and stiffens itself to such an extent that one might think it would never get soft again.   But when it has left the vulva, after having satisfied its passion, it goes to sleep.

There are members that fall asleep while inside the vulva, but the majority of them come out firm; but at that moment they get drowsy and little by little they go to sleep.

Ez zoddame (the crowbar).—It is so called because when it meets the vulva and the same will not let it pass in directly, it forces the entrance with its head, breaking and tearing everything, like a wild beast in the rutting season.

El khiate (the tailor).—It takes this name from the circumstance that it does not enter the vulva until it has manoeuvred about the entrance, like a needle in the hand of a tailor, creeping and rubbing against it until it is sufficiently roused, after which it enters.

Mochefi el relil (the extinguisher of passion).—This name is given to a member which is large, strong, and slow to ejaculate; such a member satisfies most completely the amorous wishes of a woman; for, after having wrought her up to the highest pitch, it allays her excitement better than any other.   And, in the same way, it calms the ardour of the man.   When it wants to get into the vulva, and arriving at the portal, finds it closed, it laments, begs and promises: "Oh! my love! let me come in, I will not stay long." And when it has been admitted, it breaks its word, and makes a long stay, and does not take its leave till it has satisfied its ardour by the ejaculation of the sperm, coming and going, tilting high and low, and rummaging right and left.   The vulva protests, "How about your word, you deceiver?" She says, "you said you would only stop in for a moment." And the member answers, "Oh, certainly! I shall not retire until

I have encountered your womb; but after having found it, I will engage to withdraw at once." At these words, the vulva takes pity on him, and advances her matrix, which clasps and kisses its head, as if saluting it.[1] The member then retires with its passion cooled down.

El khorrate (the turnabout).—This name was given to it because on arriving at the vulva it pretends to come on important business, knocks at the door, turns about everywhere, without shame or bashfulness, investigating every corner to the right and left, forward and back-ward, and then all at once darts right to the bottom of the vagina for the ejaculation.

Ed deukkak (the striker).—Thus called because on ar-riving at the entrance of the vulva it gives a slight knock. If the vulva opens the door, it enters; if there is no re-sponse, it begins to knock again and does not cease until it is admitted. The parasite [2] who wants to get into the house of a rich man to present at a feast does the same, he knocks at the door; and if it is opened, he walks in; but if there is no response to his knock, he repeats it again and again until the door is opened. And similarly the deukkak with the door of the vulva.

By "knocking at the door" is meant the friction of the member against the entrance of the vulva until the latter becomes moist. The appearance of this moisture is the

[1] Note of the autograph edition.—This image is drawn from a kind of salute very much in use by the lower class of Mus-sulmans when meeting a superior by seizing the head of the latter, and drawing it down so as to be able to kiss it.

[2] The word teufil of the text rendered in the translation with "parasite" is the name of a man who lived in Coufa, an impor-tant town in Irak, and whom they had nicknamed Teufil el Aaress, the wedding teufil, because he always came to a wedding feast without invitation.

phenomenon alluded to by the expression "opening the door."

El aouame (the swimmer).—Because when it enters the vulva it does not remain in one favourite place, but, on the contrary, turns to the right, to the left, goes forward, draws back, and then moves like swimming in the middle amongst its own sperm and the fluid furnished by the vulva, as if in fear of drowning and trying to save itself.

Ed dekhal (the housebreaker).—Merits that name because on coming to the door of the vulva this one asks, "What do you want?" "I want to come in!" "Impossible! I cannot take you in on account of your size." Then the member insists that the other one should only receive its head, promising not to come in entirely; it then approaches, rubs its head twice or thrice between the vulva's lips, till they get humid and thus lubricated, then introduces first its head, and after, with one push, plunges in up to the testicles.

El korradj (the coward).—So called because on approaching a vulva which has been deprived of the coitus for some time, and trying to get in, the vulva, in heat with amorous passion, says, "Yes! but on one condition, and that is, if you enter you must not leave again until you have ejaculated so and so many times." Upon which the member replies, "I promise you that I will not withdraw until I have done you three times oftener than you have named." Once in, the intense heat of the vulva promotes the enjoyment; the member goes to and fro, burning for the perfect pleasure engendered by the alternate friction against the lips of the vulva and against the matrix. As soon as one ejaculation has taken place it tries promptly to withdraw, which causes the vulva to cry out, "Why do you leave, you liar? You should be called coward and liar."

El aaouar (the one-eyed).—Because it has but one eye, which eye is not like other eyes, and does not see clearly.[1]

El fortass (the bald one).—Because there is no hair on its head, which makes it look bald.

Abou aine (he with one eye).—It has received this name because its one eye presents the peculiarity of being without pupil and eyelashes.

El atsar (the stumbler).—It is called so because if it wants to penetrate in the vulva, as it does not see the door, it beats about above and below, and thus continues to stumble as over stones in the road, until the lips of the vulva gets humid, when it manages to get inside. The vulva then says, "What has happened to you that made you stumble about so?" The member answers, "O my love, it was a stone lying in the road."

Ed dommar (the odd-headed).—Because its head is different from all other heads.

Abou rokba (the one with a neck).—That is the being with a short neck, a well developed throat, and thick at the end, a bald head, and who, moreover, has coarse and bristly hair from the navel to the pubis.

Abou guetaia (the hairy one; who has a forest of hair).—It is given this name when the hair is abundant about it.

El besiss (the impudent).—It has received this name because from the moment that it gets stiff and long it does not care for anybody, lifts impudently the clothing of its master by raising its head fiercely, and makes him ashamed while itself feels no shame. It acts in the same

[1] The epithet of one-eyed is also given by Martial to the virile member.

unabashed way with women, turning up their clothes and laying bare their thighs. Its master may blush at this conduct, but as to itself its stiffness and determination to plunge into a vulva only increase.

El mostahi (the shame-faced).—This sort of member, which is met with sometimes, is capable of feeling ashamed and timid when facing a vulva which it does not know, and it is only after a little time that it gets bolder and stiffens. Sometimes it is even so much troubled that it remains incompetent for the coitus, which happens in particular when a stranger is present, in which case it becomes quite incapable of moving.

El bekkai (the weeper).—So called on account of the many tears it sheds; as soon as it gets in erection, it weeps; when it sees a pretty face, it weeps; handling a woman, it weeps. It even weeps tears sacred to memory.

El hezzaz (the rummager).—It is named thus because as soon as it penetrates into the vulva it begins to rummage about vigorously, until it has appeased its passion.

El lezzaz (the unionist).—Received that name because as soon as it is in the vulva it pushes and works till fur meets fur, and even makes efforts to force the testicles in.

Abou laaba (the expectorant).—Has received this name because when coming near a vulva, or when its master touches a woman or plays with her or kisses her, its saliva begins to move and it has tears in its eye; this saliva is particularly abundant when it has been for some time out of work, and it will even wet then his master's dress. This member is very common, and there are but few people who are not furnished with it.

The liquid it sheds is cited by lawyers under the name

of medi.[1] Its production is the result of toyings and of
lascivious thoughts. With some people it is so abundant
as to fill the vulva, so that they may erroneously believe
that it comes from the woman.

Ech chelbak (the chopper).—So called because when
it enters a juicy vulva it makes a noise like the sounds
produced by the chopping waves of a lake.

El hattak (the staver in).—This is the vigorous member which becomes very long and hard, like a staff or a
bone. Its name signifies that it tears the membrane in
the virginal vulva, and makes the blood run abundantly.[2]

El fattache (the searcher).—From its habit when in
the vulva to turn in every direction as if in search of
something, and that something is the matrix. It will
know no rest until it has found it.

El hakkak (the rubber).—It has got this name because
it will not enter the vagina until it has rubbed its head
against the entrance and the lower part of the belly. It
is frequently mistaken for the next one.

El mourekhi (the flabby one).—The one who can
never get in because it is too soft, and which is therefore
content to rub its head against the entrance to the vulva
until it ejaculates. It gives no pleasure to woman, but
only inflames her passion without being able to satisfy
it, and makes her cross and irritable.

El motela (the ransacker).—So named because it pen-

---

[1] Note of the autograph edition.—Medi, sperm exuding by
the mere touching of a woman.—"Dictionary of Kazimirski,"
page 182. No doubt the prostatic moisture is alluded to here.

[2] The root of the word "hattak," used by the author, does not
only mean to tear a veil, but also to violate, take the flower of a
virgin. It thus becomes a membrane which is violently broken
by the efforts of the member.

etrates into unusual places, makes itself well acquainted with the state of the vulvas, and can distinguish their qualities and faults.

El mokcheuf (the discoverer).—Has been thus denominated because in getting up and raising its head, it raises the vestments which hide it, and uncovers its master's nudities, and because it is also not afraid to lay bare the vulvas which it does not yet know, and to lift up the clothes which cover them without shame. It is not accessible to any sense of bashfulness, cares for nothing and respects nothing. Nothing which concerns the coitus is strange to it; it has a profound knowledge of the state of humidity, freshness, dryness, tightness or warmth of vulvas, which it explores assiduously. There are, in fact, certain vulvas of an exquisite exterior, plump and fine outside, while their inside leaves much to wish for, and they give no pleasure, owing to their being not warm, but very humid, and having other similar faults. It is for this reason that the mokcheuf tries to find out about things concerning the coitus, and has received this name.

These are the principal names that have been given to the virile member according to its qualities. Those that think that the number of these names is not exhaustive can look for more; but I think I have given a nomenclature long enough to satisfy my readers.

CHAPTER IX

SUNDRY NAMES GIVEN TO THE SEXUAL ORGANS OF WOMEN [1]

El feurdj, the slit.

El keuss, the vulva.

El kelmoune, the voluptuous.

El ass, the primitive.

Ez zerzour, the starling.

Ech cheukk, the chink.

Abou tertour, the one with a crest. [2]

Abou khochime, the one with a little nose. [2]

El guenfond, the hedgehog.

Es sakouti, the silent one.

Ed deukkak, the crusher.

Et tseguil, the importunate.

El fechefache, the watering-can.

El becha, the horror.

El taleb, the yearning one.

El hacene, the beautiful.

En neuffakh, the one that swells.

[1] Here are some of the names given by Rabelais to the natural parts of women; le serrecropiere, le calibistris, le pertuys, le boursavitz.

[2] The word abou signifies father, and abou aine literally translated means "father of the eye,," but in reality the word used in this way indicates the possession, and means, "who has."—See the "Chrestomathie Arabe" of Bresnier, page 67, second edition, note 2 of No. xv. There are a great many similar combinations of words forming surnames or nicknames. Frequent recurrences in this sense will appear in this work.

Abou djebaha, the one with a projection.[1]
Elouasa, the vast one.
El dride, the large one.
Abou beldoum, the glutton.[1]
El mokaour, the bottomless.
Abou cheufrine, the two lipped.[1]
Abou aungra, the humpbacked.[1]
El rorbal, the seive.
El hezzaz, the restless.
El lezzaz, the unionist.
El moudd, the accommodating.
El moudine, the assistant.
El mokeubbeub, the vaulted one.
El meusboul, the long one.
El molki, the duellist.
El mokabeul, the ever ready for the fray.
Ei harrab, the fugitive.
El sabeur, the resigned.
El maoui, the juicy.
El moseuffah, the barred one.
El mezour, the deep one.
El addad, the biter.
El menssass, the sucker.
El zeunbur, the wasp.
El harr, the hot one.
El ladid, the delicious one.

As regards the vulva called el feurdi, the slit, it has got that name because it opens and shuts again when hotly yearning for the coitus, like the one of a mare in heat at the approach of the stallion. This word, how-

---

[1] See note 2 on preceding page.

ever, is applied indiscriminately to the natural parts of men and women, for God the Supreme has used this expression in the Koran, chap. xxxiii., v. 35, "El hafidine feuroudjahoum oul el hafidate." [1] The proper meaning of feurdj is slit, opening, passage; people say, "I have found a feurdj in the mountains, viz., a passage; there is then a soukoune upon the ra and a fatcha upon the djine, and in this sense it means also the natural parts of woman. But if the ra is marked with a fatcha it signifies the deliverance from misfortunes. [2]

The person who dreams of having seen the vulva, feurdj, of a woman will know that "if he is in trouble God will free him of it; if he is in a perplexity he will soon get out of it; and lastly if he is in poverty he will soon become wealthy, because feurdj, by transposing the vowels, will mean the deliverance from evil. By analogy, if he wants a thing he will get it; if he has debts, they will be paid."

It is considered more lusky to dream of the vulva as open. But if the one seen belongs to a young virgin it indicates that the door of consolation will remain closed, and the thing which is desired is not obtainable. It is a proved fact that the man who sees in his dream the vulva of a virgin that has never been touched will certainly be involved in difficulties, and will not be lucky in his af-

---

[1] The literal translation is, "men and women who are sparing with their sexual organs," feurdj being rendered by sexual organ. This quotation really proves that the word feurdj applies to both sexes. The passage may be translated, "the persons of both sexes who are chaste," and is thus given in the Koran translation of Kazimirski.

[2] In Arabic, words composed of the same letters may bear different meaning according to the marks, which affect their vowels.

fairs. But if the vulva is open so that he can look well into it, or even if it is hidden but he is free to enter it, he will bring the most difficult tasks to a successful end after having first failed in them, and this after a short delay, by the help of a person whom he never thought of.

He who has seen in his dream a man busy upon a young girl, and when the same is getting off her managed to see at that moment her vulva, will bring his business to a happy end, after having first failed to do so, by the help of the man he has seen. If it is himself who did the girl's business, and he has seen her vulva, he will succeed by his own exertions to realize the most difficult problems, and be successful in every respect. Generally speaking, to see the vulva in dreams is a good sign; so it is of good augury to dream of coition, and he who sees himself in the act, and finishing with the ejaculation, will meet success in all his affairs. But it is not the same with the man who merely begins coition and does not finish it. He, on the contrary, will be unlucky in every enterprise.

It is supposed that the man who dreams of being busy with a woman will afterwards obtain from her what he wants.

The man who dreams of cohabiting with women with whom to have sexual intercourse is forbidden by religion, as for instance his mother, sister, etc. (maharime), must consider this as a presage that he will go to sacred places (moharreme); and, perhaps, even journey to the holy house of God, and look upon the grave of the Prophet.[1]

---

[1] The word harame signifies at the same time illicit, forbidden action, and a holy thing. Moharreme indicates the holy soil of Mecca, the place of pilgrimage for Mussulmans. Maharime designates the persons whom to enjoy in coition is prohibited by religion.

As regards the virile member, it has been previously mentioned that to dream of accident occurring to the organ means the loss of remembrance and extinction of the race.

The sight of a pair of pantaloons (seronal) prognosticates the appointment to a place (aulaia), by reason of the analogy of the letters composing the word seronal with those forming by transposition the two words sir, go, and ouali, named: "go to the post to which you are named." It is related that a man who had dreamed that the Emir had given him a pair of pantaloons became Cadi. Dreaming of pantaloons is also a sign of protection for the natural parts, and foretells success in business.

The almond (louze), a word composed of the same letters as zal, to cease, seen in a dream by a man in trouble means that he will be liberated from it; to a man who is ill, that he will be cured; in short that all misfortunes will give away. Somebody having dreamed that he was eating almonds, asked a wise man the meaning of it; he received the answer, that by reason of the analogy of the letters in louze and zal, the ills that best him would disappear; and the event justified the explanation.

The sight of a molar tooth (deurss) in a dream indicates enmity. The man, therefore, who has seen his tooth drop out may be sure that his enemy is dead. This arises from the word deurss, signifying both an enemy and a molar, and one can say at the same time, "It is my tooth and it is my enemy."[1]

The window (taga)[2] and the shoe (medassa) reminds

---

[1] Deurss signifies a molar tooth and a man difficult to live with, hence enemy.

[2] The Arabs use sometimes in joke the word taga (window) for designating the sexual organ of woman.

you of women. The vulva resembles in fact, when in-
vaded by the verge, a window with a man putting his
head in to look about, or a shoe that is being put on.
Consequently, he who secs himself in dreaming in the
act of getting in at a window, or putting on a shoe, has
the certainty of getting possession of a young woman or
a virgin, if the window is newly built, or the shoe new
and in good condition; but that the woman will be old
according to the state of the window or shoe.

The loss of a shoe foretells to a man the loss of his
wife.

To dream of something folded together, and which
gets open, predicts that a secret will be divulged and
made public. The same remaining folded up indicates,
on the other hand, that the secret will be kept.

If you dream of reading a letter you will know that
you will have news, which will be, according to the
nature of the contents of the letter, good or bad.

The man who dreams of passages in the Koran or the
Traditions, Hadits, will from the subjects treated therein
draw his conclusions. For instance the passage, "He will
grant you the help of God and immediate victory," will
signify to him victory and triumph. "Certainly he (God)
has the decision in has hands." "Heavens will open and
offer its numerous portals." And other similar passages
indicate success.

A passage treating of punishments prognosticates punishment; from those treating of benefits a lucky event
may be concluded. Such is the passage in the Koran,
which says: "He who forgives sins is terrible in his in-
flictions." [1]

---

[1] "Who effaces sins, welcomes repentance, and who is terrible
in punishments." Koran, chap. xi., v. 2.

Dreams about poetry and songs contain their explanations in the contents of the objects of the dream.

He who dreams of horses, mules, or asses may hope for good, for the Prophet (God's salutation and goodness be with him!) has said, "Men's fortunes are attached to the forelocks of their horses till to the day of resurrection!" and it is written in the Koran, "God the Highest has thus willed it that they serve you for mounts and for state." [1]

The correctness of these prognostications is not subject to any doubt.

He who dreams of seeing himself mounted upon an ass as a courier, and arriving at his destination, will be lucky in all things; but he who tumbles off the ass on his way is advised that he will be subject to accidents and misfortune.

The fall of the turban from the head predicts ignominy, the turban being the Arab's crown.

If you see yourself in a dream with naked feet it means a loss; and the bare head has the same significance.

By transposing the letters other analogies may be arrived at.

These explanations are here not in their place; but I have been induced to give them in this chapter on account of the use to which they may be put. Persons who would wish to know more on this subject have only to consult the treatise of Ben Sirine. I now return to the names given to the sexual parts of women.

El keuss (the vulva). [2]—This word serves as the name of a young woman's vulva in particular. Such a vulva is

[1] "Il" (God has given you horses, mules, and asses to serve you as mounts and for pomp. He has created what you do not doubt." Koran, chap. xvi., v. 8.

[2] The word keuss, signifying the natural parts of woman, is not an original Arabic word; it is taken from the Greek.

very plump and round in every direction, with long lips, grand slit, the edges well divided and symmetrical and rounded; it is soft, seductive, perfect throughout. It is the most pleasant and no doubt the best of all the different sorts. May God grant us the possession of such a vulva! Amen. It is warm, tight and dry, so much so that one might expect to see fire burst out of it. Its form is graceful, its odour pleasant; the whiteness of its outside sets off its carmine-red middle. There is no imperfection about it.

El relmoune (the voluptuous).[1]—The name given to the vulva of a young virgin.

Ell ass (the primitive).—This is a name applicable to every kind of vulva.

Ez zerzour (the starting).—The vulva of a very young girl, or, as others pretend, of a brunette.

[1] Note of the autograph edition.—All the qualifications given in the Arab text to the sexual organs of woman are referring to the word "feurdj," which is used as masculine, and is translated with vulva and vagina. In order to avoid a fatiguing repetition of one word and the same word, the translator has used now one, now the other of these expressions, which has occasioned the following anomaly: the Arab word "feurdj" is always masculine, while of the French words for vulva and vagina the first, vulve, is feminine, and the other, vagina, is masculine. We must observe here that neither vulva nor vagina give exactly the sense of the Arab "feurdj," which designates the whole of the organ for copulation of the woman, whilst vulva means the outside parts up to the membrane, and vagina is the conduit destined for the reception of the virile member up to the matrix. Neither of these words, therefore, corresponds exactly to "feurdj"; that as it was not feasible to use in the descriptions a long paraphrase, as "the organ for copulation in woman," and still less the vulgar latin word cunnus, it has seemed more convenient to apply the rhetorical figure called synecdoche, viz., to designate the whole by a part, and to use in turns the two above mentioned words, but vulva in preference with respect to the outer parts, and vagina when the interior parts are spoken of.

Ech cheukk (the chink).—The vulva of a bony, lean woman. It is like a chink in a wall, with not a vestige of flesh. May God keep us from it!

Abou tertour (the crested one).[1]—Is the name given to a vulva furnished with a red comb, like that of a cock, which rises at the moment of the enjoyment.

Abou khochime (the snubnose).—Is a vulva with thin lips and a small tongue.[2]

El guenfond (the hedgehog).—The vulva of the old, decrepit woman, dried up with age and with bristly hair.

El sakouti (the silent one).—This name has been given to the vulva that is noiseless. The member may enter it a hundred times a day but it will not say a word, and will be content to look on without murmur.

Ed deukkak (the crusher).—So called from its crushing movements upon the member. It generally begins to push the member, directly it enters, to the right and to the left, and to grip it with the matrix, and would, if it could, absorb also the two testicles.

El tseguil (the importunate).—This is the vulva which is never tired of taking in the member. This latter might pass a hundred nights with it, and walk in a hundred times every night, still that vulva would not be sated—nay, it would want still more, and would not allow the member to come out again at all, if it was possible. With such a vulva the parts are exchanged; the vulva is the

---

[1] There is no doubt that the author wanted to designate by comb that part of the sexual organs of woman which is called clitoris, from the Greek word to tickle. The clitoris is the seat of voluptuousness; it lengthens out and hardens when tickled.

[2] The small lips, ornymphs, are spoken of here, which, in young girls, are hidden by the larger ones.

pursuer, the member the pursued. Luckily it is a rarity, and only found in a small number of women, who are wild with passion, all on fire, and in flame.

El fechefache (the watering can).—A vulva with which certain women are gifted, and which, in passing water, emits from its orifice a sonorously sounding noise.

El becha (the horror).—A vulva of such horrible and repulsive aspect that its looks alone suffices to soften a member which is in erection. It is found in some women, and God keep us from it!

El taleb (the yearning one).—This vagina is met with in a few women only. With some it is natural; with others it becomes what it is by long abstinence. It is burning for a member, and, having got one in its embrace, it refuses to part with it until its fire is extinguished.

El hacene (the beautiful).—This is the vulva which is white, plump, in form vaulted like a dome, firm and without any deformity. You cannot take your eyes off it, and to look at it changes a feeble erection into a strong one.

El neuffagh (the swelling one).—So called because a torpid member coming near it, and rubbing its head against it a few times, at once swells and stands upright. To the woman who has such a one it procures excessive pleasure, for, at the moment of the crisis it opens and shuts convulsively, like the vulva of a mare.

Abou djbaha (one with a projection).—Some women have this sort of vulva, which is very large, with a pubis prominent like a projecting, fleshy forehead.

El ouasa (the vast one).—A vulva surrounded by a

---

[1] Note in the autograph edition.—The author used two expressions belonging to the law, "el mentloub" and "el taleb," signifying the defendant and the plaintiff.

very large pubis. Women of that build are said to be of large vagina, because, although on the approach of the member it appears firm and impenetrable to such a degree that not even a meroud [1] seems likely to be passed in, as soon as it feels the friction of its gland against its centre it opens wide at once.

El aride (the large one).—This is the vulva which is as wide as it is long; that is to say, fully developed all round, from side to side, and from the pubis to the perineum. It is the most beautiful to look upon. As the poet has said:

"It has the splendid whiteness of a forehead,
In its dimensions it is like the moon,
The fire that radiates from it is like the sun's,
And seems to burn the member which approaches;
Unless first moistened with saliva the member cannot enter,
The odour it emits is full of charms."

It is also said that this name applies to the vagina of women who are plump and fat. When such a one crosses her thighs one over the other the vulva stands out like the head of calf. If she lays it bare it resembles a saa [1] for corn placed between her thighs; and, if she walks, it is apparent under her clothes by its wavy movement at each step. May God, in his goodness and generosity, let us enjoy such a vagina! It is of all the most pleasing, the most celebrated, the most wished for.

Abou belaoum (the glutton).—The vulva of a vast

[1] Note in the autograph edition.—The meroud is a little stick or tsylus which the Ahabian women use for blackening their eyelids, or for introducing an eye salve.

[1] Note in autograph edition.—The "saa" is a measure for cereals, and which will contain, according to the localities in which it is used, different quantities, from three to eight decaltries. It is certain that the author in making this comparison had in view the round form of the sack containing the grain, and not the volume of a "saa."

capacity of swallowing. If such a vulva has not been able to get to the coitus for some time it fairly engulfs a member that then comes near it, without leaving any trace of it outside, like as a man who is famished flings himself upon viands that are offered to him and would swallow them without mastication.

El mokaour (the bottomless).—This is the vagina of indefinite length, having in consequence, the matrix ly-ing very far back. It requires a member of the largest dimensions; any other could not succeed in rousing its amorous sensibilities.

Abou cheufrine (the two lipped).—This name is giv-en to the amply developed vagina of an excessively stout woman. Also to the vagina the lips of which having be-come flaccid, owing to weakness, are long and pendulous.

Abou aungra (the humpbacked).—This vulva has the mount of Venus prominent and hard, standing out like the hump on the back of a camel, and reaching down to between the thighs like the head of a calf. May God let us enjoy such a vulva! Amen!

El rorbal (the sieve).—This vulva on receiving a mem-ber seems to sift it all over, below, right and left, fore and aft, until the moment of pleasure arrives.

El hezzaz (the restless).—When this vagina has re-ceived the member it begins to move violently and with-out interruption until the member touches the matrix, and then knows no repose till it has hastened on the enjoyment and finished its work.

El lezzaz (the unionist).—The vagina which, having taken in the member, clings to it and pushes itself for-ward upon it so closely that, if the thing were possible, it would enfold the two testicles.

El moudd (the accommodating).—This name is applied to the vagina of a woman who has felt for a long
time an ardent wish for coition. In rapture with the
member it sees, it is glad to second its movements of
come and go; it offers to the member its matrix by pressing its forward within reach, which is after all, the best
gift it can offer. Whatever place inside of it the member wants to explore, this vulva will make him welcome
to, gracefully according to its wish; there is no corner it
will not help the member to get to.

When the crisis arrives, and the member is ready to
ejaculate, it grips its head with matrix and womb, sucking the last drop of sperm into the matrix. And the
woman does not feel happy until floods of the spermal
fluid pour into the recesses of her matrix.

El mouaine (the assistant).—This vulva is thus named
because it assists the member to go in and out, to go up
and down, in short, in all its movements, in such a way
that if it desires to do a thing, to enter or to retire, to
move about, etc., the vulva hastens to give it all facilities,
and answers to its appeal. By this aid the ejaculation is
facilitated, and the enjoyment heightened; even a
member that is tardy in ejaculation arrives rapidly at it,
and soon spurts its sperm.

El mokeubbeub (the vaulted one).—This is a vulva of
large size, surmounted by a protuberance, brawny, dry,
and shaped like a vault, a compact mass of hard flesh
and gristle. God preserve us from such a one!

El meusboul (the long one).—This name applies only
to some vulvas; everyone knows that the vulvas are far
from being all of the same conformation and aspect.
This vulva extends from the pubis to the anus. It

lengthens out when the woman is lying down or standing, and contracts when she is sitting, differing in this
respect from the vulva of a round shape.   It looks like a
splendid cucumber lying between the thighs.[1]   With
some women it shows projecting under light clothing, or
when they are bending back.

El molki (the duelist).—This is the vulva which, on
the introduction of a member, executes the movement of
coming and going, pushes itself upon it for fear of its
retiring before the pleasure arrives.   There is no enjoyment for it but the shock given to its matrix by the member, and it is for this that it projects its matrix to grip
and suck the member's gland when the ejaculation takes
place.   Certain vulvas, wild with desire and lust, be it
natural or a consequence of long abstention, throw themselves upon the approaching member, opening the mouth
like a famished infant to whom the mother offers the
breast.   In the same way this vulva advances and retires
upon the member to bring it face to face with the matrix
as if in fear that, unaided, it could not find the same.

The vulva and the member resemble thus two skilful
duelists, each time that one of them rushes upon its an-
tagonist, the latter opposes its shield to parry the blow
and repulse the assault.   The member represents the
sword, and the matrix the shield.   The one who first
ejaculates the sperm is vanquished; while the one who is
slowest is the victor; and, assuredly, it is a fine fight!   I
should like thus to fight without stopping to the day of
my death.

----

[1] Note in the autograph edition.—This comparison of the
vulva to a cucumber cannot seem otherwise than ridiculous to
us, nevertheless it is often used by the Arabs.   It serves to
designate a vulva gifted with desirable qualities.

As the poet says:

> I have let them see the effect of a subtle shadow,
> Spinning like an ever busy spider.
> They said to me, "How long will you go on?"
> I answered them, "I will work till I am dead."

El mokabeul (ever ready for the fray). — Thus is called the vagina of the woman that is always hot after the virile member. Far from being afraid of a rigid and hard member, it looks upon it with contempt and asks for one that is still stiffer.

This is the vulva which is not shocked, nor does it blush as the others do, when the vestments are lifted up that cover it; which, on the contrary, makes the member heartily welcome, lets it repose upon its vaulted dome, and introduces it into its core as if to swallow it entirely; so far, indeed, that the testicles are crying out, "Oh, what a misfortune! Our brother has disappeared! We are uneasy about him, for he has boldly thrown himself into that abyss! He must certainly be foolhardy to penetrate like a dragon into such a cavern!" The vulva hearing those lamentations, and desirous to dispel their chagrin, tells them, "Have no fear about this, he is alive, and his ears hear your words." Upon which they reply, "If what you say is true, O master of the beautiful countenance, let him come out, that we may see him." The vulva then says, "I shall not let him come out living; not till death has struck him down." The two testicles implore then, "What sin has he committed, that he should pay for it with his life? Imprisonment and blows should be sufficient punishment." The vagina, "By the existence of him who has created the heavens, there is no way out of me until he is dead!" Then addressing the member, "Do you hear the words of your two brothers? Hasten to show yourself to them, for your absence has plunged them into great affliction!" After the ejaculation, the member returns to them reduced to nothing and like a shadow; but they do not know him, saying, "Who are you, you wonder of leanness?" "I am your brother, and have been ill," says the member; "did you not see in what state I was when I entered? I have knocked at the doors of all the physicians to get advice. But what a prime physician have I found here! He has treated my complaint, and cured it without either auscultation or examination!" The two testicles answer, "O brother of ours, we suffer the same as you, for we are as one with you. Why did not God allot us the same cure?" Forthwith the sperm fills them and augments their volume. They then wish for the same treatment, saying, "Oh, hasten to take us to the same physician, that he may cure our illness, for he knows all maladies!" Here terminates the conversation of the two testicles with the member about its disappearance, which made them fear that he might have fallen into a silo or pit.

El harrab (the fugitive).—The vagina which, being very tight and short, is hurt by the penetration of a very large and stiff member; it tries to escape to the right and left. It is thus, people say, with the vagina of most virgins, which, not yet having made the acquaintance of the member and fearful of its approach, tries to get out of its way, when it glides in between the thighs to be admitted.

Es sabeur (the resigned).—This is the vulva which, having admitted the member, submits patiently to all its whims and movements. This vulva is strong enough to suffer resignedly the most violent and prolonged coition. If it were assaulted a hundred times it would not be vexed or annoyed; and instead of venting reproaches, it would give thanks to God. It will show the same patience if it has to do with several members who visit it successively.

This kind of vagina is found in women of a glowing temperament. If they only knew how to do it, they would not allow the man to dismount, nor his member to retire for a single moment.

El maoui (the juicy).—The vagina thus named has one of the four most abominable defects which can affect a vagina; nay, the most repulsive of all, for the too great abundance of secretions detracts from the pleasures of coition. This imperfection grows still worse when the man by preliminary caresses provokes the issue of the moisture. God preserve us from them! Amen.

El moseuffah (the barrel one).—This kind of vagina is not often met with. The defect which distinguishes it is sometimes natural, sometimes it is the result of an unskilfully executed operation of circumcision upon the woman.[1] It can happen that the operator makes a false move with his instrument and injures the two lips, or even only one of them. In healing there forms a thick scar, which bars the passage, and in order to make the vagina accessible to the member, a surgical operation and the use of the bistouri will have to be resorted to.

El merour (the deep one).—The vagina which has always the mouth open, and the bottom of which is beyond sight. The longest members only can reach it.

[1] Note in the autograph edition.—In certain countries in Africa an operation is made upon girls, analogous to the circumcision, consisting in the partial excision of the lesser lips of the vulva, which attain in that climate sometimes a disproportional development.—(Dictionnaire de Dedecine, Littre et Robin, page 306.

El addad (the biter).—The vulva which, when the member has got into it and is burning with passion, opens and shuts again upon the same fiercely. It is chiefly when the ejaculation is coming that the man feels the head of his member bitten by the mouth of the matrix. And certainly there is an attractive power in the same when it clings, yearning for sperm, to the gland, and draws it in as far as it can. If God in his power has decreed that the woman shall become pregnant the sperm gets concentrated in the matrix, where it is gradually vivified; but if, on the contrary, God does not permit the conception, the matrix expels the seed, which then runs over the vagina.

El meusass (the sucker).—This is a vagina which in its amorous heat in consequence of voluptuous toyings, or of long abstinence, begins to suck the member which has entered it so forcibly as to deprive it of all its sperm, dealing with it like a child draws the breast of the mother.

The poets have described it in the following verses:

"She—the woman—shows in turning up her robe
An object—the vulva—developed full and round,
In semblance like a cup turned upside down.
In placing thereupon your hand, you seem to feel
A well formed bosom, springy, firm, and full.
In boring in your lance it gets well bitten,
And drawn in by a suction, as the breast is by a child
And after having finished, if you wish to re-commence,
You'll find it flaming hot as any furnace."

Another poet (may God grant all his wishes in Paradise!) has composed on the same theme the following:

"Like to a man extended on his chest, she—the vulva—fills
    the hand
which has to be well stretched to cover it.
The place it occupies is standing forth
Like an unopened bud of the blossom of a palm tree.
Assuredly the smoothness of its skin.

Is like the beardless cheek of adolescence;
Its conduit is but narrow,
The entrance to it is not easy,
And he who essays to get in
Feels as though he was butting against a coat of mail.
And at the introduction it emits a sound
Like to the tearing of a woven stuff.
The member having filled its cavity,
Receives the lively welcome of a bite,
Such as the nipple of the nurse receives
When placed between the nursling's lips for suction.
Its lips are burning,
Like a fire that is lighted,
And how sweet it is, this fire!
How delicious for me."

El zenubour (the wasp).—This kind of vulva is known by the strength and roughness of its fur. When the member approaches and tries to enter it gets stung by the hairs as if by a wasp.

El harr (the hot one).—This is one of the most praise-worthy vulvas. Warmth is in fact very much esteemed in a vulva, and it may be said that the intensity of the enjoyment afforded by it is in proportion to the heat it develops. Poets have praised it in the following verses:
"The vulva possesses an intrinsic heat;

Shut in a solid heart (interior) and pent up breast (matrix).—
Its fire communicates itself to him that enters it;
It equals in intensity the fire of love.
She is as tight as a well-fitting shoe,[1]
Smaller than the circle of the apple of the eye."

El ladid (the delicious).—It has the reputation of pro-curing an unexampled pleasure, comparable only to the one felt by the beasts and birds of prey, and for which

---

[1] Note of the autograph edition.—This comparison is some-what vulgar for poetry, and may even appear incomprehensible; nevertheless it finds its explanation in the fact that the shoes of the Arabs are kept fast to the foot by their upper borders being narrower than the foot itself, which has to be forced in.

they fight sanguinary combats. And if such effects are produced upon animals, what must they be for man. And so it is that all the wars spring from the search of the voluptuous pleasure which the vagina procures, and which is the highest fortune of this world; it is a part of the delights of paradise awarded to us by God as a fore-taste of what is waiting for us, namely, delights a thousand times superior, and above which only the sight of the Benevolent (God) is to be placed.

More names might certainly be found applicable to the sexual organs of woman, but the number of those mentioned above appears to me ample. The principal object of this work is to collect together all the remarkable and attractive matters concerning the coitus, so that he who is in trouble may find a conclusion in it, and the man to whom erection offers difficulties may be able to look into it for a remedy against his weakness. Wise physicians have written that people whose members have lost their strength, and are afflicted with impotence, should assiduously read books treating of coition, and study carefully the different kind of lovemaking, in order to recover their former vigour. A certain means of provoking erection is to look at animals in the act of coition. As it is not always everywhere possible to see animals whilst in the act of copulation, books on the subject of generation are indispensable. In every country, large or small, both the rich and poor have a taste for this sort of books, which may be compared to the stone of philosophy transforming common metals into gold.

It is related (and God penetrates the most obscure matters, and he is the most wise!) that once upon a time, before the reign of the great Kalif Haroun er Rachid,

there lived a buffoon, who was the amusement of women, old people and children. His name was Djoaidi.[1]
Many women granted him their favours freely, and he
was much liked and well received by all. By princes,
vizirs and caids he was likewise very well treated; in
general all the world pampered him; at that time, indeed,
any man that was a buffoon enjoyed the greatest consideration, for which reason the poet has said:

"Oh, Time! Of all the dwellers here below
You only elevate buffoons or fools,
Or him whose mother was a prostitute,
Or him whose anus as an inkstand serves,[2]
Or him who from his youth has been a pander;
Who has no other work but to bring the two sexes together."

Djoaidi related the following story:

THE HISTORY OF DJOAIDI AND FADEHAT EL DJEMAL

I was in love with a woman who was all grace and perfection, beautiful of shape, and gifted with all imaginable charms. Her cheeks were like roses, her forehead
lily white, her lips like coral; she had teeth like pearls,
and breasts like pomegranates. Her mouth opened round
like a ring; her tongue seemed to be incrusted with precious gems; her eyes, black and finely slit, had the lan-
gour of slumber, and her voice the sweetness of sugar.
With her form pleasantly filled out, her flesh was mellow like fresh butter, and pure as the diamond.

---

[1] "Djoaidi" signifies a man of the people. The root djaa
points to crisp, naturally curling hair.

[2] Note in the autograph edition.—Paraphrase for a designing
minion, a giton. It takes its origin from the comparison, very
common with Arabs, of the pen and the inkstand and the verge
and the vulva.

As to her vulva, it was white, prominent, round as an arch; the centre of it was red, and breathed fire, and without a trace of humidity; for, sweet to the touch, it was quite dry. When she walked it showed in relief like a dome or an inverted cup. In reclining it was visible between her thighs, looking like a kid couched on a hillock.

This woman was my neighbour. All the others played and laughed with me, jested with me, and met my sug-gestions with great pleasure. I revelled in their kisses, their close embraces and nibblings, and in sucking their lips, breasts, and necks. I had coition with all of them, except my neighbour, and it was exactly her I wanted to possess in preference to all the rest; but instead of being kind to me, she avoided me rather. When I contrived to take her aside to trifle with her and try to rouse her gaiety, and spoke to her of my desires, she recited to me the following verses, the sense of which was a mystery to me:

"Among the mountain tops I saw a tent placed firmly,
Apparent to all eyes high up in mid-air.
But, oh, the pole that held it up was gone.
And like a vase without a handle it remained,
With all its cords undone, its centre sinking in,
Forming a hollow like that of a kettle."

Every time I told her of my passion she answered me with these verses, which to me were void of meaning, and to which I could make no reply, which, however, only excited my love all the more. I therefore inquired of all those I knew—amongst wise men, philosophers, and savants—the meaning, but not one of them could solve the riddle for me, so as to satisfy my heat and appease my passion.

Nevertheless I continued my investigations, when at

last I heard of a savant named Abou Nouass,[1] who lived in a far-off country, and who, I was told, was the only man capable of solving the enigma. I betook myself to him, apprised him of the discourses I had with the woman, and recited to him the above-mentioned verses.

Abou Nouass said to me, "This woman loves you to the exclusion of every other man. She is very corpulent and plump." I answered, "It is exactly as you say. You have given her likeness as if she were before you, excepting what you say in respect of her love for me, for, until now, she has never given me any proof of it." "She has no husband." "This is so," I said. Then added, "I have reason to believe that your member is of small dimensions, and such a member cannot give her pleasure nor quench her fire; for what she wants is a lover with a member like that of an ass. Perhaps it may not be so. Tell me the truth about this!" When I had reassured him on that point, affirming that my member, which began to rise at the expression of his doubtings, was full-sized, he told me that in that case all difficulties would disappear, and explained to me the sense of the verses as follows:

The tent, firmly planted, represents the vulva of grand dimension and placed well forward, the mountains, between which it rises, are the thighs. The stake which supported its centre and has been torn up, means that she has no husband, comparing the stake or pole that supports the tent to the virile member holding up the lips of the vulva. She is like a vase without handle; this

---

[1] The real name of Abou Nouass was Abou Hali Hacene. He also had the surname d'el Hakemi. He was born of obscure parents towards 135 or 136 of the Hegira, and acquired a great reputation as a poet and a philosopher.

means if the pail is without a handle to hang it up by it is good for nothing, the pail representing the vulva, and the handle the verge. The cords are undone and its centre is sinking in; that is to say, as the tent without a supporting pole caves in at the center, inferior in this respect to the vault which remains upright without sup- port, so can the woman who has no husband not enjoy complete happiness. From the words, It forms a hollow like that of a kettle, you may judge how lascivious God has made that woman in her comparisons: she likens her vulva to a kettle, which serves to prepare the tserid.[1] Listen; if the tserid is placed in the kettle, to turn out well it must be stirred by means of a medeleuk [2] long and solid, whilst the kettle is steadied by the feet and hands. Only in that way can it be prepared properly. It cannot be done with a small spoon; the cook would burn her hands, owing to the shortness of the handle, and the dish would not be well prepared. This is the symbol of this woman's nature, O Djoaidi. If your member has not the dimensions of a respectable mede- leuk, serviceable for the good preparation of the tserid, it will not give her satisfaction, and, moreover, if you do not hold her close to your chest, enlacing her with your hands and feet, it is useless to solicit her favours; finally if you let her consume herself by her own fire, like the bottom of the kettle which gets burnt if the medeleuk is not stirred upon it, you will not gratify her desire by the result.

You see now what prevented her from acceding to

---

[1] The tserid, or more commonly tserida, is an Arabian dish.

[2] Note in the autograph edition.—Medeleuk, from deleuk, to pound, mash. This is a large wooden spoon, corresponding in shape and size to a pouch. This latter expression, however, being vulgar, has not been employed.

your wishes; she was afraid that you would not be able to quench her flame after having fanned it.

But what is the name of this woman, O Djoaidi?

"Fadehat el Djemal (the sunrise of beauty)," I replied.

"Return to her," said the sage, "and take her these verses and your affair will come to a happy issue, please God! You will then come back to me, and inform me of what will have come to pass between you two."

I gave my promise, and Abou Nouass recited to me the following lines:

"Have patience now, O Fadehat el Djemal,
I understand your words, and all shall see how I obey them.
O you! beloved and cherished by whoever
Can revel in your charms and glory in them!
O apple of my eye! You thought I was embarrassed
About the answer which I had to give you.
Yes, certainly! It was the love I bore you
Made me look foolish in the eyes of all you know.
They thought I was possessed of a demon;
Called me a Merry Andrew and buffoon.
For God! What of buffoonery I've got,
        Should it be, that
No other member is like mine? Here! see it, measure it!
What woman tastes it falls in love with me,
In violent love. It is a well known fact
That you from far may see it like a column.
If it erects itself it lifts my robe and shames me.
Now take it kindly, put it in your tent,
Which is between the well-known mountains placed.
It will be quite at home there, you will find it
Not softening while inside, but sticking like a nail;
Take it to form a handle to your vase.
Come and examine it, and notice well
How vigorous it is and long in its erection!
If you but want a proper medeleuk,
A medeleuk to use between your thighs,
Take this to stir the centre of your kettle.
It will do good to you, O mistress mine!
Your kettle be it plated will be satisfied!"[1]

[1] Note in the autograph edition.—The Arabs have a vulgar saying of a man who is not easily satisfied that he is mokeus deur, plated. Doubtless it refers in a similar sense to the vulva.

Having learnt these verses by heart, I took my leave of Abou Nouass and returned to Fadehat el Djemal. She was, as usual, alone. I gave a slight knock at her door; she came out at once, beautiful as the rising sun, and coming up to me, she said, "Oh! enemy of God, what business has brought you here to me at this time?"

I answered her, "O my mistress! a business of great importance."

"Explain yourself, and I will see whether I can help you," she said.

"I shall not speak to you about it until the door is locked," I answered.

"Your boldness to-day is very great," she said.

And I, "True, O my mistress! boldness is one of my qualities."

She then addressed me thus, "O enemy of yourself! O you most miserable of your race! If I were to lock the door, and you having nothing wherewith to satisfy my desires, what should I do with you? face of a Jew!"

"You will let me share your couch, and grant me your favours."

She began to laugh; and after we had entered the house, she told a slave to lock the house door. As usual, I asked her to respond to my proposals; she then recited to me again the above mentioned verses. When she had finished I recited to her those which Abou Nouass had taught me.

As I proceeded I saw her move and more moved, I observed her giving way, to yawn, to stretch herself, to sigh. I knew now I should arrive at the desired result. When I had finished my member was in such a state of erection that it became like a pillar, still lengthening. When Fadehat el Djemal saw it in that condition she precipitated herself upon it, took it into her hands, and drew it towards her thighs. I then said, "O apple of my eyes! this may not be done here, let us go into your chamber."

She replied, "Leave me alone, O son of a debauched woman! Before God! I am losing my sense in seeing your member getting longer and longer, and lifting your robe. Oh, what a member! I never saw a finer one! Let it penetrate into this delicious, plump vulva, which maddens all who heard it described; for the sake of which so many died of love; and of which your superiors and masters themselves could not get possession."

I repeated, "I shall not do it anywhere else than in your chamber."

She answered, "If you do not enter this minute this tender vulva I shall die."

As I still insisted upon repairing to her room, she cried, "No, it is quite impossible; I cannot wait so long!"

I saw in fact her lips tremble, her eyes filling with tears. A general tremour ran over her, she changed colour, and laid herself down upon her back, baring her thighs, the whiteness of which made her flesh appear like crystal tinged with carmine.

Then I examined her vulva—a white cupola with a purple centre, soft and charming. It opened like that of a mare on the approach of a stallion.

At that moment she seized my member and kissed it, saying, "by the religion of my father it must penetrate into my vulva!" and drawing nearer to me she pulled it towards her vagina.

I now hesitated no longer to assist her with my member, and placed it against the entrance to her vulva. As soon as the head of my member touched the lips, the

whole body of Fedehat el Djemal trembled with excitement. Sighing and sobbing, she held me pressed to her
bosom.

Again I profited by this moment to admire the beauties of her vulva. It was magnificent, its purple centre
setting off its whiteness all the more. It was round, and
without any imperfection; projecting like a splendidly
curved dome over her belly. In one word, it was a
masterpiece of creation as fine as could be seen. The
blessing of God, the best creator, upon it.

And the woman who possessed this wonder had in
her time no superior.

Seeing her then in such transports, trembling like a
bird, the throat of which is being cut, I pushed my dart
into her. But thinking she might not be able to take in
the whole of my member, I had gone about cautiously,
but she moved her buttocks furiously, saying to me,
"This is not enough for my contentment." Making a
strong push, I lodged my member completely in her,
which made her utter a painful cry, but the moment
after she moved with greater fury than before. She
cried, "Do not miss the corners, neither high nor low,
but above all things do not neglect the centre! The centre!" she repeated. "If you feel it coming, let it go into
my matrix so as to extinguish my fire." Then we moved
alternately in and out, which was delicious. Our legs
were interlaced, our muscles unbent, and so we went on
with kisses and claspings until the crisis came upon us
simultaneously. We then rested and took breath after
this mutual conflict.

I wanted to withdraw my member, but she would not
consent to this and begged of me not to take it out. I
acceded to her wish, but a moment later she took it out

herself, dried it, and replaced it in her vulva. We re-
newed our game, kissing, pressing, and moving in
rhythm. After a short time, we rose and entered her
chamber, without having this time accomplished the enjoyment. She gave me now a piece of an aromatic root,[1]
which she recommended me to keep in my mouth, as-
suring me that as long as I had it there my member
would remain on the alert. Then she asked me to lie
down, which I did. She mounted upon me, and taking
my member into her hands, she made it enter entirely
into her vagina. I was astonished at the vigour of her
vulva and at the heat emitted from it. The opening of
her matrix in particular excited my admiration. I never
had any experience like it: it closely clasped my member
and pinched the gland.

With the exception of Fadehat el Djemal no woman
had until then taken in my member in its full length.
She was able to do so, I believe, owing to her being very
plump and corpulent, and her vulva being large and
deep.

Fadehat el Djemal, astride upon me, began to rise and
descend; she kept crying out, wept, went slower, then
accelerated her movements again, ceased to move altogether; when part of my member became visible she
looked at it, then took it out altogether to examine it
closely, then plunged it in again until it had disappeared
completely. So she continued until the enjoyment overcame her again. At last, having dismounted from me,
she now laid herself down, and asked me to get on her.
I did so, and she introduced my member entirely into
her vulva.

We thus continued our caresses, changing our posi-

[1] Probably cinnamon or the root of the cubeb-plant.

tion in turns, until night came on. I thought it proper to show a wish to go now, but she would not agree to this, and I had to give her my word that I would remain. I said to myself, "this woman will not let me go at any price, but when daylight comes God will advise me." I remained with her, and all night long we kept caressing each other, and took but scanty rest.

I counted during that day and night, I accomplished twenty-seven times the act of coition, and I became afraid that I should never be able to leave the woman's house.

Having at last made good my escape, I went to visit Abou Nouass again, and informed him of all that had happened. He was surprised and stupefied, and the first words were ,"O Djoaidi, you can have neither authority nor power over such a woman, and she would make you do penance for all the pleasure you have had with other women!"

However, Fadehat el Djemal proposed to me to be-come her legitimate husband, in order to put a stop to the vexatious rumours that were circulating about her conduct. I, on the other hand, was only on the look out for adultery. Asking the advice of Abou Nouass about it, he told me, "If you marry Fadehat el Djemal you will ruin your health, and God will withdraw his protection [1] from you, and the worst of all will be that she will cuckold you, for she is insatiable with respect to the coitus, and would cover you with shame." And I answered him, "Such is the nature of women; they are insatiable as far as their vulvas are concerned, and so that their lust gets satisfied they do not care whether

[1] The Arab word seteur signifies veil, window-blind, and by extension, protection or even shield, buckler. It was in this latter sense that the author has used the word here.

it be with a buffoon, a negro, a valet, or even with a man that is despised and reprobated by society."

On this occasion Abou Nouass depicted the character of women in the following verses:

"Women are demons, and were born as such;
No one can trust them, as is known to all;
If they love a man, it is only out of caprice;
And he to whom they are most cruel loves them most.
Beings full of treachery and trickery, I aver
The man that loves you truly is a lost man;
He who believes me not can prove my word
By letting woman's love get hold of him for years!
If in your own generous mood you have given them
Your all and everything for years and years,
They will say afterwards, 'I swear by God! my eyes
Have never seen a thing he gave me!'
After you impoverished yourself for their sake,
Their cry from day to day will be for ever 'Give!
Give man, Get up and buy and borrow.' [1]
If they cannot profit by you they'll turn against you;
They will tell lies of you and calumniate you.
They do not recoil to use the slave in the master's absence,
If once their passions are aroused, and they play tricks;
Assuredly, if once their vulva is in rut,
They only think of getting in some member in erection.
Preserve us God! from woman's trickery;
And of old women in particular. So be it."

[1] Note in the autograph edition.—Literally: "Seized by your bounty," a form of speech used to express the attentions which men show to women.

CHAPTER X

CONCERNING THE ORGANS OF GENERATION OF ANIMALS

Know, O Vizir (God's blessing be with you!), that the sexual organs of the various male animals are not analogous with the different natures of the virile members which I have mentioned.

The verges of animals are classed according to the species to which they belong, and these species are four which I have mentioned.

1. The verges of animals with hoofs as the horse, mule, ass, which verges are of large size.[1]

El remoul, the colossus.

El kass,[2] the serpent rolled up.

El fellag,[3] the splitter.

El zellate, the club.

El heurmak, the indomitable.

El meunefoukh, the swollen.

Abou dommar, the one with a head.

Abou beurnita, the one with a hat.

El keurkite,[4] the pointed staff.

El keuntra, the bridge.

El rezama, the mallet.

---

[1] Note in the autograph edition.—Literally, magnificent creation.

[2] The word kass, from the root kass, means to pierce a female; in the coitus, enwrapping her like a serpent.

[3] This name comes from the root felleg, to split, to divide.

[4] Keurkite is the name of a staff with a long, pointed ferule, as carried by the Marabouts. In some texts this name is replaced by kneurite, the Arabian name for lobster, and also for a sort of cuttle fish abounding on the African coast.

Abou sella, the fighter.[1]

2. The verges of animals which have the kind of feet called akhefaf,[2] as, for instance, the camel.

El maloum, the well-known.
El tonil, the long one.
Ech cherita, the riband.[3]
El mostakinme, the firm one.
El heurkal, the swinging one.
El mokheubbi, the hidden one.
Ech chaaf, the tuft.
Tsequil el ifaha, the slow-coach.

3. The verges of animals with split horns, like the ox, the sheep, etc.

El aceub, the nerve.
El heurbadj, the rod.
El sonte, the whip.
Requig ed ras, the small head.
El tonil, the long one.

For the ram.
El aicoub, the nervous.

And lastly, the members of animals with claws, as the lion, fox, dog, and other animals of this species.

El kedib, the verge.
El kibouss, the great gland.
El metemerole, the one that will lengthen.

[1] See note 2 on page 129.

[2] Note in the autograph edition.—Akhefaf has no equivalent in French. It is a foot showing rudimentary hoofs or toes united at the sole by a thick and callous epidermis, as seen in the camel.

[3] Id.—Cherita means a plaited riband or flat cord.

[4] Id.—The only sense which can be found in chaaf is that of tuft, frieze, hair in general.

It is believed that of all the animals of God's creation the lion is the most expert in respect to coition. If he meets the lioness he examines her before copulation. He will know if she has already been covered by a male. When she comes to him he smells her, and if she has allowed herself to be crossed by a boar he knows it immediately by the odour that animal has left upon her. He then smells her urine, and if the examination proves unfavourable, he gets into a rage, and begins to lash with his tail right and left. Woe to the animal that comes at that time near him; it is certain to be torn to pieces. He then returns to the lioness, who, seeing that he knows all, trembles with terror. He smells again at her, utters a roar which makes the mountains shake, and, falling upon her, lacerates her back with his claws. He even will go so far as to kill her, and then befoul her body with his urine.

It is said that the lion is the most jealous and most intelligent of all animals. It is also averred that he is generous, and spares him who gets round him by fair words.

A man who on meeting a lion uncovers his sexual parts causes him to take flight.

Whoever pronounces before a lion the name of Daniel (Hail be to him!)[1] also sends him flying, because the prophet (Hail be to him!) has enjoined this upon the lion in respect to the invocation of his name. Therefore, when this name is pronounced, the lion departs without doing any harm. Several cases which proves this fact are cited.

---

[1] It is probable that this belief originates with the sojourn of Daniel in the lions' den.

CHAPTER XI

ON THE DECEITS AND TREACHERIES OF WOMEN

Know, O Vizir (to whom God be good!) that the stratagems of women are numerous and ingenious. Their
tricks will deceive Satan himself, for God, the Highest,
has said (Koran, chap. xii., verse 28), that the deceptive
faculties of women are great, and he has likewise said
(Koran chap. vi., verse 38), that the stratagems of
Satan are weak. Comparing the word of God as to the
ruses of Satan and woman, contained in those two verse,
it is easy to see how great these latter ones are.[1]

STORY OF A DECEIVED HUSBAND BEING
CONVICTED HIMSELF OF INFIDELITY

It is related that a man fell in love with a woman of
great beauty, and possessing all perfections imaginable.
He had made many advances to her, which were repulsed; then he had endeavoured to seduce her by rich
presents, which were likewise declined. He lamented,
complained, and was prodigal with his money in order
to conquer her, but to no purpose, and he grew lean as
a spectre.

This lasted for some time when he made the acquaintance of an old woman, whom he took into his confidence,
complaining bitterly about it. She said to him, "I shall
help you, please God."

Forthwith she made her way to the house of the
woman, in order to get an interview with her; but on
arriving there the neighbors told her that she could not
get in, because the house was guarded by a ferocious

---

[1] "The nature of woman is such." (Rabelais, Book iii., chap.
33.)

bitch, which did not allow anyone to come in or depart, and in her malignity always flew at the face of people.

Hearing this, the old woman rejoiced, and said to herself, "I shall succeed, please God." She then went home, and filled a basket with bits of meat. Thus provided she returned to the woman's house, and went in.

The bitch, on seeing her, rose to spring at her; but she produced the basket with its contents, and showed it her. As soon as the brute saw the viands, it showed its satisfaction by the movements of its tail and nostrils. The old woman putting down the basket before it, spoke to it as follows, "Eat, O my sister. Your absence has been painful to me; I did not know what had become of you, and I have looked for you a long time. Appease your hunger!"

While the animal was eating, and she stroked its back, the mistress of the house came to see who was there, and was not a little surprised to see the bitch, which would never suffer anybody to come near her, so friendly with a strange person. She said, "O old woman, how is it that you know our dog?" The old woman gave no reply, but continued to caress the animal, and utter lamentations.

Then said the mistress of the house to her, "My heart aches to see you thus. Tell me the cause of your sorrow."

"This bitch," said the woman, "was formerly a woman, and my best friend. One fine day she was invited with me to a wedding; she put on her best clothes, and adorned herself with her finest ornaments. We then went together. On our way we were accosted by a man, who at her sight was seized with the most violent love; but she would not listen to him. Then he offered brilliant presents, which she also declined. This man,

meeting her some days later, said to her, 'Surrender yourself to my passion, or else I shall conjure God to change
you into a bitch.' She answered, 'Conjure as much as
you like.' The man then called the maledictions of
heaven upon that woman, and she was changed into a
bitch, as you see here."

At these words the mistress of the house began to cry
and lament, saying, "O, my mother! I am afraid that I
shall meet the same fate as this bitch." "Why, what
have you done," said the old woman. The other answered, "There is a man who has loved me since a long
time, and I have refused to accede to his desires, nor did
I listen to him, though the saliva was dried up in his
mouth by his supplications; and in spite of the large ex-
penses he had gone to in order to gain my favour I have
always answered him that I should not consent, and
now, O my mother, I am afraid he might call to God to
curse me."

"Tell me how to know this man," said the old woman,
"for fear that you might become like this animal."

"But how will you be able to find him, and whom
could I send to him?"

The old woman answered, "Me, daughter of mine! I
shall render you this service, and find him." "Make
haste, O my mother, and see him before he conjures
God against me." "I shall find him still this day," answered the old woman, and, please God, you shall meet
him to-morrow."

With this, the old woman took her leave, went on
the same day to the man who had made her his confidant, and told him of the meeting arranged for the next
day.

So the next day the mistress of the house went to the

old woman, for they had agreed that the rendezvous should take place there. When she arrived at the house she waited for some time, but the lover did not come. No doubt he had been prevented from making his appearance by some matter of importance.

The old woman reflecting upon this mischance, thought to herself, "There is no might nor power but in God, the Great." But she could not imagine what might have kept him away. Looking at the woman, she saw that she was agitated, and it was apparent that she wanted coition hotly. She got more and more restless, and presently asked, "Why does he not come?" The old woman made answer, "O my daughter, some serious affair must have interfered, probably necessitating a journey. But I shall help you under these circumstances." She then put on her melahfa,[1] and went to look for the young man. But it was to no purpose, as she could not get to hear anything about him.

Still continuing her search, the old woman was thinking, "This woman is at this moment eagerly coveting a man. Why not try to-day another young man, who might calm her ardour? To-morrow I shall find the right one." As she was thus walking and thinking she met a young man of very pleasing exterior. She saw at once, that he was a fit lover, and likely to help her out of her perplexity, and she spoke to him, "O my son, if I were to set you in connection with a lady, beautiful, graceful and perfect, would you make love to her?" "If your words are truth, I would give to you this golden dinar!" said he. The old woman, quite enchanted, took the money, and conducted him to the house.

[1] The melahfa is a large veil, generally of white cotton web, used by women to wrap themselves in, both body and head, when they walk out.

Now, it so happened that this young man was the husband of the lady, which the old woman did not know till she had brought him, and the way she found it out was this: She went first into the house and said to the lady, "I have not been able to find the slightest trace of your lover; but failing him, I have brought you somebody to quench your fire for to-day. We will save the other for to-morrow. God has inspired to do so."

The lady then went to the window to take a look at him whom the old woman wanted to bring to her, and, getting sight of him, she recognized her husband, just on the point of entering the house.[1] She did not hesitate, but hastily donning her melahfa, she went straight to meet him, and striking him in the face, she exclaimed, "O! enemy of God and of yourself, what are you doing here? You surely came with the intention to commit adultery. I have been suspecting you for a long time, and waited here every day, while I was sending out the old woman to enveigle you to come in. This day I have found you out, and denial is of no use. And you always told me that you were not a rake! I shall demand a divorce this very very day, now I know your conduct!"

The husband, believing that his wife spoke the truth, remained silent and abashed.

Learn from this the deceitfulness of woman, and what she is capable of.

---

[1] Note in the autograph edition.—An analogous situation is found in the "Tales of Boccacio," Tale Six of the Third Day, done into verse by La Fontaine, in the story of Richard Minutolo (First Book of the Tales). It must be added that the groundwork of the Arabian tale is different from Boccaccio's. Observe, however, that the means employed by the old woman to gain for the young man the lady's favours is not without analogy to those described in Tale Eight of the Fifth Day of the same book.

STORY OF THE LOVER AGAINST HIS WILL

A story is told of a certain woman who was desperately in love with one of her neighbours, whose virtue and piety were well known. She declared to him her passion; but, finding all her advances constantly repulsed, in spite of all her wiles, she resolved to have her satisfaction nevertheless, and this is the way she went to work her purpose:

One evening she apprised her negress that she intended to set a snare for that man, and the negress, by her order, left the street door open; then in the middle of the night, she called the negress and gave her the following instructions: "Go and knock with this stone at our street door as hard as you can, without taking any notice of the cries which I shall utter, or the noise I make; as soon as you hear the neighbor opening his door, come back and knock the same way at the inner door.[1] Take care that he does not see you, and come in at once if you observe somebody coming." The negress executed this order punctually.

Now, the neighbour was by nature a compassionate man, always disposed to assist people in distress, and his help was never asked in vain. On hearing the noise of the blows struck at the door and the cries of his neighbour, he asked his wife what this might mean, and she replied, "It is our neighbour so and so, who is attacked in her house by thieves." He went in great haste to her aid; but scarcely had he entered the house when the negress closed the door upon him. The woman seized him, and uttered loud screams. He protested, but the

---

[1] Note in the autograph edition.—The Arabian houses are generally situated in an inner court, which communicates by a door with the street, while a second door leads to the rooms.

mistress of the house put, without any more ado, this condition before him. "If you do not consent to do with me so and so, I shall tell that you have come in here to violate me, and hence all this noise." "The will of God be done!" said the man, "nobody can go against Him, nor escape from His might." He then tried sundry subterfuges in order to escape, but in vain, for the mistress of the house recommended to scream and make a row, which brought a good many people to the spot. He saw that his reputation would be compromised if he continued his resistance, and surrendered, saying, "Save me, and I am ready to satisfy you!" "Go into this chamber and close the door behind you," said the lady of the house, "if you want to leave this house with honour, and do not attempt to escape unless you wish those people to know that you are the author of all this commotion." When he saw how determined she was to have her way, he did as she had told him. She, on her part, went out to the neighbors that had come to help her, and giving them some kind of explanation, dismissed them. They went away condoling with her.

Left alone, she shut the doors and returned to her unwilling lover. She kept him in sequestration for a whole week, and only set him free after she had completely drained him.

Learn from this the deceitfulness of women, and what they are capable of.

STORY OF A MAN WHO WAS MADE A CUCKOLD BY HIS ASS

The story goes that a man, a street porter who was married, had an ass which he employed in his business. His wife was very fat and corpulent, and had a very plump, deep, and excessively large vulva. Her husband, on the contrary, was furnished with a verge which was both little and soft. She simply held him in contempt, in the first place on account of his weak member, and then because he but rarely fulfilled his conjugal duty. He was, in fact not vigorous enough for that work; whilst she, burning for the coitus, would never have had enough of it, not even if she could have revelled in it day and night; in fact, no man could have satisfied her, and she would have coped with the whole race of males. If she had contrived to lay her hand upon a man of metal she would not have allowed him to draw his member out of her vulva, no, not for a moment.

This woman brought every night the ass its fodder. As she often kept her husband waiting, he would say when she returned: "What made you stay so long?" And she answered: "I have sat myself down by the side of the ass, and saw it take its meal; it appeared to be so tired that I was sorry for it."

This went on for some time, and the husband had no suspicion of anything being wrong. Moreover, he returned home every evening tired with his day's work, and went to lie down directly, leaving it to his wife to look after the ass. She, however, had become very intimate with the animal in the following manner (how abominable God had made her!). When the time came for feeding him she took off his pack-saddle and placed it on her own back, buckling the girths round her body. Then she took a little of his dung and of his urine, mixed them together, and rubbed the entrance of her vulva with it. This done, she placed herself on her hands and feet within range of the ass, and took position, her vulva facing him. He would approach, smell at her vulva, and thinking to have a beast of burden before him, spring upon her. As soon as he was thus placed, she seized his member with one of her hands and introduced its head into her vulva. The vulva got more and more enlarged, so that the member, penetrating little by little, finished with being lodged in its full length, and brought on the crisis of the pleasure.

So the woman took her pleasure with the ass for a long time. But one night when her husband had been asleep for some time he awoke suddenly, and felt a desire to caress his wife. Not finding her by his side, he rose very softly and went to the stable. What was his astonishment when he saw her under the ass, the latter working up and down her croup. "What does this mean, O you so-and-so?" he cried. But she quickly disengaged herself from under the ass, and said, "May God curse you for not pitying your ass!" But, come, what does all this mean?" the husband repeated. "That," said the woman, "when I came and brought his fodder he refused to eat; I saw by that how tired he was. I passed my hand over his back and his back nearly gave way under him. I then thought his pack-saddle was too heavy and in order to make sure of it, I tried it on my back and found it very heavy. Now I know the reason of his excessive fatigue. Believe me, if you want to preserve your ass, do not work him so hard."

Learn from this the deceitfulness of women, and what they are capable of.

A LARCENY OF LOVE

The following story is told of two women who inhabited the same house. The husband of one of them had a member long, thick and hard; while the husband of the other had, on the contrary, that organ little, insignificant and soft. The first one rose always pleasant and smiling; the other one got up in the morning in tears and vexation.

One day the two women were together, and spoke of their husbands.

The first one said, "I live in the greatest happiness. My bed is a couch of bliss. When my husband and I are together in it it is the witness of our supreme pleasure; of our kisses and embraces, of our joys and amorous sighs. When my husband's member is in my vulva it stops it up completely; it stretches itself out until it touches the bottom of my vagina, and it does not take its leave until it has visited every corner—threshold, vestibule, ceiling and centre. When the crisis arrived it takes its position in the very centre of the vagina, which it floods with tears. It is in this way we quench our fire and appease our passion."

The second answered, "I live in the greatest grief; our bed is a bed of misery, and our coition is a union of fatigue and trouble, of hate and malediction. When my husband's member enters my vulva there is a space left open, and it is so short it cannot touch the bottom. When it is in erection it is twisted all ways, and cannot procure any pleasure. Feeble and meagre, it can scarcely ejaculate a drop, and its service gives no pleasure to any woman."

Such was the almost daily conversation which the two women had together.

It happened, however, that the woman who had so much cause for complaint thought in her heart how delightful it would be to commit adultery with the other one's husband. She thought to herself, "It must be brought about, if it be only for once." Then she watch-

ed her opportunity until her husband had to be absent
for a night from home.

In the evening she made preparation to get her project
carried out, and perfumed herself with sweet scents and
essences. When the night was advanced to about a third
of its duration, she entered noiselessly the chamber in
which the other woman and her husband were sleeping,
and groped her way to their couch. Finding that there
was a free space between them, she slipped in. There
was scant room, but each of the spouses thought it was
the pressure of the other, and gave way a little; and so
she contrived to glide between them. She then quietly
waited until the other woman was in a profound sleep,
and then, approaching the husband, she brought her
flesh in contact with his. He awoke, and smelling the
perfumed odours which she exhaled, he was in erection
at once. He drew her towards him, but she said in a
low voice, "Let me go to sleep!" He answered, "Be
quiet, and let me do! The children will not hear anything!" She then pressed close up to him, so as to get
him farther away from his wife, and said, "Do as you
like, but do not waken the children, who are close by."
She took these precautions for fear that his wife should
wake up.

The man, however, roused by the odour of the perfumes, drew her ardently towards himself. She was
plump and mellow, and her vulva projecting. He
mounted upon her and said, "Take it (the member) in
your hand, as usual!" Se took it, and was astonished at
its size and magnificence, then introduced it into her
vulva.

The man, however, observed that his member had
been taken in entirely, which he had never been able to

do with his wife. The woman, on her part, found that
she had never received such a benefit from her husband.

The man quite surprised. He worked his will upon
her a second and third time, but his astonishment only
increased. At last he got off her, and stretched himself
along side her.

As soon as the woman found that he was asleep, she
slipped out, left the chamber, and returned to her own.

In the morning, the husband, on rising, said to his
wife, "Your embraces have never seemed so sweet to me
as last night, and I never breathed such sweet perfumes
as those you exhaled." "What embraces and what perfumes are you speaking of? asked the wife. "I have not
a particle of perfume in the house." She called him
storyteller, and assured him that he must have been
dreaming. He then began to consider whether he might
not have deceived himself, and agreed with his wife that
he must actually have dreamed it all.

Appreciate, after this, the deceitfulness of women,
and what they are capable of.

STORY OF THE WOMAN WITH TWO HUSBANDS

It is related that a man, after having lived for some time
in a country to which he had gone, became desirous of
getting married. He addressed himself to an old woman
who had experience in such matters, asking her whether
she could find him a wife, and who replied, "I can find
you a girl gifted with great beauty and perfect in shape
and comeliness. She will surely suit you, for, besides
having these qualities, she is virtuous and pure. Only
mark, her business occupies her all the day, but during
the night she will be yours completely. It is for this
reason she keeps herself reserved, as she apprehends that
a husband might not agree to this."

The man replied, "This girl need not be afraid. I, too am not at liberty during the day, and I only want her for the night."

He then asked her in marriage. The old woman brought her to him, and he liked her. From that time they lived together, observing the conditions under which they had come together.

This man had an intimate friend whom he introduced to the old woman who had arranged his marriage according to the conditions mentioned, and which friend had requested the man to ask her to do him the same service. They went to the old woman and solicited her assistance in the matter. "This is a very easy matter," she said. "I know a girl of great beauty, who will dissipate your heaviest troubles. Only the business she is carrying on keeps her at work all night, but she will be your friend all day long." "This shall be no hindrance," replied the friend. She then brought the young girl to him. He was well pleased with her, and married her on the conditions agreed upon.

But before long the two friends found out that the two wives which the old harridan had procured for them were only one woman.

Appreciate, after this, the deceitfulness of women, and what they are capable of.

STORY OF BAHIA

It is related that a married woman of the name of Bahia (splendid beauty) had a lover whose relations to her were soon a mystery to no one, for which reason she had

to leave him.   Her absence affected him to that degree that he fell ill, because he could not see her.

One day he went to see one of his friends, and said to
him, "Oh, my brother! an ungovernable desire has seized
me, and I can wait no more. Could you accompany me
on a visit I am going to pay to Bahia, the well-beloved
of my heart?" The friend declared himself willing.

The next day they mounted their horses; and after a
journey of two days, they arrived near the place where
Bahia dwelt. There they stopped. The lover said to his
friend, "Go and see the people that live about here, and
ask for their hospitality, but take good care not to divulge our intentions, and try in particular to find the
servant-girl of Bahia, to whom you can say that I am
here, and whom you will charge with the message to her
mistress that I would like to see her." He then described the servant-maid to him.

The friend went, met the servant, and told her all
that was necessary.   She went at once to Bahia, and
repeated to her what she had been told.

Bahia sent to the friend the message, "Inform him
who sent you that the meeting will take place to-night,
near such and such a tree, at such and such an hour."

Returning to the lover, the friend communicated to
him the decision of Bahia about the rendezvous.

At that hour that had been fixed, the two friends were
near to the tree.   They had not to wait long for Bahia.
As soon as her lover saw her coming, he rushed to meet
her, kissed her, pressed her to his heart, and they began
to embrace and caress each other.

The lover said to her, "O Bahia, is there no way to
enable us to pass the night together without rousing the

suspicions of your husband?" She answered, "Oh, before God! if it will give you pleasure, the means to contrive this are not wanting." "Hasten," said her lover,
"to let me know how it may be done." She then asked
him, "Your friend here, is he devoted to you, and intelligent?" He answered, "Yes." She then rose, took off her
garments, and handed them to the friend, who gave her
his, in which she then dressed herself; then she made the
friend put on her clothes. The lover said, surprised
"What are you going to do?" "Be silent," she answered,
and, addressing herself to the friend, she gave him the
following explanations: "Go to my house and lie down
in my bed. After a third part of the night is passed, my
husband will come to you and ask you for the pot into
which they milk the camels. You will then take up the
vase, but you must keep it in your hands until he takes it
from you. This is our usual way. Then he will go and
return with the pot filled with milk, and say to you,
'Here is the pot!' But you must not take it from him
until he has repeated the words. Then take it out of his
hands, or let him put it on the ground himself. After
that, you will not see anything more of him till the
morning. After the pot has been put on the ground, and
my husband is gone, drink the third part of the milk,
and replace the pot on the ground."

The friend went, observed all these recommendations,
and when the husband returned with the pot full of
milk he did not take it out of his hands until he had said
twice, "Here is the pot!" Unfortunately he withdrew his
hands when the husband was going to set it down, the
latter thinking the pot was being held, let it go, and the
vase fell upon the ground and was broken. The husband, in the belief that he was speaking to his wife, ex-

claimed, "What have you been thinking of?" and beat him with it till it broke; then took another, and continued to batter him stroke on stroke enough to break his back. The mother and sister of Bahia came running to the spot to tear her from his hands. He had fainted. Luckily they succeeded in getting the husband away.

The mother of Bahia soon came back, and talked to him so long that he was fairly sick of her talk; but he could do nothing but be silent and weep. At last she finished, saying, "Have confidence in God, and obey your husband. As for your lover, he cannot come now to see and console you, but I will send in your sister to keep you company." And so she went away.

She did send, indeed, the sister of Bahia, who began to console her and curse him who had beaten her. He felt his heart warming towards her, for he had seen that she was of resplendant beauty, endowed with all perfections, and like the full moon in the night. He placed his hand over her mouth, so as to prevent her from speaking and said to her, O lady! I am not what you think. Your sister Bahia is at present with her lover, and I have run into danger to do her a service. Will you not take me under your protection? If you denounce me, your sister will be covered with shame; as for me, I have done my part, but may the evil fall back upon you!"

The young girl then began to tremble like a sheaf, in thinking of the consequences of her sister's doings, and then beginning to laugh, surrendered herself to the friend who proved himself so true. They passed the remainder of the night in bliss, kisses, embraces, and mutual enjoyment. He found her the best of the best. In her arms he forgot the beating he had received, and they did not cease to play, toy, and make love till daybreak.

He then returned to his companion. Bahia asked him how he had fared, and he said to her, "Ask your sister. By my faith! she knows it all! Only know, that we have passed the night in mutual pleasures, kissing and enjoying ourselves until now."

Then they changed clothes again, each one taking his own, and the friend told Bahia all the particulars of what had happened to him.

Appreciate, after this, the deceitfulness of women, and what they are capable of.

THE STORY OF THE MAN WHO WAS AN EXPERT IN STRATAGEMS, AND WAS DUPED BY A WOMAN

A story is told of a man who had studied all the ruses and all the stratagems invented by women for the deception of men, and pretended that no woman could dupe him.

A woman of great beauty, and full of charms, got to heart of her conceit. She, therefore, prepared for him in the medjeles [1] a collation, in which several kinds of wine figured, and nothing was wanting in the way of rare and choice viands. Then she sent for him, and invited him to come and see her. As she was famed for her great beauty and the rare perfection of her person, she had roused his desires, and he hastened to avail himself of her invitation.

She was dressed in her finest garments, and exhaled the choicest perfumes, and assuredly whoever had thus seen her would have been troubled in his mind. And thus, when he was admitted into her presence, he was

---

[1] The medjeles, from djeleuss, to sit down, is the name of a saloon in Arab houses, generally situated on the ground floor. It is the vestibule, the saloon for visitors.

fascinated by her charms, and plunged into admiration by her marvellous beauty.

This woman, however, appeared to be preoccupied on account of her husband, and allowed it not to be seen that she was afraid of his coming back from one minute to another. It must be mentioned that this husband was very proud, very jealous, and very violent, and would not have hesitated to shed the blood of anyone whom he would have found prowling about his house. What would he have done, and, with much more reason, to the man whom he might have found inside?

While the lady and he, who flattered himself that he should possess her, were amusing themselves in the medjeles, a knock at the house-door filled the lover with fear and trouble, particularly when the lady cried, "This is my husband, who is returning." All in a tremble, she hid him in a closet, which was in the room, shut the door upon him, and left the key in the medjeles; then she opened the house-door.

Her husband, for it was he, saw, on entering, the wine and all the preparations that had been made. Surprised, he asked what it meant. "It means what you see," she answered. "But for whom is all this?" he asked. "It is for my lover whom I have here." "And where is he?" "In this closet," she said, pointing with her finger to the place where the suffered was confined.

At these words the husband started. He rose and went to the closet, but found it locked. "Where is the kay?" he siad. She answered, "Here!" throwing it to him. But as he was putting it into the lock she burst out laughing uproariously. He turned towards her, and said, "What are you laughing at?" "I laugh," she answered, "at the weakness of your judgment, and your want of reason and reflection. Oh, you man without sense, do you think that if I had in reality a lover, and had admitted him into this room I should have told you that he was here and where he was hidden? This is certainly not likely. I had no other thought than to offer you a collation on your return, and wanted only to have a joke with you in doing as I did. If I had a lover I should certainly not have made you my confidant."

The husband left the key in the lock of the closet without having turned it and returned to the table, and said, "True! I rose; but I had not the slightest doubt about the sincerity of your words." Then they ate and drank together, and then made love.

The man in the closet had to stop there until the husband went out. Then the lady went to set him free, and found him quite undone and in a bad state. When he came out after having escaped an imminent peril, she said to him, "Well, you wiseacre, who know so well the stratagems of women, of all those you know is there one to equal this?" He made answer, "I am now convinced that your stratagems are countless."

Appreciate after this the deceits of woment and what they are capable of.

STORY OF THE LOVER WHO WAS SURPRISED BY THE UNEXPECTED ARRIVAL OF THE HUSBAND

It is related that a woman who was married to a violent and brutal man, having her lover with her on the unexpected arrival of her husband, who was returning from a journey, had only just time to hide him under the bed. She was compelled to let him remain in this dangerous and unpleasant position, knowing of no expedient which might enable him to leave the house. In her restlessness she went to and fro, and having gone to the street-door, one of her neighbours, a woman, saw that she was in trouble, and asked her the reason of it. She told her what had happened. The other one then said, "Return into the house. I will charge myself with the safety of your lover, and I promise you that he shall come out unharmed." Then the woman re-entered her house.

Her neighbour was not long in joining her, and they together prepared the meal, and then they all sat down to eat and drink. The woman sat facing her husband, and the neighbour opposite the bed. The latter began to tell stories and anecdotes about the tricks of women; and the lover under the bed heard all that was going on.

Pursuing her tales, the neighbour told the following one: "A married woman had a lover, whom she loved tenderly, and by whom she was loved the same. One day the lover came to see her in the absence of her husband. But the latter happened to return home unexpectedly just as they were together. The woman, knowing of no better place, hid her lover under the bed, then sat down by her husband, who was taking some refreshment, and joked and played with him. Amongst other playful games, she covered her husband's eyes with a napkin, and her lover took this opportunity to come out from under the bed and escape unobserved."

The wife understood at once how to profit by this tale; taking a napkin and covering the eyes of her husband with it, she said, "Then it was by means of this ruse that the lover was helped out of his dilemma." And the lover, taking the opportunity, succeeded in making good his escape unobserved by the husband. Unconscious of what had happened this latter laughed at the story, and his merriment was still increased by the last words of his wife and by her action.

Appreciate after this the deceitfulness of women, and what they are capable of.

THE STORY OF THE USELESS PRECAUTIONS
It is related that a man had a wife who was endowed with all beauties and perfections; she was like the full moon. He was very jealous for he knew all the deceits and ways of women. He therefore never left the house without carefully locking the street door and the door of the terrace.

One day his wife asked him "Why do you do this?" "Because I know your ruses and fashions," said he. "It is not by acting in this way that you will be safe," she said, "for certainly, if a woman has set her heart upon a thing, all precautions are useless." "Well, well!" replied he; "it is always wise to keep the doors locked." She said, "Not at all; the fastenings of the doors are of no avail, if a woman once thinks of doing what you mean." "Well, then," said he, "if you can do it, you may!"

As soon as her husband had gone out, the woman mounted to the top of the house, and, through a small hole, which she made into the wall, she looked to see what was going on outside. At that moment a young man was passing by, who, looking up, saw her, and desired to possess her. He said to her, "How can I come to you?" She told him that it could not be done, and that the doors were locked. "How could we get together"; he asked. She answered him, "I shall make a hole in the house door. Be on the watch for my hus-

[1] Note in the autograph edition.—Compare this with the tale of La Fontaine (Book ii.): "One does not Think of Every-thing," reproduced from the "Cent Nouvelles Nouvelles."

band when he returns to-night, and after he shall have passed in, put your member through the hole, and it shall meet my vulva, and you can then do my business; any other way it is impossible."

The young man watched until he had seen the husband return from evening prayer; and after he had entered the house and locked the door, he went to find the hole made in it, and passed his member through it. The wife also was on the look out. Her husband had barely got into the house, and was still in the courtyard, when she went to the door, and appearing to satisfy herself that the door was fast, she placed her vulva to the member, which appeared through the hole, and introduced it into her vagina.

This done, she extinguished the lamp, and called to her husband, asking him to bring a light. He asked, "Why?" "I have dropped a trinket and cannot find it," she answered. He then came with a lamp. The member of the young man was still in her vulva, and at that moment ejaculating. "Where did you drop your trinket?" asked the husband. "Here!" she cried, drawing back and leaving the verge of her lover naked and covered with sperm.

At this sight the husband fell to the ground with rage. When he was up again, the wife said to him: "Well! and those precautions?" "God grant me repentance!" he said.

After this appreciate the deceits of women, and what they are capable of.

Women have such a number of ruses at their disposal, that they cannot be counted. They would succeed to make an elephant mount upon the back of an ant, and do work there. How detestable in their doings God has made them!

CHAPTER XII

CONCERNING SUNDRY OBSERVATIONS USEFUL TO KNOW FOR MEN AND WOMEN

Know, O Vizir (to whom God be good), that the information contained in this chapter is of the greatest utility, and it is only in this book that such can be found. Assuredly to know things is better than to be ignorant of them. Knowledge may be bad, but ignorance is more so.

The knowledge in question concerns matters unknown to you, and relating to women.

There was once a woman, named Moarbeda, who was considered to be the most knowing and wisest person of her time. She was a philosopher. One day various queries were put to her, and among them the following, which I shall give here with her answers.

"In what part of a woman's body does her mind reside?"—"Between her thighs."

"And where her enjoyment?"—"In the same place."

"And where the love of men and the hatred of them?"

—"In the vulva," she said; adding, "to the men whom we love we give our vulva, and we refuse it to him we hate. We share our property with the man we love, and are content with whatever little he may be able to bring to us; if he has no fortune, we take him as he is. But, on the other hand, we keep at a distance him whom we hate, were he to offer us wealth and riches."

"Where, in a woman, are located knowledge, love and taste?"—"In the eye, the heart, and the vulva."

When asked for her explanations on this subject she replied: "Knowledge dwells in the eye, for it is the woman's eye that appreciates the beauty of form and of appearance. By the medium of this organ love penetrates into the heart and dwells in it, and enslaves it. A woman in love pursues the object of its love, and lays snares for it. If she succeed, there will be an encounter between the beloved one and her vulva. The vulva tastes him and then knows his sweet or bitter flavour. It is in fact, the vulva which knows how to distinguish by tasting the good from the bad."

"Which virile members are preferred by women? What women are most eager for the coitus and which are those who detest it? Which are the men preferred by women, and which are those whom they abominate?" —She answered, "Not all women have the same conformation of vulva, and they also differ in their manner of making love, and in their love for and their aversion to things. The same disparities are existing in men, both with regard to their organs and their tastes. A woman of plump form and with as hallow uterus will look out for a member which is both short and thick, which will completely fill her vagina, without touching the bottom of it; a long and large member would not suit her. A woman with a deep lying uterus, and consequently a long vagina, only yearns for a member which is long and thick and of ample proportions, and thus fills her vagina in its whole extension; she will despise the man with a slender member, for he could never satisfy her in coition."

"The following distinctions exist in the temperaments of women: The billious, the melancholy, the sanguine, the phlegmatic, and the mixed. Those with a billious or melancholy temperament are not much given to the coitus, and like it only with men of the same disposition. Those who are sanguine or phlegmatic love coition to excess, and if they encounter a member, they would never let it leave their vulva if they could help it. With these also it is only men of their own temperament who can satisfy them, and if such a woman were married to a billious or melancholy man, they should lead a sorry life together. As regards mixed temperaments, they exhibit neither a marked predilection for, nor aversion against the coitus.

"It has been observed that under all circumstances little women love the coitus more and evince a stronger affection for the virile member than women of a large size. Only long and vigorous members suit them: in them they find the delight of their existence and of their couch.

"There are also women who love the coitus only on the edge of their vulva, and when a man lying upon them wants to get his member into the vagina, they take it out with the hand and place its gland between the lips of the vulva.

"I have reason to believe that this is only the case with young girls or with women not used to men. I pray God to preserve us from such, or from women for whom it is an impossibility to give themselves up to men.[1]

"There are women who will do their husband's behests, and will satisfy them and give them voluptuous

[1] Note in the autograph edition.—This is a parenthesis introduced by the author in the discourse of Moarbeda, giving vent to his indignation. This paragraph, the preceding one, and the two that follow, are not to be found in some of the Arab texts, and on close examination we are convinced that they are interpolated.

pleasure by coition, only if compelled by blows and ill-treatment. Some people ascribe this conduct to the aversion they feel either against coition or against the husband; but this is not so; it is simply a question of temperament.

"There are also women who do not care for coition because all their ideas turn upon the grandeurs, personal honours, ambitious hopes, or business-cares of the world. With others this indifference springs, as it may be, from purity of the heart, or from jealousy, or from a pronounced tendency of their souls towards another world, or lastly from past violent sorrows. Furthermore, the pleasures which they feel in coition depend not alone upon the size of the member, but also upon the particular conformation of their own natural pars. Amongst those the vulva called from its form el morteba, the square one, and el mortafa, the projecting, is remarkable. This vulva has the peculiarity of projecting all round when the woman is standing up and closes her thighs. It burns for the coitus, its slit is narrow, and it is also called el keulihimi, the pressed one. The woman who has such a one likes only large members, and they must not let her wait long for the crisis. But this is a general characteristic of women.

"As to the desire of men for coition, I must say that they are also addicted to it more or less according to their different temperaments, five in number,[1] like the women's, with the difference that the hankering of the

"What are the faults of women?" Moarbeda replied to this question, "The worst of women is she who imme-

---

[1] Note in the autograph edition.—The text says four, the author, no doubt, not taking the mixed temperament into account. It has been considered right to make this slight modification in the translation.

woman after the member is stronger than that of a man after a vulva."

diately cries out loud as soon as her husband wants to touch the smallest amount of her property for his necessities. In the same line stands she who divulges matters which her husband wants to be kept secret."—"Are there any more?" she is asked. She adds, "The woman of a jealous disposition and the woman who raises her voice so as to drown that of her husband; she who disseminates scandal: the woman that scowls, the one who is always burning to let men see her beauty, and cannot stay at home; and with respect to this last let me add that a woman who laughs much, and is constantly seen at the street door, may be taken to be an arrant prostitute.

"Bad also are those women who mind other people's affairs; those who are always complaining; those who steal things belonging to their husbands; those of a disagreeable and imperious temper; those who are not grateful for kindness received: those that will not share the conjugal couch, or who incommode their husbands by the uncomfortable positions they take in it; those who are inclined to deceit, treachery, calumny and ruse.

"Then there are still women who are unlucky in whatever they undertake: those who are always inclined to blame and censure; those who invite their husbands to fulfil their conjugal duty only when it is convenient for them; those that make noises in bed; and lastly those who are shameless, without intelligence, tattlers and curious.

"Here you have the worst specimens amongst women."

CHAPTER XIII

CONCERNING THE CAUSES OF ENJOYMENT IN THE ACT OF GENERATION

Know, O Vizir (to whom God be Good!), that the causes which tend to develop the passion for coition are six in number: the fire of an ardent lover, the super-abundance of sperm, the proximity of the loved person whose possession is eagerly desired, the beauty of the face, exciting viands, and contact.

Know also, that the causes of the pleasure in cohabitation, and the conditions of the enjoyment are numerous, but that the principal and best ones are: the heat of the vulva; the narrowness, dryness, and sweet exhalation of the same. If any one of these conditions is absent, there is at the same time something wanting in the voluptuous enjoyment. But if the vagina unites the required qualifications, the enjoyment is complete. In fact, a moist vulva relaxes the nerves, a cold one robs the member of all its vigour, and bad exhalations from the vagina detract greatly from the pleasure, as is also the case if the latter is very wide.

The acme of enjoyment, which is produced by the abundance and impetuous ejaculation of the sperm, depends upon one circumstance, and this is, that the vulva is furnished with a suction-pump (orifice of the uterus), which will clasp the virile member, and suck up the sperm with an irresistible force. The member once seized by the orifice, the lover is powerless to retain the sperm, for the orifice will not relax its hold until it has extracted every drop of sperm, and certainly if the crisis arrives before this gripping of the gland takes place, the pleasure of the ejaculation will not be complete.

Know that there are eight things which give strength to any favour the ejaculation. These are: bodily health, the absence of all care and worry, an unembarrassed mind, natural gaiety of spirit, good nourishment, wealth, the variety of the faces of women, and their complexions.

If you want to acquire strength for the coitus, take fruit of the mastic-tree (derou),[1] pound them and macerate them with oil and honey; then drink of the liquid first thing in the morning: you will thus become vigorous for the coitus, and there will be abundance of sperm produced.

The same result will be obtained by rubbing the virile member and the vulva with gall from the jackel. This rubbing stimulates those parts and increases their vigour.

A savant of the name of Djelinouss[2] has said: "He who feels that he is weak for coition should drink before going to bed a glassful of very thick honey and eat twenty almonds and one hundred grains of the pine tree. He must follow this regime for three days. He may also pound onion-seed, sift it and mix it afterwards with honey, stirring the mixture well, and take of this mixture while still fasting."

[1] The mastic is a tree with many branches, the fruit of which are little red berries, which get black when they ripen. There is an oil extracted from them, which is reputed to have the property of strengthening and hardening the flesh.

[2] The savant in question was Galien, also called Galenos, meaning sweet in Greek. The name was given him in his youth on account of his extreme pleasantness; and from this is derived the Arab name Djelinouss.

A man who would wish to acquire vigour for coition may likewise melt down fat from the hump of a camel, and rub his member with it just before the act; it will then perform wonders, and the woman will praise it.

If you would make the enjoyment still more voluptuous masticate a little cubeb-pepper or cardamon-grains of the large species; put a certain quantity of it upon the head of your member, and then go to work. This will procure for you, as well as for the woman, a matchless enjoyment. The ointment from the balm of Judea or of Mecca [1] produces a similar effect.

If you would make yourself very strong for the coitus, pound very carefully pyrether [2] together with ginger, [3] mix them while pounding with ointment of lilac, [4] then rub with this compound your abdomen, the testicles, and the verge. This will make you ardent for the coitus.

You will likewise predispose yourself for cohabitation, sensibly increase the volume of your sperm, gain increased vigour for the action, and procure for yourself extraordinary erections, by eating of chrysocolla [5] the

[1] Note in the autograph edition.—Amyris gileadensis, or the Canadian pine.

[2] Idem.—Anthemis pyrethrum.

[3] Zeundjebil, the amomum zingiber.

[4] The ointment here mentioned is undoubtedly composed of fat or oil and lilac leaves, mixed and pounded. These leaves are held to be tonic and astringent, and the capsules produced by the shrub give an extract which serves as a febrifuge.

[5] The chrysocolla is a substance used when soldering metals, and gold in particular, and which in all probability is borax. The word tinkal, as the raw borax is called in India, is very like the Arab name teunkar. As to the name chrysocolla, it is derived from the Greek words for gold and glue, viz., gold-glue.

size of a mustard-grain.[1] The excitement resulting from the use of this nostrum is unparalleled, and all your qualifications for the coitus will be increased.

If you wish the woman to be inspired with a great desire to cohabit with you, take a little of cubebs, pyr-ether, ginger and cinnamon, which you will have to masticate just before joining her; then moisten your member with your saliva and do her business for her. From that moment she will have such an affection for you that she can scarcely be a moment without you.

The virile member rubbed with ass's milk, will become uncommonly strong and vigorous.

Green peas, boiled carefully with onions, and powd-ered with cinnamon, ginger and cardamoms, well pound-ed, create for the consumer considerable amorous passion and strength for the coitus.

---

[1] By the expression of "the size of a mustard grain" the Arabs mean a very minute quantity.

Observations in the autograph edition upon the notes one and two.—The translator might easily have been misled by the texts before him, for three texts were found to say, "by eating chryso-colla and mustard grain." This latter substance is exciting enough to seem deserving of recommendation for the purpose. Several texts have besides instead of teunkar, the word takra, which is, according to Abel er Rezeug, synonymous with fer-bioune, and signifies the powdered fruit of veratrum sabadilla, a corrosive and dangerous medicine. Ferbioune is also used for inphorbia.

CHAPTER XIV

DESCRIPTION OF THE UTERUS OF STERILE WOMEN
AND TREATMENT OF THE SAME

Know, O Vizir (God be good to you!), that wise physicians have plunged into this sea of difficulties to very
little purpose. Each one has looked at the matter with
his own point of view, and in the end the question has
been left in the dark.

Amongst the causes which determine the sterility of
women may be taken the obstruction in the uterus by
clots of blood, the accumulation of water,[1] the want of
or defective sperm of the man, organic malformation of
in women that are very corpulent, so that their uterus
stagnation of the courses and the corruption of the men-
strual fluid, and the habitual presence of wind in the
uterus. Other savants attribute the sterility of women
to the action of spirits and spells. Sterility is common
in women that are very corpulent, so that their uteurs
gets compressed and cannot conceive, not being able to
take up the sperm, especially if the husband's member is
short and his testicles are very fat; in such a case the act
of copulation can only be imperfectly completed.

One of the remedies against sterility consists of the
marrow from the hump of a camel, which the woman

---

[1] There is reason to believe that the author is speaking here
of so-called "whites," which occasions protuberances in the
genital organs of women.

spreads on a piece of linen, and rubs her sexual parts with it, after having been purified subsequently to her courses. To complete the cure, she takes some fruits of the plant called jackal's grapes,[1] squeezes the juice out of them into a vase, and then adds a little vinegar; of this medicine she drinks fasting for seven days, during which time her husband will take care to have copulation with her.

The woman may besides pound a small quantity of sesame-grain and mix its juice with a bean's weight of sandarach [2] powder; of this mixture she drinks during three days after her periods; she is then fit to receive her husband's embraces.

The first of these beverages is to be taken separately, and in the first instance; after this the second, which will have a salutary effect, if so it pleases the Almighty God!

There is still another remedy. A mixture is made of nitre, gall from a sheep or a cow, a small quantity of the plant named el meusk,[3] and of the grains of that plant. The woman saturates a plug of soft wool with this mixture, and rubs her vulva with it after menstruation; she then receives the caresses of her husband, and, with the will of God the Highest, will become pregnant.

---

[1] The jackal's-grape, also called foxgrape and meuknina, is simply the black nightshade (solanum nigrum). This name has been translated erroneously bear's-grape (uva ursi), which is nothing but the arbute tree, which furnishes an anodyne.

[2] Note in the autograph edition.—Sandarach, zemikh el ahmeur, red arsenic. Dictionary of Kazimirski.

[3] The word meusk used by the author designates a plant, and signifies also musk. The plant is no doubt the tuberose, called in Arabic meusk el roumi, the musk of the Christian.

CHAPTER XV

CONCERNING MEDICINES WHICH PROVOKE ABORTION

Know, O Vizir (God be good to you!) that the medicines which will bring on abortion, and the ejection of the foetus, are innumerable. But I shall speak of those to you which I have proved, and therefore acknowledge as good, so that everybody may learn what may benefit and what may do harm.

I shall in the first place speak of the madder-root[1] A small quantity of this substance freshly gathered, or even dried, but in the latter case bruised and moistened at the time when it is to be used, vitiates the virile sperm or kills the foetus, bringing abortion on and provoking the menstruation when introduced in the woman's vagina. The same end may be obtained by means of a decoction of the same plant taken fasting by the woman, and used at the same time by an external application to moisten the vagina.

Fumigation with the smoke of burnt cabbage seeds cause abortion, if the woman introduces the vapour into her vagina by means of a tube or reed.

I now come to alum. This substance, powdered, and introduced into the vagina, or sprinkled on the verge before coition, prevents the woman from conceiving by obstructing the arrival of the sperm in the uterus; for it has the property of drying up and contracting the vagina.

[1] Certain texts have araoua, which would mean the buphtalmum silvestram; but there is reason to believe that it is madderroot which is meant, as according to the work of Abd er Rezeug el Djezairi this is an abortive.

But the too frequent use of it will make the woman barren and annihilate all her capability of conception.

The man who at the moment of copulation coats his member with tar,[1] deprives his sperm of its generative faculty. This is the most powerful of all applications, and if a woman during her pregnancy introduces some of the substance repeatedly into her vagina, she will be sterile, and the child will be born dead.

The woman who drinks the weight of a mitskal of laurel water, with a little pepper, will cause her courses to flow again, and clear her uterus from the clots of blood which sometimes lodge there. If she makes use of this medicine when she is already pregnant, the embryo will be expelled; and taken after confinement, this medicine has the property of causing the expulsion from the matrix of all deleterious matter and of the after-birth.

The woman who drinks an infusion of coarse cinnamon[2] mixed with red myrth, and then introduces into her vagina a plug of wool saturated with the mixture, kills the foetus and provokes its expulsion, with the will of God the Highest!

If the foetus dies in the womb, a decoction of yellow wall-flowers in water will cause the expulsion of the same, with the will of God the Highest!

All the above enumerated medicines are efficacious and their effect is certain.

---

[1] The Arabs have known since a long period the vegetable tar, guetrane, and, in fact the French name for it has been derived from their language. They obtain it by distillation in rough furnaces from the wood of the resinous trees found in their country, the pine and the cedar.

[2] Note in the autograph edition.—The common name of cinnamon is keurfa. Dar sini is the name of an inferior quality.

CHAPTER XVI

CONCERNING THE CAUSES OF IMPOTENCE IN MEN

Know, O Vizir (God be good to you!) that there are men whose sperm is vitiated by the inborn coldness of their nature, by diseases of their organs,[1] by purulent discharges, and by fevers. There are also men with the urinary canal in their verge deviating owing to a downward curve; the result of such conformation is that the seminal liquid cannot be ejected in a straight direction, but falls downward.[2]

Other men have the member too short and too small to reach the neck of the matrix, or their bladder is ulcerated or they are affected by other infirmities, which prevent them from coition.

Finally, there are men who arrive quicker at the crisis than the women, in consequence of which the two emissions are not simultaneous; there is in such cases no conception.

All these circumstances serve to explain the absence of conception in women; but the principal cause of all is the shortness of the virile member.

As another cause of impotence may be regarded the sudden transmission from hot to cold, and vice versa, and a great number of analogous reasons.

---

[1] Note in the autograph edition.—The word seulss signifies more particularly the emission of the urine or diabetes; but in the present case it seems to be applied to genital-urinary maladies in general.

[2] This abnormity is called hyposadias. Where, on the contrary, the opening of the urethra is turned upwards it bears the name of epispadias.

Men whose impotence is due either to the corruption of their sperm owing to their cold nature, or to maladies of the organs, or to discharges or fevers and similar ills, or to their excessive promptness in ejaculation, can be cured. They should eat stimulant pastry containing honey, ginger, pyrether, syrup of vinegar, hellebore, garlic, cinnamon, nutmeg, cardamoms,[1] sparrows' tongues,[2] Chinese cinnamon, long pepper, and other spices. He will be cured by using them.

As to the other afflictions which we have indicated—the curvature of the urethra, the small dimensions of the virile member, ulcers on the bladder, and the other infirmities which are adverse to coition—God only can cure them.

[1] Cardamom, already mentioned, is a very aromatic medicinal seed which comes from Italy, and is used in the preparation of theriac. It is the fruit of several kinds of the amomum tree, and especially of the amomum cardamomum.

[2] Sparrow's tongue, stallena panerina, sparrow-wort.

Observations in the autograph edition.—We are not of that opinion. The sparrow's tongue, as above, seems to be nothing else than the seed of the ash tree. (See the dictionaries of Kazimirski and Beaussier, and the book on medicines of Abd er Rezeug.)

CHAPTER XVII

UNDOING OF AIGUILLETTES (IMPOTENCE FOR A TIME)

Know, O Vizir (God be good to you!), that impotence arises from three causes:

Firstly, from the tying of aiguillettes.[1]

Secondly, from a feeble and relaxed constitution.

And thirdly, from too premature ejaculation.

To cure the tying of aigullettes you must take ga-langa,[2] cinnamon from Mecca, cloves, Indian cachou,[3] nutmeg, Indian cubebs, sparrow-wort,[4] cinnamon, Per-sian pepper, Indian thistle,[5] cardamoms,[6] pyrether, laurel-seed, and gilly-flowers. All these ingredients must be pounded together carefully, and one drinks of it as much as one can, morning and night, in broth, particu-larly in pigeon broth; fowl broth may, however, be sub-

---

[1] It happens sometimes at the encounter of a man and woman that the former, though burning with desire, cannot accomplish the act of coition, owing to the state of inertia resisting all in-citement to which his member is reduced. It is then said of him that his aiguillette (needle) is tied.

[2] The galanga is an Indian root. There are two kinds: the galanga major and the galanga minor.

[3] The cachou, from the Indian catche, or the Brazilian cajou, is a vegetable substance which comes to us from India.

Observation in the autograph edition.—Certain texts have it, Indian tartar or Indian harehar. It cannot be exactly determined to what substances these two names belong.

[4] See Note 2, page 199.

[5] This is the thistle which grows in the West Indies. Taken as a decoction, this plant acts as a pectoral and an aperient.

Observation in the autograph edition.—The texts which have been consulted give as the name of the plant, the use of which is recommended, chelass el heundi, a name for which an Eng-l:sh equivalent could not be found.

[6] See Note 1, page 199.

stituted just as well. Water is to be drunk before and after taking it. The compound may likewise be taken with money, which is the best method, and gives the best results.

The man whose ejaculation is too precipitate must take nutmeg and incense (oliban)[1] mixed together with honey.

If the impotence arises from weakness, the following ingredients are to be taken in honey: viz., pyrether, net-tle-seed,[2] a little spurge (or cevadille), ginger, cinnamon of Mecca, and cardamon. This preparation will cause the weakness to disappear and effect the cure, with the permission of God the Highest!

I can warrant the efficacy of all these preparations, the virtue of which has been tested.

The impossibility of performing the coitus, owing to the absence of stiffness in the member, is also due to other causes. It will happen, for instance, that a man with his verge in erection will find it getting flaccid just when he is on the point of introducing it between the thighs of the woman. He thinks this is impotence, while it is simply the result, may be, of an exaggerated respect for the woman, may be of a misplaced bashfulness, may be because one has observed something disagreeable, or on account of an unpleasant odour; finally, owing to a feeling of jealousy, inspired by the thought that the woman is no longer a virgin, and has served the pleasure of other men.

---

[1] Oliban is mentioned in the Journal Asiatique, in connection with the Greek fire and gunpowder, by Messrs. Reynaud and Favet.

[2] Nettle-seed is considered by the Arabs as a remedy against the inflammation of the urethral canal.

CHAPTER XVIII

PRESCRIPTION FOR INCREASING THE DIMENSIONS OF SMALL MEMBERS AND FOR MAKING THEM SPLENDID

Know, O Vizir (God be good to you!), that this chapter which treats of the size of the virile member, is of the first importance both for men and women. For the men, because from a large and vigorous member there spring the affection and love of the women; for the women, because it is by such members that their amorous passions get appeased, and the greatest pleasure is procured for them. This is evident from the fact that many men, solely by reason of their insignificant member, are, as far as the coition is concerned, objects of aversion to the women, who likewise entertain the same sentiment with regard to those whose members are soft, nerveless, and relaxed. Their whole happiness consists in the use of robust and strong members.

A man, therefore, with a small member, who wants to make it grand or fortify it for the coitus, must rub it before the copulation with tepid water, until it gets red and extended by the blood flowing into it, in consequence of the heat; he must then anoint it with a mixture of honey and ginger, rubbing it in sedulously. Then let him join the woman; he will procure for her such pleasure that she objects to him getting off her again.

Another remedy consists in a compound made of a moderate quantity of pepper, lavender, galanga, and musk, reduced to powder, sifted and mixed up with honey and preserved ginger. The member, after having been first washed in warm water, is then vigorously rubbed with the mixture; it will then grow large and brawny, and afford to the woman a marvellous feeling of voluptuousness.

A third remedy is the following: wash the member in warm water until it becomes red, and enters into erection. Then take a piece of soft leather, upon which spread hot pitch, and envelop the member with it. It will not be long before the member raises its head, trembling with passion. The leather is to be left on until the pitch grows cold, and the member is again in a state of repose. This operation, several times repeated, will have the effect of making the member strong and thick.

A fourth remedy is based upon the use made of leeches, but only of such as live in water (sic). You put as many of them into a bottle as can be got in, and then fill it up with oil. Then expose the bottle to the sun, until the heat of the same has effected a complete mixture. Then, with the fluid thus obtained the member is to be rubbed several consecutive days, and it will, by being thus treated, become of a good size and of full dimensions.

For another procedure I will here note the use of an ass's member. Procure one and boil it, together with onions and a large quantity of corn. With this dish feed fowls, which you eat afterwards. One can also macerate the ass's verge with oil, and use the fluid thus obtained afterwards for anointing one's member with it, and drinking of it.

Another way is to bruise leeches with oil, and rub the verge with this ointment; or, if it is preferred, the leeches may be put into a bottle, and, thus enclosed, buried in a warm dunghill until they are dissolved into a coherent mass and form a sort of liniment, which is used for repeatedly anointing the member. The member is certain to greatly benefit by this.

One may likewise take rosin and wax, mixed with tubipore,[1] asphodel,[2] and cobbler's glue,[3] with which mixture rub the member, and the result will be that its dimensions will be enlarged.

The efficacy of all these remedies is well known, and I have tested them.

[1] The tubipore is a calcareous polypus composed of cylindrical tubes, and forming round masses, often of great size, in the sea. Its medical properties are much doubted.

Observations in the autograph edition.—This substance is called in certain texts deum el akhouine, and is, according to the book of the physician Abd-er-Rezeug, the juice of a plant called chiane, alias hei el aleum; the juice goes also by the name deum et tsabane. We have ascertained that hei el aleum signifies also the sempervivum (a name given to a kind of house-leek, and the literal translation of deum et tsabane is dragon's blood. This is all the information we could gather.

[2] The asphodel (daffodil) is a plant with lilaceous flowers, coming from Italy. There is a yellow and a white kind.

Observation in the autograph edition.—Boureouk signifies also borax and nitre.

[3] The glue used by the Mussulman cobblers to glue their leather is made of a single substance, the spleen of cattle or sheep, which they call tihal.

Note in the autograph edition.—The only text which gives this passage calls this substance annzeronte or annezeronte, the rosin of the sarcocollus, which was credited with the property to make the flesh firm and heal wounds.

CHAPTER XIX

OF THINGS THAT TAKE AWAY THE BAD SMELL FROM THE ARMPITS AND SEXUAL PARTS OF WOMEN AND CONTRACT THE LATTER

Know, O Vizir (God be good to you!), that bad exhalations from the vulva and of the armpits are, as also a wide vagina, the greatest of evils.

If a woman wants this bad odour to disappear she must pound red myrrh, then sift it, and knead this powder with myrtle-water,[1] and rub her sexual parts with this wash. All disagreeable emanation will disappear from her vulva.

Another remedy is obtained by pounding lavender, and kneading it afterwards with musk-rose-water. Saturate a piece of wollen-stuff with it, and rub the vulva with the same until it is hot. The bad smell will be removed by this.

If a woman intends to contract her vagina, she has only to dissolve alum in water, and wash her sexual parts with the solution, which may be made still more efficacious by the addition of a little bark of the walnut-tree, the latter substance being very astringent.

Another remedy to be mentioned is the following, which is well known for its efficacy: Boil well in water carobs (locusts),[2] freed from their kernels, and bark of

---

[1] The author designates here, under the name of ass, the myrtus communis of Linuaeus; the more usual name is reund, which serves also to designate the laurel tree.

[2] The carob is the fruit of the locust-tree, a well-known tree, the flowers of which emit a penetrating odour like that of the virile sperm. The fruit is considered to have aperient and pectoral properties, and the leaves are astringent.

the pomegrante tree. The woman takes a sitz bath in the decoction thus obtained, and which must be as hot as she can bear it; when the bath gets cold, it must be warmed and used again, and this immersion is to be repeated several times. The same result may be obtained by fumigating the vulva with cow-dung.

To do away with the bad smell of the armpits, one takes antimony [1] and mastic, which are to be pounded together, and to be put with water into an earthen vase. The mixture is then rubbed against the sides of the vase until it turns red; when it is ready for use rub it into the armpits, and the bad smell will be removed. It must be used repeatedly until a radical cure is effected.

The same result may be arrived at by pounding together antimony (hadida) and mastic, setting the mixture afterwards into a stove over a low fire, until it is of the consistency of bread, and rubbing the residue with a stone until the pellicle, which will have formed, is removed. Then rub it into the armpits, and you may be sure that the bad smell will soon be gone.

[1] Note in the autograph edition.—The texts, which were consulted, name the substance in question hadida, by which name goes the oxide of copper of commeric, which, exposed to the action of fire, pulverised, and mixed with gall-nut, is used for dyeing the hair black.

CHAPTER XX

INSTRUCTIONS WITH REGARD TO PREGNANCY AND
HOW THE GENDER OF THE CHILD THAT IS TO
BE BORN MAY BE KNOWN—THAT IS TO SAY,
KNOWLEDGE OF THE SEX OF THE FOETUS.

Know, O Vizir (God be good to you!), that the certain
indications of pregnancy are the following: the dryness
of the vulva immediately after the coitus, the inclination
to stretch herself, accesses of somnolency, heavy and
profound sleep, the frequent contraction of the opening
of the vulva to such an extent that not even a meroud
could penetrate, the nipples of the breast become darker,
and lastly, the most certain of all the marks is the cessa-
tion of the menstruation.

If the woman remains always in good health from the
time that her pregnancy is certain, if she preserves the
good looks of her face and a clear complexion, if she
does not become freckled, then it may be taken as a sign
that the child will be a boy.

The red colour off the nipples also point to a child of
the male sex. The strong development of the breasts,
and bleeding from the nose, if fit comes from the right
nostril,[1] are signs of the same purport.

The signs pointing to the conception of a child of the
female sex are numerous. I will name them here: frequent indisposition during pregnancy, pale complexion,

[1] The right side is considered by Mussulmans as the side of
good augury. See the Koran, chap. lvi., verse 26.

spots and freckles, pains in the matrix, frequent night-mares, blackness of the nipples, a heavy feeling on the left side, nasal hemorrhage on the same side.

If there is any doubt about the pregnancy, let the woman drink, on going to bed, honey-water, and if she has a feeling of heaviness in the abdomen, it is a proof that she is with child. If the right side feels heavier than the left one, it will be a boy. If the breasts are swelling with milk, this is similarly a sign that the child she is bearing will be of the male sex.

I have received this information from savants, and all the indications are positive and tested.

CHAPTER XXI

FORMING THE CONCLUSION OF THIS WORK, AND TREATING OF THE GOOD EFFECTS OF THE REGULATION OF EGGS AS FAVOURABLE TO THE COITUS

Know, O Vizir (God be good to you!), that this chapter contains the most useful instructions—how to increase the intensity of the coitus—and that the latter part is profitable to read for an old man as well as for the man in his best years and for the young man.

The Cheikh, who gives good advice to the creatures of God the Great! he the sage, the savant, the first of the men of his time, speaks as follows on this subject; listen then to his words.

He who makes it a practice to eat every day fasting the yolks of eggs, without the white part, will find in this ailment an energetic stimulant for the coitus. The same is the case with the man who during three days eats of the same mixed with onions.

He who boils asparagus,[1] and then fries them in fat,

---

[1] Note in the autograph edition.—The Arab text has heiloun. The medical dictionary of Abd el Rezeug says about heiloun: "Helioun and in placing the ia (in) more forward, making it heiloun, is in the medical, but not in the general sense, asparagus." So we have adopted this meaning, in preference to boiled meal as translated, and which meaning we could not find, although we searched carefully for it in the Arab books.

and then pours upon them the yolks of eggs with pounded condiments and eats every day of this dish, will grow
very strong for the coitus, and find in it a stimulant for
his amorous desires.

He who peels onions, puts them into a saucepan, with
condiments and aromatic substances, and fries the mixture with oil and yolk of eggs, will acquire a surpassing
and invaluable vigour for the coitus, if he will partake
of this dish for several days.

Camel's milk mixed with honey and taken regularly
develops a vigour for copulation which is unaccountable,
and causes the virile member to be on the alert night
and day.

He who for several days makes his meals upon eggs
boiled with myrrh, coarse cinnamon, and pepper, will
find his vigour with respect to coition and erections
greatly increased. He will have a feeling as though his
member would never return to a state of repose.

A man who would wish to copulate during a whole
night, and whose desire, having come on suddenly, will
not allow him to prepare himself and follow the regimen
just mentioned, may have recourse to the following
recipe. He must get a great number of eggs, so that he
may eat to surfeit, and fry them with fresh fat and butter; when done he immerses them in honey, working the
whole mass well together. He must eat of them as much
as possible with a little bread, and he may be certain that
for the whole night his member will not give him any
rest.

On this subject the following verses have been composed:—

"The member of Abou el Heiloukh has remained erect
For thirty days without a break, because he did eat onions.
Abou el Heidja has deflowered [1] in one night
Once eighty virgins, and he did not eat nor drink between,
Because he'd surfeited himself first with chick-peas,
And had drunk camel's milk with honey mixed.
Mimoun, the negro, never ceased to spend his sperm, while he
For fifty days without a truce the game was working.
How proud he was to finish such a task!
For ten days more he worked it,[2] nor was he yet surfeited,
But all this time he ate but yolk of eggs and bread." [3]

The deeds of Abou el Heiloukh Abou el Heidja, and Mimoun, just cited, have been justly praised, and their history is truly marvelous. So I will make you acquainted with it, please God, and thus complete the signal services which this work is designed to render to humanity.

THE HISTORY OF ZOHRA

The Cheikh, the protector of religion (God, the Highest, be good to him!) records that there lived once in remote antiquity an illustrous King, who had numerous armies and immense riches.

This King had seven daughters remarkable for their beauty and perfections. These seven had been born one after another, without any male infant between them.

The Kings of the time wanted them in marriage, but

---

[1] The text says, Abou el Heidja deflowered eighty virgins straight, that is to say, from the front in the natural way.

Observations in the autograph edition.—The texts, which we have consulted, say "entirely."

[2] "Depuys luy Aristoteles," etc. Rabelais, Book iii., chap. 27.

[3] Note.in the autograph edition.—It is to be observed that in these verses, as similarly in all the other verses which appear in the work, the line is always broken at the hemistitch, and not at the verse, as the Arab language admits in the verse two quite distinct parts, which are, in theory, equal in rhythm.

they refused to be married. They wore men's clothing, rode on magnificent horses covered with gold-embroidered trappings, knew how to handle the sword and the spear, and bore men down in single combat. Each of them possessed a splendid palace with the servants and slaves necessary for the service for the preparation of meat and drink, and other necessities of the kind.

Whenever a marriage-offer for one of them was presented to the King, he never failed to consult with her about it; but they always answered, "That shall never be."

Different conclusions were drawn from these refusals; some in a good sense, some in a bad one.

For a long time no positive information could be gathered of the reasons for this conduct, and the daughters preserved in acting in the same manner until the death of their father. Then the oldest of them was called upon to succeed him, and receives the oath of fidelity from all his subjects. This accession to the throne resounded through all the countries.

The name of the eldest sister was Fouzel Djemal (the flower of beauty); the second was called Soltana el Agmar (the queen of moons); the third, Bediaat el Djemal (the incomparable in beauty); the fourth, Quarda (the rose); the fifth, Mahmouda (the praiseworthy); the sixth, Kamela (the perfect); and, finally, the seventh, Zohra (the beauty).

Zohra, the youngest, was at the same time the most intelligent and judicious.

She was passionately fond of the chase, and one day as she was riding through the fields she met on her way a cavalier, who saluted her, and she returned his salute; she had some twenty men in her service with her. The cavalier thought it was the voice of a woman he had heard, but as Zohra's face was covered by a flap of her haïk, he was not certain, and said to himself, "I would like to know whether this is a woman or a man." He asked one of the princes's servants, who dissipated his doubts. Approaching Zohra, he then conversed pleasantly with her till they made a halt for breakfast. He sat down near her to partake of the repast.

Disappointing the hopes of the cavalier, the princess did not uncover her face, and, pleading that she was fasting, ate nothing. He could not help admiring secretly her hand, the gracefulness of her waist, and the amorous expression of her eyes. His heart was seized with a violent love.

The following conversation took place between them:

The Cavalier: "Is your heart insensible for friendship?"

Zohra: "It is not proper for a man to feel friendship for a woman; for if their hearts once incline towards each other, libidinous desires will soon invade them, and with Satan enticing them to do wrong, their fall is soon known by everyone."

The Cavalier: "It is not so, when their affection is true and their intercourse pure without infidelity or treachery."

Zohra: "If a woman gives way to the affection she feels for a man, she becomes an object of slander for the whole world, and of general contempt, whence nothing arises but trouble and regrets."

The Cavalier: "But our love will remain secret, and in this retired spot, which may serve us as our place of

---

[1] The haïk is a long piece of a light and white material, generally of wool or silk, with which the Arabs envelop body and head, and over which they wear the burnous.

meeting, we shall have intercourse together unknown to all."

Zohra: "That may not be. Besides, it could not so easily be done, we should soon be suspected, and the eyes of the whole world would be turned upon us."

The Cavalier: "But love, love is the source of life. The happiness, that is, the meeting, the embraces, the caresses of lovers. The sacrifice of the fortune, and even of the life for your love."

Zohra: "These words are impregnated with love, and your smile is seductive, but you would do better to refrain from similar conversation."

The Cavalier: "Your word is emerald and your counsels are sincere. But love has now taken root in my heart, and no one is able to tear it out. If you drive me from you I shall assuredly die."

Zohra: "For all that you must return to your place and I to mine. If it pleases God we shall meet again."[1]

They then separated, bidding each other adieu, and returned each of them to their dwelling.

The cavalier's name was Abou el Heidja. His father, Kheiroun, was a great merchant and immensely rich, whose habitation stood isolated beyond the estate of the princess, a day's journey distant from her castle. Abou el Heidja returned home, could not rest, and put on again his teneur[2] when the night fell, took a black turban, and buckled his sword on under his teneur. Then he mounted his horse, and, accompanied by his favorite, negro,

---

[1] Note in the autograph edition.—The greater part of this dialogue is written in rhymed prose.

[2] The teneur is a woolen vestment used by Orientals to keep off the cold on their journeys. They are generally old vestments which are used on such occasions and thus called.

Mimoun, rode away secretly under cover of the night.

They travelled all night without stopping until, on the approach of daylight the dawn came upon them in sight of Zohra's castle. They then made a halt among the hills, and entered with horses into a cavern which they found there.

Abou el Heidja left the negro in charge of the horses, and went in the direction of the castle, in order to examine its approaches; he found it surrounded by a very high wall. Not being able to get into it, he retired to some distance to watch those who came out. But the whole day passed away and he saw no one come out.

After sunset he sat himself down at the entrance of the cavern and kept watch until midnight; then sleep overcame him.

He was lying asleep with his head on Mimoun's knee, when the latter suddenly awakened him. "What is it?" he asked. "O my master," said Mimoun, "I have heard some noise in the cavern, and I saw the glimmer of a light." He rose at once, and looking attentively, he perceived indeed a light, toward which he went, and which guided him to a recess in the cavern. Having ordered the negro to wait for him while he was going to find out where it proceeded from he took his sabre and penetrated deeper into the cavern. He discovered a subterranean vault, into which he descended.

The road to it was nearly impracticable, on account of the stones which encumbered it. He contrived, however, after much trouble to reach a kind of crevice, through which the light shone which he had perceived. Looking through it, he saw the princess Zohra, surrounded by about a hundred virgins. They were in a magnificent palace dug out in the heart of the mountain, splendidly furnished and resplendent with gold everywhere. The maidens were eating and drinking and enjoying the pleasures of the table.

Abou el Heidja said to himself, "Alas! I have no companion to assist me at this difficult moment." Under the influence of this reflection, he returned to his servant, Mimoun, and said to him, "Go to my brother before God,[1] Abou el Heiloukh, and tell him to come here to me as quickly as he can." The servant forthwith mounted upon his horse, and rode through the remainder of the night. Of all his friends, Abou el Heiloukh was the one whom Abou el Heidja liked best; he was the son of the Vizir. This young man and Abou el Heidja and the negro, Mimoun, passed as the three strongest and most fearless men of their time, and no one ever succeeded in overcoming them in combat.

When the negro Mimoun came to his master's friend, and had told him what had happened, the latter said, "Certainly, we belong to God and shall return to him." Then he took his sabre, mounted his horse, and taking his favourite negro with him, he made his way, with Mimoun, to the cavern.

Abou el Heidja came out to meet him and bid him welcome, and having informed him of the love he bore to Zohra, he told him of his resolution to penetrate forcibly into the palace, of the circumstances under which he had taken refuge in the cavern, and the marvellous scene he had witnessed while there. Abou el Heiloukh was dumb with surprise.

---

[1] Among the Arabs the name of "brother" is very usual between friends.

At nightfall they heard singing, boisterous laughter, and animated talking. Abou el Heidja said to his friend, "Go to the end of the subterranean passage and look. You will then make excuse for the love of your brother." Abou el Heiloukh stealing softly down to the lower end of the grotto, looked into the interior of the palace, and was enchanted with the sight of these virgins and their charms. "O brother," he asked, "which among these women is Zohra?"

Abou el Heidja answered, "The one with the irre-proachable shape, whose smile is irresistible, whose cheeks are roses, and whose forehead is resplendently white, whose head is encircled by a crown of pearls, and whose garments sparkle with gold. She is seated on a throne encrusted with rare stones and nails of silver, and she is leaning her head upon her hand."

"I have observed her of all the others," said Abou el Heiloukh, "as though she were a standard or a blazing torch. But, O my brother, let me draw your attention to a matter which appears not to have struck you." "What is it?" asked Abou el Heidja. His friend replied, "It is very certain, O my brother, that licentiousness reigns in this place. Observe that these people come here only at night time, and that this is a retired place. There is every reason to believe that it is exclusively consecrated to feasting, drinking and debauchery, and if it was your idea that you could have come to her you love by any other way than the one on which we are now, you would have found that you had deceived yourself, even if you had found means to communicate with her by the help of other people." "And why so?" asked Abou el Heidja. "Because," said his friend, "as far as I can see, Zohra solicits the affection of young girls, which is proof that she can have no inclination for men, nor be responsive to their love."

"O Abou el Heiloukh," said Abou el Heidja, "I know the value of your judgment, and it is for that I have sent for you. You know that I have never hesitated to follow your advice and counsel!" "O my brother," said the son of the Vizir, "if God had not guided you to this entrance of the palace, you would never have been able to approach Zohra. But from here, we can find our way."

Next morning, at sunrise, they ordered their servants to make a breach in that place, and managed to get everything out of the way that could obstruct the passage. This done they hid their horses in another cavern, safe from wild beasts and thieves; then all the four, the two masters and the two servants, entered the cavern and penetrated into the palace, each of them armed with sabre and buckler. They then closed up again the breach and restored its former appearance.

They now found themselves in darkness, but Abou el Heiloukh, having struck a match, lighted one of the candles, and they began to explore the place in every sense. It seemed to them the marvel of marvels. The furniture was magnificent. Everywhere there were beds and couches of all kinds, rich candlebras, splendid lustres, sumptuous carpets, and tables covered with dishes, fruits and beverages.

When they had admired all these treasures, they went on examining the chambers, counting them. There was a great number of them, and in the last one they found a secret door, very small, and of appearance which attracted their attention. Abou el Heiloukh said, "This is very probably the door which communicates with the palace. Come, O my brother, we will await the things that are to come in one of these chambers." They took their position in a cabinet of difficult access, high up, and from which one could see without being seen.

So they waited till night came on. At that moment the secret door opened, giving admission to a negress carrying a torch, who set alight all the lustres and cande-labra, arranged the beds, set the plates, placed all sorts of meats upon the tables, with cups and bottles, and perfumed the air with the sweetest scents.

Soon afterwards the maidens made their appearance. Their gait denoted at the same time indifference and lan-guor. They seated themselves upon the divans, and the negress offered them meat and drink. They ate, drank, and sang melodiously.

Then the four men, seeing them giddy with wine, came down from their hiding place with their sabres in their hands, brandishing them over the heads of the maidens. They had first taken care to veil their faces with the upper part of their haik.

"Who are these men," cried Zohra, "who are invading our dwelling under cover of the shades of the night. Have you risen out of the ground, or did you descend from the sky? What do you want?"

"Coition!" they answered.

"With whom!" asked Zohra.

"With you, O apple of my eye!" then said Abou el Heidja, advancing.

Zohra: "Who are you?"

"I am Abou el Heidja."

Zohra: "But how is it you know me?"

"It is I who met you while out hunting at such and such a place."

Zohra: "But what brought you hither?"

"The will of God the Highest!"

At this answer Zohra was silent, and set herself to think of a means by which she could rid herself of these intruders.

Now among the virgins that were present there were several whose vulvas were like iron barred,[1] and whom no one had been able to deflower; there was also present a woman called Mouna (she who appeases passion), who was insatiable as regards coition. Zohra thought to herself, "It is only by a stratagem I can rid of these men. By means of these women I will set them tasks which they will be unable to accomplish as conditions for my consent." Then turning to Abou el Heidja, she said to him, "You will not get possession of me unless you fulfil the conditions which I shall impose upon you." The four cavaliers at once consented to this without knowing them, and she continued, "But, if you do not fulfil them, will you pledge your word that you will be my prisoners, and place yourselves entirely at my disposition?" "We pledge our words!" they answered.

She made them take their oath that they would be faithful to their word, and then, placing her hand in that of Abou el Heidja, she said to him, "As regards you I impose upon you the task to deflower eighty virgins without ejaculating. Such is my will! He said, "I accept."

She let him then enter a chamber where there were several kinds of beds, and sent to him the eighty virgins

[1] Literally, "ironbound," mouseahate.

in succession. Abou el Heidja deflowered them all, and so ravished in a single night the maidenhood of eighty young girls without ejaculating the smallest drop of sperm. This extraordinary vigour filled Zohra with as- tonishment, and likewise all those who were present.

The princess, turning to the negro Mimoun, asked, "And this one, what is his name?" They said "Mimoun." "Your task shall be," said the princess, pointing to Mouna, "to do this woman's business without resting for fifty consecutive days; you need not ejaculate unless you like; but if the excess of fatigue forces you to stop, you will not have fulfilled your obligations." They all cried out at the hardness of such a task; but Mimoun pro- tested, and said, "I accept the condition, and shall come out of it with honour!" The fact was that this negro had an insatiable appetite for the coitus. Zohra told him to go with Mouna to her chamber, impressing upon the latter to let her know if the negro should exhibit the slightest trace of fatigue."

"And you, what is your name?" she asked the friend of Abou el Heidja. "Abou el Heiloukh," he replied. "Well, then, Abou el Heiloukh, what I require of you is to remain here, in the presence of these women and virgins, for thirty consecutive days, with your member during this period always in erection during day and night.

Then she said to the fourth, "What is your name?"

"Felah (good fortune)," was his answer. "Very well, Felah," she said, "you will remain at our disposition for any services which we may have to demand of you."

However, Zohra, in order to leave no motive for any excuse and so that she might not be accused of bad faith,

had asked them, first of all, what regimen they wished
to follow during the period of their trial. Abou el Heidja
had asked for the only drink—excepting water—camel's
milk with honey, and, for nourishment, chick-peas cooked with meat and abundance of onions; and, by means of
these aliments he did, by the permission of God, accomplish his remarkable exploit. Abou el Heiloukh de-
manded, for his nourishment, onions cooked with meat,
and, for drink, the juice pressed out of pounded onions
mixed with honey. Mimoun, on his part, asked for yolks
of eggs and bread.

However, Abou el Heidja claimed of Zohra the favour
of copulating with her on the strength of the fact that
he had fulfilled his engagement. She answered him,
"Oh, impossible! the condition which you have fulfilled
is inseparable from those which your companions have to
comply with. The agreement must be carried out in its
entirety, and you will find me true to my promise. But
if one amongst you should fail in his task, you will all
be my prisoners by the will of God!"

Abou el Heidja gave way in the face of this firm
resolve, and sat down amongst the girls and women, and
ate and drank with them, whilst waiting for the conclusion of the tasks of his companions.

At first Zohra, feeling convinced that they would soon
all be at her mercy, was all amiability and smiles. But
when the twentieth day had come she began to show
signs of distress; and on the thirtieth she could no longer restrain her tears. For on that day Abou el Heiloukh
had finished his task, and, having come out of it honour-
ably, he took his seat by the side of his friend amongst
the company, who continued to eat tranquilly and to
drink abundantly.

From that time the princess, who had now no other hope than in the failure of the negro Mimoun, relied upon his becoming fatigued before he finished his work. She sent every day to Mouna for information, who sent word that the negro's vigour was constantly increasing, and she began to despair, seeing already Abou el Heidja and Abou el Heiloukh coming off as victors in their enterprises. One day she said to the two friends, "I have made inquiries about the negro, and Mouna has let me know that he was exhausted with fatigue." At these words Abou el Heidja cried, "In the name of God! if he does not carry out his task, aye, and if he does not go beyond it for ten days longer, he shall die the vilest of deaths!"

But his zealous servant never during the period of fifty days took any rest in his work of copulation, and kept going on, besides, for ten days longer, as ordered by his master. Mouna, on her part, had the greatest satisfaction, as this feat had at last appeased her ardour for coition.[1] Mimoun, having remained victor, could then take his seat with his companions.

Then said Abou el Heidja to Zohra, "See, we have

---

[1] Note in the autograph edition.—In certain texts the following version is found: "Mouna, at the end of fifty days, was glad to have come to the end of the trial, for she had become sick of the coitus; but as Mimoun kept going on, she sent to Zohra the message, 'O my mistress, the time has lapsed, and he will not part with me! I conjure you, by God the Magnificent, withdraw me from this grievous situation. My thighs are like broken, and it becomes impossible for me to keep lying down.' But Mimoun swore that he would not retire until the ten days ordered by his master were gone, and he kept his word."

fulfilled all the conditions you have imposed upon us. It is now for you to accord me the favours which, according to our agreement, was to be the price if we succeeded." "It is but too true!" answered the princess, and she gave herself up to him, and he found her excelling the most excellent.[1]

As to the negro, Mimoun, he married Mouna. Abou el Heïloukh chose, amongst all the virgins, the one whom he had found most attractive.

They all remained in the palace, giving themselves up to good cheer and all possible pleasures, until death put an end to their happy existence and dissolved their union. God be merciful to them[2] as well as to all Mussulmans! Amen!

It is to this story that the verses cited previously make allusion.[3] I have given it here, because it testifies to the efficacy of the dishes and remedies, the use of which I have recommended, for giving vigour for coition, and all learned men agree in acknowledging their salutary effects.

There are still other beverages of excellent virtue. I will describe the following: "Take one part of the juice pressed out of pounded onions, and mix it with two parts of purified honey. Heat the mixture over a fire until the

---

[1] Note in the autograph edition.—Another version says here: "The performance of Mimoun filled all the world with admiration. They then took possession of everything contained in the castle; treasures, women, servants, the girls and all. They divided the whole into equal parts, of which each took his share; then Abou el Heidja had his pleasure with Zohra, and he found her, etc."

[2] When pronouncing the name of a dead co-religionist, the Mussulmans never fail to add, "God be merciful to him!"

[3] Note in the autograph edition.—It must be observed that certain particulars as given in the verses are not in perfect accordance with the corresponding parts in the story.

onion-juice has disappeared and the honey only remains. Then take the residue from the fire, let it cool, and preserve it for use when wanted. Then mix of the same one aukia[1] with three aouak of water, and let chick-peas be macerated in this fluid for one day and one night.

This beverage is to be partaken of during winter and on going to bed. Only a small quantity is to be taken, and only for one day. The member of him who has drunk of it will not give him much rest during the night that follows. As to the man who partakes of it for several consecutive days, he will constantly have his member rigid and upright without intermission. A man with an ardent temperament ought not to make use of it, as it may give him a fever. Nor should the medicine be used three days in succession except by old or cold-tempered men. And lastly, it should not be resorted to in summer.

I certainly did wrong to put this book together;
But you will pardon me, nor let me pray in vain.
O God! award no punishment for this on judgment day!
And thou, oh reader, hear me conjure thee to say: So be it!'[2]

---

[1] Note in the autograph edition.—Aoukia, from the Greek. The meaning differs according to the countries and times. In pharmacopoeia it is twelve drachms.

[2] Id.—These verses form the end of the most complete manuscript which we had in our hands.

APPENDIX TO THE AUTOGRAPH EDITION

TO THE READER

In the year of grace 1876 some amateurs who were passionately fond of Arabian literature combined for the purpose of reproducing, by autographic process, a number of copies of a French translation of a work written by the Cheikh Nefzaoui, which book had, by a lucky chance, fallen into their hands. Each brought to the undertaking such assistance as his special knowledge allowed, and it was thus that a tedious work was achieved by amateurs, amidst obstacles which were calculated to abate the ardour of their enthusiasm.

Thus, as the reader has doubtless already divined, it was not an individual, but a concourse of individuals, who, taking advantage of a union of favourable circumstances and facilities, not of common occurrence, offered to their friends the first fruit of a work, interesting, and of such rarity that to the present time very few have had the opportunity of reading it, while they could only gather their knowledge from incorrect manuscripts, sophisticated copies, and incomplete translations! It is to this association of efforts, guided by the principle of the division of labour for the carrying out of a great undertaking, that the appearance of this book is due.

The Editor (it is under this name that the Society J. M. P. Q. has been, is, and will be designated, is assured before hand, notwithstanding the imperfection of his production, of the sympathies of his readers, who are all friends of his, or friends of his friends, and for whose benefit he has worked. For this reason he is not going to claim an indulgence which has been already extended to him, his wish only to make clear to everybody the exact value and nature of the book which he is offering, and to make known on what foundations the work has been done, in how far the remarkable translations of M——— has been respected, and, in short, what reliance may be placed in the title, "Translated from the Arabic by H———, Staff Officer."

It is, in fact, important that there should be no mis-understanding on this point, and that the reader should not imagine that he holds an exact copy of that transla-tion in his hands; for we confess that we have modified it, and we give these explanations in order to justify the alterations which were imposed by the attending circum-stances.

As far as we are aware, there have been made until now only two proper translations of the work of the Cheikh Nefzaoui. One, of which we have availed our-selves, is due, as is well known, to M———, a fanatical and distinguished Arabophile; the other is the work of Doctor L———; the latter we have never seen.

A learned expounder commenced a translation which promised to leave the others far behind. Unfortunately, death interrupted the accomplishment of this work, and there was no one to continue it.

Our intention, at the outset, was to reproduce simply the first of the aforenamed translations, making, how-ever, such rectifications as were necessitated by gross mistakes in the orthography, and in the French idiom, by which the manuscript in our possession was disfigured. Our views did not go beyond that; but we had scarcely made any progress with the book when we found that it was impossible to keep the translation as it stood. Obvious omissions, mistaken renderings of the sense, originating, no doubt, with the faulty Arab text which the translator had at his disposal, and which were patent at first sight, imposed upon the necessity of consulting other sources. We were thus induced to examine all the Arab manuscripts of the work which we could by any possibility obtain.

Three texts were to this end put under contribution. These treated of the same subjects in the same order, and presented the same succession of chapters, corresponding, however, in this respect, point by point, with the manuscript upon which our translator had to work, but while two of them gave a kind of abstract of the questions treated, the third, on the contrary, seemed to enlarge at pleasure upon every subject.

We shall expatiate to some slight extent upon this last named text, since the study of it has enabled us to clear up a certain number of points upon which M——, notwithstanding his conscientious researches, has been unable to throw sufficient light.

The principal characteristic of this text which, is not exempt from gross mistakes, is the affectation of more care as to style and choice of expressions; it enters more into fastidious, and frequently technical particulars, contains more quotations of verses—often, be it remarked, inapplicable ones— and uses, in certain circumstances, filthy images, which seem to have had a particular attraction for the author; but as a compensation for these faults, it gives, instead of cold, dry explications, pictures which are often charming, wanting neither in poetry nor originality, nor in descriptive talent, not even in a certain elevation of thought, and bearing an undeniable stamp of originality. We may cite as an example the "Chapter of Kisses," which is found neither in our translation nor in the other two texts which we have examined, and which we have borrowed.

In our character of Gauls, we must not complain about the obscenities which are scattered about, as if on purpose to excite grosser passions; but what we must deprecate are the tedious expansions, whole pages full of verbiage, which disfigure the work, and are like the reverse of the medal. The author has felt this himself, as at the conclusion of his work he requests the reader to pardon him in consideration of the good intention which has guided his pen. In presence of the qualities of first rank, which must be acknowledged to exist in the book, we should have preferred that it had not contained these defects: we should have liked, in one word, to see it more homogeneous and more earnest, and more particularly so if one considers that the circumstances which we are pointing out raises doubts as to the veritable origin of the new matters which have been discovered, and which might easily be taken for interpolations due to the fancy of one or more of the copyists through whose hands the work passed before we received it.

Everyone knows, in fact, the grave inconveniences attaching to manuscripts, and the services rendered by the art of printing to science and literature by disposing of them. No copy leaves the hands of the copyist complete and perfect, particularly if the writer is an Arab, the least scrupulous of all. The Arab copyist not only

involuntary scatters about mistakes which are due to
his ignorance and carelessness, but will not shrink from
making corrections, modifications, and even additions
according to his fancy. The literary reader himself,
carried way by the charm of the subject, often annotates
the text in margin, inserts an anecdote or idea which
is just current, or some puffed-up medical recipe; and all
this, to the great detriment of its purity, finds its way
into the body of the work through the hands of the next
copyist.

There can be no doubt that the work of the Cheikh
Nefzaoui has suffered in this way. Our three texts and
the one upon which the translator worked, offer striking
dissimilarities, and of all kinds; although, by the way,
one of the translations seems to approach more nearly in
style to the extended text of which we have spoken. But
a question of another sort comes before us with respect
to this last, which contains more than four times as much
it not be possible that a third work, still more complete
Cheik Nefzaoui, always bearing in mind the modification
to which manuscripts are exposed, and does it so stand
by itself as a work for the perusal of voluptuaries, while
the others are only abridged copies for the use of the
vulgar, serving them as an elementary treatise? Or might
it not be the product of numerous successive additions
to the original work, by which, as we have already sug-
gested, its bulk has been considered increased.

We have no hesitation in pronouncing in favour of
the first of these hypotheses. In the record which the
Cheikh gives of it, he says that this is the second work
of the kind which he has composed, and that it is in fact
only the first one, entitled the "Torch of the Universe,"

considerably increased in pursuance of the advice given by the Vizir Mohammed ben Ouana ez Zouaoui. Might it not be possible that third work, still more complete than the second, had been the outcome of new studies of the author? Subjects of a particular specialty have certainly been treated in the work of which we speak. translation, we find reproaches addressed by the transla- tor to the author, because he has merely hinted at two questions of more than ordinary interest, viz., tribady and paederasty. Well, then, the Chiekh would meet his critic triumphantly by appearing before him with the work in question, for the chapter which constitutes by itself more than half of its whole volume is the twenty- first, and bears the superscription: "The twenty-first and last chapter of the book, treating of the utility of eggs and some other substances which favour the coitus; of tribady and the woman who first conceived this de- scription of voluptuousness; of paederasty and matters concerned with it; of procuresses and the sundry ruses by which one may get possession of a woman; of facetiae, jokes, anecdotes and several questions concerning the coitus in general."

What would be the surprise of the translator to find a community of views and sentiments existing between himself, a representative of modern civilization, and this Arab, who lived more than three hundred years ago. He could only express his regret for having entertained so bad an opinion of his master, for having believed for one moment in an omission on his part, and for having doubted his competency to deal with the various ques- tions spoken of.

Does not the discovery of a text so complete authorise

us to admit the existence of two works, one elementary, the other learned? And might it not be by reason of a little remnant of bashfulness, that the author has reserv- ed for the twenty-first chapter without any previous al- lusion, the remarkable subjects which we do not find hinted at in any other place?

To put the question in this fashion is at the same time to solve it, and to solve it in the affirmative. That inter- minable chapter would not be a product of interpola- tions. It is too long and too serious a work to admit of such a supposition. The little that we have seen of it seems to bear the stamp of well-pronounced originality, and to be composed with too much method, not to be the work—and entirely the work—of the master.

One may be surprised that this text is so rare, but the answer is very simple. As the translator judiciously ob- serves in his notice, the matters treated in the twenty- first chapter are of a nature to startle many people. See! an Arab, who practises in secret paederasty, affects in public rigid an austere manners, while he discusses with- out constraint in his conversation everything that con- cerns the natural coitus. Thus you will easily under- stand that he would not wish to be suspected of reading such a book, by which his reputation would be compro- mised in the eyes of his co-religionists while he would, without hesitation exhibit a book which treated of the coitus only. Another consideration, moreover, suffices to completely explain the rarity of the work; its compass makes it very expensive, and the manuscript is not attain- able by everybody on account of the high price it reaches.

However it may be regards the origin of the text, hav- ing the three documents in our possession we have given

careful revision to the translation of M——. Each doubtful point has been the object of minute research, and has
been generally cleared up by one or the other. When
there were several acceptable versions, we chose that
which was the most fit for the context, and many muti-
lated passages were restored. Nor were we afraid to
make additions in borrowing from the extended text
what appeared to us worthy of reproduction, and for
the omission of which we should have been blamed by
the reader. We were careful, however, not to overload
the work, and to introduce no new matter which would
militate against the peculiar character of the original
translation. It is partly for this last reason, and still
more so because the work required for this undertaking
surpassed our strength that we could not bring to light,
to our great regret, the treasures concealed in the twenty-first chapter, as well as a certain number of new tales
not less acceptable than those which we have given, and
with which we have enriched the text.

We must not conceal that, leaving out of sight these
alterations, we have not scrupled to refine the phrases,
round off the periods, correct the phraseology, and, in
short, to amend even the form of the translation which,
in many instances, left much to be desired. It was a
matter of necessity that the perusal of the contents of
the book should be made agreeable. Now, the translator, with the most praiseworthy intentions, had been too
anxious to render the Arabic text, with its short jum-
bled sentences as clearly as possible, and had thus made
the reading painfully laborious. Looking at some passages, it may even be supposed that he had only jotted
them down, particularly towards the end, and had not

been able, for some reason or other, to revise them until it was too late.

The new matter introduced has compelled us to make modifications in the notes of the translator, and to add new notes for the better elucidation of the subjects which have not been treated before. We have been, with respect to these notes, as careful as we were with respect to the text, endeavouring to respect as much as possible the personal work of the translator.

Now that the reader has all the necessary information about the French edition of the Cheikh Nefzaoui's work, he will permit us to make, in conclusion, a few remarks upon the ensemble of the book.

There are found in it many passages which are not attractive. The extraordinary ideas displayed—for instance those about medicines and concerning the meanings of dreams—clash too directly with modern thought not to awaken in the reader a feeling more of boredom than of pleasure.

The work is certainly encumbered with a quantity of matter which cannot but appear ridiculous in the eyes of the civilized modern reader; but we should not have been justified in weeding it out. We were bound to keep it intact as we had received it from our translator. We have held with the Italian proverb, Traduttore, traditore, that a work loses sufficient of its originality by being conveyed from its own tongue into another, and we hope that the plan we have adopted will meet with general approval. Those oddities are, moreover, instructive, as they make us acquainted with the manner and character of the Arab under a peculiar aspect, and not only of the Arab who was contemporary with our author, but also with the Arab of our own day. The latter is, in fact, not much more advanced than was the former. Although our contact with the race becomes closer every day in Tunis, Morocco, Egypt, and other Mussulman countries, they hold to their old medical prescriptions, have the same belief in divination, and honour the same mass of ridiculous notions, in which sorcery and amulets play a large part, and which appear to us supremely absurd. At the same time, one may observe from the very passages which we here refer to, that this people was not so averse as one might believe to witticisms, for the pun (calembour) occupies an important position in the explanation of dreams with which the author has studied the chapters on the sexual organs, apparently for no particular reason but no doubt with the idea that no matter of interest should be absent from his work.

The reader will perhaps also find that probability is frequently sacrificed to imagination. This is a distinct mark of the Arabic literature, and our work could not otherwise but exhibit the faults inherent to the genius of this race, which revels in the love for the marvellous, and amongst whose chief literary productions are to be counted the "Thousand and One Nights." But if these tales show such defaults very glaringly, they exhibit on the other hand, charming qualities, simplicity, grace, delicacy; a mine of precious things which has been explored and made use of by modern authors. We have pointed out, in some notes, the relationship which we found between these tales and those of Boccaccio and La Fontaine, but we could not draw attention to all. We had to pass over many with silence, and amongst them some of the most striking, as for instance in the case of "The Man Expert in Stratagems Duped by his Wife," which we find reproduced with all the perfect mastership of Balzac at the end of the "Physiologie du Mariage."

We will not pursue this sketch any further. If instead of commencing the book with a preface we have preferred to address the reader at the end, this was done in order not to impose our views upon him and thus to stand between him and the work. Whether these additional lines will be read by him or not, we believe that we have done our duty by informing him of the direction we gave to our work. We tried, on the one hand, to prove the merits of the translator who furnished the basis for our labours, that is to say, the part which required the most science and study, while, on the other hand, we desired our readers to know in how far this translation had to be recast.

To the Arabophile who would wish to produce a better translation the way is left open; and in perfecting the work he is free to uncover the unknown beauties of the twenty-first chapter to his admiring contemporaries.

THE END

www.ingramcontent.com/pod-product-compliance
Lightning Source LLC
Chambersburg PA
CBHW030815020726
47499CB00006B/1926